Gambling
with
Murder

Gambling
with
Murder

A Southern California Mystery

Lida Sideris

Lida Sideris

LEVEL
BEST BOOKS

First published by Level Best Books 2022

Author Photo Credit: Shane Sideris

First edition

ISBN: 978-1-68512-086-3

Cover art by Level Best Designs

This book was professionally typeset on Reedsy.
Find out more at reedsy.com

To MomV who steadfastly reads and re-reads all of my drafts until I get it right

Praise for GAMBLING WITH MURDER

"Jaunty banter...laugh-inducing escapades, and a genuinely compelling plot makes this a welcome blend of adventure, humor, and romance."—*Kings River Life* Magazine

Chapter One

Luck be a Lady

I maneuvered around shattered glass, splintered picture frames, and fragments of bubble wrap strewn along the cracked cement floor. Something crunched or crackled beneath my every step. Empty spaces joined hands to form a footpath meandering through the old warehouse. The beam of my flashlight circled around stacks of crates, blankets, old tires—

"Ninja One, see anything yet?" Veera Bankhead's voice sputtered through the walkie-talkie cinched onto my belt.

Dressing up like ninjas had been Veera's idea. To help us blend into the night. We wore matching black tunics over black slacks. The hood hid my long hair. A facemask rendered me incognito. Only the slit across my eyes kept me from tripping. Veera was posted in the parking lot outside to discourage unwelcome visitors.

"Looks like a hoarder's paradise." I stepped over a pile of well-used sneakers.

"Any idea of what we're looking for?" she asked.

"Oh, the usual hidden-in-a-warehouse items. A barrel labeled 'TNT'. A nondescript briefcase filled with rolls of cash. Dorothy's ruby slippers would be nice."

By day, Veera and I worked in the legal department of Ameripictures Film Studios. Tonight's side gig was connected to our day job...by a

1

nearly invisible thread. Props had gone missing from a high-budget movie currently in production. A police investigation was underway, but Veera suspected an inside job. She'd convinced studio security into letting us take a look. An anonymous tip led to a Los Angeles warehouse hidden beneath the 405- freeway. I stepped gingerly over dented soda cans to stay on the path between the heaps.

"We gotta find something," Veera said. "Our reputation's at stake."

She didn't mean our reputation in the legal department. She meant our reputation as quasi-professional, unlicensed private investigators. I had my father to thank for showing me the P.I. ropes. Investigating suspicious deaths was what I did best, with help from Veera. It had earned us a level of respect from the studio security crew. That's how we got the nosing around for missing props gig.

"I still say that new intern is behind the thefts," Veera said. "He's been hangin' out at the prop house every day."

"Isn't he inventorying the props?" I asked.

"So he says," Veera replied.

I had low hopes of finding anything tonight but I had to admit, this was the perfect location to hide stolen goods. A baby elephant could get lost in here. "Did you find out who owns this place?" I asked.

"Working on it," she replied.

It didn't hurt matters that Veera had handled parking lot security before becoming my legal assistant. She had connections far and wide in the Southern California security guard world.

I pinned the beam of my light into a dark corner. "That's strange." Four large pieces of luggage lay side-by-side atop a long folding table. Everything surrounding me was in stacks and piles. I quick-stepped closer. The luggage exteriors, aluminum handles, and zippers looked new. Why store unused luggage in a place with worn-out, broken-down stuff?

"Oh-oh," Veera said.

"Hold on." I grabbed a suitcase and slid it closer to me. I shone my light on a combination lock. Next to it sat a small keyhole. Pulling out a paperclip from my pants pocket, I shoved it into the keyhole and jiggled it around.

"Two unmarked vehicles drove up," Veera whispered.

We'd parked my BMW behind the warehouse. I'd left Veera hiding behind a bottle brush shrub near the entry.

I popped open the lid of the suitcase. Folded bedsheets lay on top. Easing them aside, I gaped at the blood-red cape with a stylized golden "S" on the back. "It's Superman."

"The cars parked next to each other," Veera said.

To the side of the cape lay a pillowcase. I ran my fingers over something odd-shaped and bulky inside. I unwrapped it to find a one-of-a-kind, golden gun.

"No way." A cigarette case formed the handle. The trigger was a cufflink and a fountain pen served as the barrel. It was a prop gun from a James Bond film.

"Two muscular guys came out of a van," Veera said. "There's a third-person taking his sweet time exiting a Prius. Looks to be someone smaller, older by the way he moves. And he's wearing a dress, which means he could be a female. Headed your way. If there's a backdoor, I'd use it."

"Can't. I hit the jackpot." I spun around. Where to hide?

I slammed shut the suitcase and yanked off a blanket covering a wooden trunk nearby. Unfolding the blanket, I stuffed the ends of the top portion beneath the luggage and draped the rest over the table. The metal door at the entry of the warehouse rattled open. I shut off my walkie-talkie and flashlight and dove under the table. A three-inch gap between the floor and the blanket meant I'd see them coming...and they might see me if anyone noticed the blanket over the table was a new addition.

Two pairs of footsteps thumped fast and hard, growing louder by the moment. Another pair padded along rapidly, with a short pause in between. What did that mean? The third person was likely smaller, like Veera said, and not as nimble-footed. A circle of light smacked into the blanket in front of me, spreading its rays along the floor.

"I've got the pirate map from *Goonies*, too."

The voice was high and squeaky, like it had bubbled up through a glass of champagne. Was a kid behind the prop thefts? That would explain the quick, short footsteps.

Two pairs of shoes pulled up. A size fourteen men's work boot and a size tenish Nike sneaker. Where was the third pair?

"All this junk yours?" The voice was growly and deep like it belonged to a tree-dwelling iguana with powerful jaws. Must be the man in the size fourteens.

"The junk's a ruse. I'm a collector of fine movie memorabilia," came the squeaky reply. "I have my daughter to thank for that."

Daughter? This was no kid. Who was her daughter?

"When my late husband's pension fund went belly-up, I became a serious collector," she continued. "It's called survival of the smartest."

Something banged against the table and a suitcase snapped open.

"I expect seventy-five grand per suitcase," she said. "I'll throw in the luggage so you can wheel everything out of here."

"We only brought fifty thou," the third wheel spoke in a harsh, nasally voice.

Stifling silence followed.

"Hey," the shorter guy said. "Get rid of that thing."

"This gun isn't a prop, boys," the lady said. "The price went up to a hundred grand per suitcase."

"Crazy old bag," the big guy said.

"You have one minute to decide."

She didn't fool around. Which meant this could get messy. They could overpower her in seconds.

I got on my knees and edged closer to the thugs' shoes. Flexing my fingers, I thrust my hands forward and cupped an ankle on each guy, jerking my grip hard toward me. The smaller guy landed flat on his back and howled long and loud. But the big guy landed on his rump, sitting up. I rocketed out from beneath the table and hopped to my feet, Glock in hand. I slid to the big guy's left and pointed the gun at his chest.

"Who are you?" he asked.

"Hands above your heads." I reached beneath my tunic for a second gun which I aimed at the other guy. "Now!"

4

Their arms slowly rose, but the .45 in the old lady's hand didn't budge. Small and plump, her pixie cut brimmed with frosty curlicues. She gazed at me with wide-set, pale blues. She was a knockout in a pink satin, floral jacket buttoned to the top over a matching skirt. Red pumps completed her fashionable, pistol-packing granny look.

"Black market props must sell like hotcakes," I said.

"You a copper?" she asked.

"I work for Ameripictures."

"Like I believe that. I've been collecting movie memorabilia for four years and the studio wasn't any wiser. Why would they suddenly come to their senses?"

"You took a cyber laser gun from a movie currently in production," I said.

"Oh." She lowered her weapon. "They don't have duplicates? They always make at least three of each prop. How about I pay you a little something and you disappear? That's tax-free spending money."

I didn't need to look down to see the big guy's creeping hand, inches away from my foot. I slammed my sneaker against his fingers. He clenched his teeth and hissed.

"Tempting, but I'll pass." I glanced around the jam-packed warehouse. "Where did you get all this—"

The front and back doors flew open and cops swarmed in, guns drawn. I raised my arms above my head while four uniforms charged toward us, climbing over the endless piles. Veera brought up the rear.

"Looks like you didn't need any help." Veera stopped by me, breathless.

The old lady's gun dropped to the floor with a clang and she braced herself against the nearest suitcase. "They forced me to do it." Her chin fell to her chest and she sobbed. "I feel so battered. This is elder abuse."

"She's the fence," the big thug said.

"Liar!" She pointed to him. "They brought me here against my will."

"In a separate vehicle?" Veera asked. "That you drove?" She clicked her tongue. "Shame on you."

An officer helped the lady to a chair, while two others handled the thugs.

"After I found out who owned the place, I called the police," Veera whispered to me. "She's Ida Schlamberger."

"Isn't the director of the studio archive—" I started.

"Bonnie Schlamberger. Ida's daughter," Veera said. "Ida's been pilfering stuff while Bonnie's been working in the archive. I'm thinking Bonnie doesn't know how busy her mother's been."

"How's an old broad supposed to live on social security these days?" Ida asked the cops. "Who's going to hire an eighty-six-year-old former pin-up girl?" She stooped over and whispered to an officer, "How'd you like an original Indiana Jones bullwhip?"

An hour later, Ida was carted away in the back of a squad car. We provided our statements and hightailed it to the parking lot.

"Ida's owned the warehouse for years," Veera said. "No one would have suspected a little old lady was behind the thefts."

We'd nearly reached my car when a Ford Explorer zipped through the lot, screeching to a stop in front of us. The driver's side door flew open and a large man stepped out. His thick salt and pepper beard was a contrast to his shaved head. A diamond stud glinted in his ear beneath the glow of streetlights.

"We need to talk," he said.

Chapter Two

Respect

Veera and I leaned against the tail end of a Ford Explorer. Ameripictures director of security, Wayne Curry, folded his arms over his massive chest.

"I got Veera's text and rushed over. You did good, ladies." Wayne took a step closer. "But this has to be on the down-low."

The 405-freeway buzzed like a giant beehive above us, gridlock free. The temperature held steady at seventy.

"Meaning what?" I asked.

"Can't give you the credit you deserve," Wayne replied.

Veera crossed her arms and advanced toward Wayne. "Let me summarize what Corrie just did for you. She risked her life to take down a dangerous criminal and find your stolen props. More props than you ever anticipated."

"The thief's in her eighties. And not exactly a hardened criminal."

Veera took another step.

"I'm not saying you didn't make things right—" Wayne held up his hands.

"I didn't take you for a credit hog," Veera said. "We earned the bragging rights."

"We're getting paid for this, right?" The studio didn't need our charity.

"You two aren't legit," he said. "Which means we can't pay you."

The mercury in my inner thermometer was about to shoot out the top of my head. Good thing I wore black.

"You've got no liability insurance, no license to investigate," Wayne said, "which means no credibility."

"Yet, you gave us the go-ahead." My turn to breathe up his neck.

"If it were up to me—"

I slammed my shoe down a hair's breadth away from his high-top sneakers. He jerked his foot up and away. This was the second time tonight I'd managed to scare a guy nearly a foot taller than I was. "It *is* up to you, Wayne. You should've thought it through before you hired us."

"Hired you? I did you a favor."

I grabbed Veera's arm to keep her from walloping Wayne. Topping out at six feet, she stood a fighting chance of wrestling him to his knees.

He held up his hand. "I'll make it up to you." He turned to leave, then pivoted around to face us again. "How'd you know the stuff was in this warehouse?"

I'd contacted one of my P.I. Dad's former informants to get the word on the street. There was talk of an old warehouse that was a hotbed for movie memorabilia. I'd narrowed it down to the shabbiest structure. "We're not legitimate enough to answer that question."

"Okay. You don't have to tell me." He wagged a finger at us and backed away. "I won't forget what you did tonight."

"Neither will we," Veera said.

"I'll make things right." Wayne backed up, climbed into his SUV, and disappeared into the night.

"I had a feeling he'd stiff us." I knew what he thought. Veera and I were on the Ameripictures payroll and in the legal department. Investigating could fall in as part of our job description, if he stretched things around enough.

"All I know is he'd better make it up to us," Veera said. "But now I don't feel so bad about borrowing a few souvenirs from inside that warehouse. I got bored waiting on the officer to take our statements." She unzipped her purse, pried it open, and slanted it toward me.

"Whoa." Inside were stacks and stacks of Benjamins. Props from the warehouse.

"Thought these might come in handy."

"If we ever need to bribe our way into a place," I said. "We'll flash the play money and see what happens."

"You know we will."

* * *

Veera and I lounged around the reception area of our Ameripictures office suite. A whole week had plodded by since we'd located the missing props. No one was the wiser about the role we'd played in capturing the thief.

"Scrawny vulture coming in for a landing," Veera said.

That was code for brace yourself for a drop-in visit from our former boss. Veera lounged on her desk chair, but instead of facing the computer screen, she'd swiveled around to view the walkway below our second-story window. Her sharp eyes scanned all passers-by about to enter our haloed building. We were housed in the oldest structure on the studio lot: the Otis building, an art deco palace where the original movie moguls reigned when presiding over this glittering slice of tinsel town. Veera and I worked for a legendary actress currently producing a documentary overseas. A documentary that had skyrocketed way over budget.

"I wouldn't get the respect I deserve if I didn't go over budget," Lacy Halloway had said in one of her rare calls to the office.

I was Lacy's latest and youngest studio lawyer, her rainmaker, although I was currently stuck in a dry spell. No deals had been signed since she took off nearly two months ago. I made it rain alright, but not in the legal field. P.I. cases kept rolling my way, like the missing prop incident. I'd cracked a few big ones with Dad, which made me a decent case-cracker. Veera threw herself into working the P.I. gig right alongside me. When she wasn't window-gazing, she was planning the grand opening of our very own investigation agency. There was the small problem of funding and the unlicensed part, but those were minor stumbling blocks.

With Lacy gone, our old boss, Marshall Cooperman, habitually checked up on us. He was the vulture Veera eyed, no offense to the members of nature's feathery clean-up crew.

"It'd be just like him to hand us our lay-off notices, right before we clocked out for the day," Veera said.

As the studio V.P. in charge of legal affairs, Marshall had been threatening to shut down our unit for a while now. Something about Lacy's unreliable production schedule and the fact that we'd abandoned his department to work for her.

Veera rose to her feet. "Every time he pops in, I worry you're gonna land a solid punch where you shouldn't. Then we won't get our severance pay."

"I would never jeopardize our seed money." We'd saved some funds for our upcoming business venture, but we needed more. I got up from the white leather sofa I'd stretched out upon.

"The vulture has landed." Veera angled her chair closer to her desk. She pounded the keys behind her computer screen and made a call.

I strolled into my office and sank onto my desk chair, opening a file. We made a good show of doing our work, but the truth was, there wasn't much to do in Lacy's absence.

"Veera Bankhead here, following up on that memo sent to your office." Veera stuck a pen behind her ear. "Wanna tell me why I haven't received a response?"

I skimmed a talent agreement that needed finishing touches. I'd barely made it to page two when the door to our suite rattled open.

"Call you back." Veera disconnected, pushed her chair away, and stood. "Buddy? What're you doing up here?"

I quick-stepped toward Veera. The elderly security guard who manned the lobby didn't make it upstairs too often. Must be important. He ambled inside, reached around Veera, and handed me an envelope.

"Good afternoon, Miss Locke, Miss Bankhead. Mr. Cooperman dropped off this letter. Went to his office by mistake."

"Thank you." I took the envelope and Veera closed the door behind him. We inspected the envelope.

Veera pointed to the return address. "Any idea who she is?"

The letter came from Holly Lee in Santa Barbara, California, a two-hour drive north of Ameripictures. "Probably a screenwriter pitching an idea that Lacy won't be interested in." Lacy was only interested in her own ideas.

"But it's addressed to you," Veera said.

"Maybe Holly's working her way up the studio ladder." I was the lowest lawyer on the totem pole. Aspiring writers and producers hoped I would recognize their pure, raw talent and shoot the manuscript to the chief sitting at the tippy top.

I ripped open the envelope and pulled out a letter. I read out loud,

Dear Corrie Locke:

"At least she spelled my name right."

I'm a former client of your father's in desperate need of your help.

"What?" Veera moved in closer.

I know you're a big-time lawyer, but can you help me?

"Reading between the lines," I said. "What do you get out of this so far?"

"That Holly's playing the flattery card so you'll pay her some serious attention."

"You've got a keen eye for detail," I said. "But it also says she can't get anyone else to help, and she can't go to the cops. Which is why she's contacting me."

"Where do you get all that from?" Veera asked.

"One word," I said. "'Desperate'."

"I gotta watch what I say around you," Veera said. "Go on."

My dear friend Dominic Rosetti has been missing for four days and I'm worried. He's never left without telling me. His driver's license, passport, credit cards, and Triple-A card were left at home.

"I'm a card carryin' Triple-A member myself," Veera said.

Dominic's a retired UN ambassador who hasn't been himself lately. He recently confided that he has enemies who've been threatening him. My business card is enclosed. Please call.

"Is she for real?" Veera asked.

I hurried into my office. "If we leave now, we'll be in Santa Barbara in a little over two hours."

"I'll take that as a yes." Veera raced to her desk and lifted a handbag the size of the Griffith Observatory. "What makes you wanna check her out?"

"Her business card," I said. "She works for a posh retirement community."

"Which means we'll get paid," Veera said.

That was part of the reason, but I had another, bigger reason for wanting to meet Holly.

Chapter Three

Stand by Me

We chugged along in my twelve-year-old BMW in L.A. traffic that hissed and snarled while it ambled slower than a sleepy turtle. Typical this time of day.

While Veera snoozed, I played back a little incident in my mind. The incident that made me say yes to Holly so quickly.

Last night, I'd practiced throwing shuriken against the dartboard on the wall of my living room. My wrists and fingers got a heavy-duty workout while I sharpened my aim. I flicked the five-pointed Japanese throwing star from different positions; crouching, kneeling, lying down, even over my shoulder. I missed on the last try, but I came close. Before I could throw again, my cell phone rang. The number was restricted. I debated answering, but curiosity grabbed hold. A woman with a softened Asian accent spoke at the other end.

"You are Corrie Locke?"

"How did you get this number?" I'd asked.

"Someone at your father's office gave it to me."

My jaw hit the hardwood floor of my compact living room. There was no rug to break the fall. I was so stunned I didn't feel any pain. Dad had an office, it's true, but that closed up after he—

"Can you help?" the lady asked. "I work at Villa Sunset in Santa Barbara. My friend is missing."

What a cruel prankster. "Wrong number." I swallowed the golf ball-sized lump in my throat and disconnected before I'd asked questions I should have asked if I truly was an experienced P.I. Why did I let my emotions get the best of me?

An internet search displayed Dad's former office address and phone number. I called and nearly hung up after the fourth ring, but someone answered. It was a recorded message.

"You've reached Locke Private Investigations. Leave your name and number and someone will return your call."

Why would the phone still be working? Did someone really give out my number? I left a voicemail. Now that I had a second chance, I'd find out how Holly really got my number.

* * *

It was the perfect night for a little undercover work. Low lying fog stretched its wispy arms from the sandy shore, lingering over neatly trimmed hedges. I was ready for anything and carried items in my trunk to prove it. Veera and I had stopped for a pizza and changed our clothes so we'd be dressed to match the night. I wore head-to-toe black from my baseball cap to boots. Veera set a more chic example in a black cardigan, charcoal gray joggers, and slip-on sneakers. Her honey-colored hair was pulled back into a high ponytail that danced behind her as she crouched next to me, glancing from side to side. Her deep skin tone blended into the night.

We'd parked off Channel Drive, a spunky little road that began and ended in the lap of Santa Barbara luxury. Stately trees raised their arms along a narrow, leafy lane that sloped away from the rustling waves of the blue Pacific. As we edged closer to our destination, elegant manor homes hid deeper behind lush greenery.

"Something doesn't feel right," Veera whispered.

Just the opposite in my opinion. Everything felt right about sneaking around in the dark. We'd done our due diligence and made sure our route avoided security cameras.

"These tennis shoes are brand spanking new," Veera said. "Why are they pinching my toes like a bunch of guerilla crabs battling inside? I can't do my best work if my feet aren't comfortable."

"I get that." My powers of concentration scattered when my shoes weren't comfy. "I'll go it alone from here if the pain's too much."

"I'm not abandoning you," Veera said. "This is our first official paying job as private investigators and we're doing it together."

We knelt behind a mature cypress tree. I peeked around one side of the trunk while Veera peered around the other. I pressed my night-vision goggles to my eyes. A lone figure strolled just inside the tall iron gates of our destination: Villa Sunset. As soon as he disappeared from view, we tiptoe-trotted across the street.

I'd called Holly on the drive up from L.A. We arranged a meeting for tomorrow and, more importantly, confirmed we'd be paid. In the meantime, we were scoping out the Villa.

I stopped in my tracks. We'd neared the north side of the property where it could get a little tricky. The compound was surrounded by a show-stopping display of perfectly maintained bushes and trees. But we had it on good authority that the shrubs on the north side were spindly, meaning we could push through them easily. And the best part? This was a deserted section of the facility. Deserted this time of night, anyway. That's what I'd read on *Yelp*.

"You sure about the security guard?" I asked Veera.

She'd made a few calls to figure out the timing of the patrol in this place. Her connections always came in handy. She kneeled beside me and scanned the area. "No live security watch at this end."

I pressed my night vision goggles against my eyes. I'd inherited the goggles from Dad, along with practical, but not necessarily legal, tools and weapons that also came in handy. A perk of being the daughter of a private investigator with plenty of hardware. Veera wore a scaled-down version of my goggles which she'd purchased online at a sketchy site. They overheated after five minutes, so her window for viewing was short. We faced the side of the facility that offered a small, fenced-in parking lot for staff. The side that security would be least interested in.

"Visitors park in the lot on the opposite side," Veera said, "and VIPs use the valet service. This is our best bet for going in stealth mode after hours."

"That's the point of entry." I pointed to the weak spot. The bushes at the very edge of the property seemed leggier and sparse. "Let's go." I shot forward.

Veera mimicked my moves. I dove between hedges and rolled onto the leafy ground. Veera slid on her stomach next to me, like a baseball player gliding to home plate. We'd landed on a wood chip path running alongside the chain-link fence surrounding the parking lot. I had less than three minutes to mask the camera lens, climb over the high fencing and hustle through to the grounds. I'd take a quick look and shoot back out.

We slipped behind a cluster of hydrangea bushes. Reaching into the pocket of my joggers, I pulled on a pair of latex gloves. Between us, we had plenty of pockets. And I kept a little something extra on me: my shuriken sat in a star-shaped buckle, custom made for me by Dad.

A car cruised behind us and we ducked until it disappeared. I pulled out a small can of black spray paint.

"I'll hoot if I see anyone," Veera said. "I'll give these owls a run for their money." She cupped a hand next to her mouth and hooted. We heard another, faraway hoot. "We're off to a promising start."

I sprinted toward the camera, jumped up on a boulder, and sprayed my heart out over the glass lens. I hopped down and onto the wood chip border. I motioned toward Veera. She slid to my side.

"Oh-no," she said.

"What's wrong?" I looked around.

She whipped off the goggles and blinked past me. She pointed to a sign running on top of the fence. Large, leathery leaves from a tree nearly hid the words.

I crouched and squinted. "Caution, electric fence," I read out loud. I put on my goggles. A thin wire stretched along the top of the fence.

"I take electrocution very seriously," Veera said." You know how long it took me to straighten my hair this morning?"

"Ninety percent of high voltage signs are bogus." That was a semi-professional guess on my part. "See." I rose and stretched out a hand.

Veera grabbed my arm and held me back. "I'm not going to stand by and watch you sizzle right in front of me."

"At most, I'll get a small jolt."

"This place is a fortress. They don't do anything small around here."

"Hold on." I pulled out my cell phone. It was nearly ten, but my question couldn't wait.

"Who're you calling?"

"Michael." My sweetie had the answers to anything technical, mechanical, and culinary. There was a reason Michael rose quickly to the head of the computer science department at L.A. Tech College. "He'll know whether this fence would cause serious damage." He answered on the first ring.

"Corrie? You okay? Should I come over?"

His first thought was only of my safety. My heart fluttered. "I'm fine. Veera and I have a question."

Veera moved in closer to listen.

"No one ever died from touching an electric fence, right?" I asked. "Hypothetically speaking."

Veera spoke into my phone, "And if it doesn't kill you, does it leave any scars?"

"Where are you two?" Michael's voice had gone up a notch.

I didn't want to worry him. Not that there was anything to worry about. "In Santa Barbara," I said.

"What? I love Santa Barbara," he said. "I would've come. Didn't you work at the studio today?"

"We left right after," I said. "We're on a little excursion." That part was nearly true.

"You never go on little excursions unless..." he said. "Don't touch the fence. Please."

"I tried to tell her," Veera said.

"Isn't it true that it'll hurt for ten minutes tops afterwards, but won't leave any marks or cause permanent damage?" I kicked into cross-examination mode. Even though I was a newbie lawyer who'd never stepped foot in a courtroom, the hibernating trial lawyer in me acted out now and then.

"No, no, no," he said. "An electric fence gives out a high voltage, low current shock. It'll pass through your surface tissue, and there will be pain. Maybe lots of it. I really like your surface tissue, Corrie. Please don't mess with it."

Veera clicked her tongue. I'd been in riskier situations and came out okay. What's the worst that could happen?

"Are you not convinced?" Michael asked. "Listen to me. You'll feel queasy like you were punched in the stomach. Your fingers will tingle and burn and your taste buds…"

"I've heard enough." Veera stepped back.

If I didn't respect Michael's opinion, it might mean the end of us. Especially if my surface tissue exploded. "Thank you, Michael. Sweet dreams." I blew kisses into the phone and stuffed it back in my pocket. I'd made friends with pain a long time ago. Michael was the one who couldn't handle it. I lifted my hand. "If I touch the wire while I jump, I won't be grounded. That should count for something."

"Don't even."

"I'll be quick."

"No, you won't," a voice boomed behind us.

Chapter Four

Sugar Pie, Honey Bunch

Veera and I swung around. Taller than the fence and far meaner looking, a uniformed security guard glared down at us, head cocked to one side. His top lip curled in a snarl. I half expected his mouth to be filled with steel-capped teeth.

"Can you point us to the ladies' room, please?" I asked. The name on his badge was Kyle.

"Get off this property." He blinded us with his flashlight.

"Technically, this is city property." Sounded legit to me.

"Out now."

"Any wiggle room in the 'now' part?" I took a step back and limped. I stalled, hoping to conjure up a way to get in. "I hurt my foot."

Veera pointed at my boot. "Could be a sprain. You got a doctor inside those buildings?"

"Get out before I physically toss you out," he said.

Kyle could probably pick me up and hurl me across the street with one hand, but Veera? It wouldn't be so easy. Together, we could take him.

He leaned forward with a grunt, just as I leaned toward Veera.

"You thinking what I'm thinking?" I whispered. I was betting his knees were his weak point.

Veera rolled her eyes over him and whispered back, "I'm thinking we should get going." She spoke louder, "Consider us gone, Kyle." Grabbing my arm, she steered me toward the car. "No good arguing with that man. He's a play-by-the-rules type of guard."

"We haven't broken any rules." The paint on the camera lens didn't count. Nothing a little glass cleaner wouldn't fix.

"The only way for us to get inside is to make the security team believe we belong there," Veera said.

Why didn't I think of that? "Brilliant. Come on." I dashed up toward our car.

"Where are we going?"

"To get in legitimately."

"Last time I checked we weren't exactly senior citizens. Villa Sunset is a high-end retirement community."

"We'll just have to find ourselves a cooperative senior," I said.

"Know someone willing to go in on the sly?"

If it were only that easy. I didn't know any seniors who'd willingly to work with us on this case. Or did I? "Our new team member."

"What new team member?"

"My mother."

* * *

We made a beeline for L.A. and planned how we'd fit Mom in.

"She'll call Villa Sunset and schedule a tour and we'll go with her," Veera said.

"That'll get us on the inside track."

Was that a solid enough plan to convince her into joining us? We stood a fifty-fifty chance, and if she said no, I'd get down on my knees and promise to return every stitch of elegant clothing I'd ever borrowed from her treasure trove of designer clothes.

"We'll figure it out," I said. We needed more than just a few hours at Villa Sunset to find the missing senior.

I dropped Veera off at Ameripictures and waited until she fired up her VW bug before accelerating to my pad in Hermosa Beach. Traffic was fairly light after midnight, which gave me a chance to think through various scenarios with Mom. She could schedule a tour and wait in the car while we snooped around. Or she could distract the tour guide while Veera and I conducted our own tour. How long would that last if Kyle recognized us? If Mom refused to help, what then? We'd have to pose, but as who? The cleaning crew? Gardeners? Traveling musicians? I parked in my garage and hurried up to my duplex.

I read somewhere that before you fall asleep, convince yourself you'll wake up with a solution, and you will. And that's exactly what I got the next morning.

* * *

I waited until a decent hour to call Michael. Seven a.m. sharp. He answered on the first ring.

"Just the way I like to start my day," he answered, "with a call from my sweetheart."

"Aww, thank you. Do you know how I like to start my day?" I asked.

"With a kiss, a hug, and a short stack of pancakes topped with blueberries and whipped cream."

He nailed that one. I drooled picturing that breakfast, but it evaporated when I thought of my real meal: a peanut butter and jelly sandwich.

"Kind of chilly out here with the fog and the breeze," he said.

"Where are you?" If I didn't know that answer, I'd have to give up P.I. work. I opened the front door and there he stood, tall, dark, a little geeky and a lot of handsome.

"Thought I'd take a little spin and next thing I know, I spun my way here." He planted a kiss on my lips, wrapped me in a warm hug, and stepped inside. He wore a blue bomber jacket over his T-shirt and his favorite olive-green chinos. He loved his chinos and they loved him right back.

"Don't you have school today?" I asked.

"Not until eleven." He checked his watch. "Until then, I'm all yours."

He headed for the kitchenette, which took all of five strides since my compact digs could fold up neatly and be stored in a shoebox. He held a large paper bag in one hand.

"Is that—?" My stomach rumbled before I could finish.

He pulled out a container filled with batter.

"I even brought my own pan." A frying pan materialized as did a small basket of blueberries.

My heart did a backflip.

"I figured you worked up an appetite after last night's investigation."

"You know about that?"

"Not yet. You can tell me while I whip up breakfast."

"Do you have time for a little side job afterward?" I asked.

"Who are we taking down?"

Another reason why I loved him. He stepped up whenever he thought I needed him, and not just for cooking.

"We've just about signed our first client," I said.

Michael's hazel eyes lit up. "Someone hired us?"

"She will today." It was practically in the bag. "We're going to track down a resident that went missing a few days ago from Villa Sunset."

Michael blew out a low whistle. "That exclusive independent living community near Butterfly Beach in Santa Barbara? You were trying to break-in there last night?"

"We were conducting a little assessment." I liked the sound of that. Vague yet professional.

"Villa Sunset is like Fort Knox. Great aunt Charlotte lived there for a year. You can't get inside without being on some kind of an approved list."

"That's where you come in."

He stopped mid-way flipping a pancake and turned serious. "I'll do it."

"But you don't even know—"

"If it means helping you in your new venture..." He ran a hand through his dark waves and gulped. "...I'll risk getting thrown in the slammer."

"Michael!"

"Just saying."

"I need you to gather intel," I said.

His eyes lit up again. "Is that all? Gee, at first I thought..."
"It involves breaking into the Villa Sunset computer system."
"Oh, boy."

Chapter Five

At Last

Michael dashed off after breakfast to start his assignment, and Veera arrived in time to help me prepare part two of my plan. I'd called Mom earlier to tell her we were stopping by for lunch. Nothing unusual about that, except it was Friday. Not only would Mom ask why we weren't at the office, but there'd be at least one other person who'd miss us as well.

"Anyone besides Marshall who could make trouble for us taking the day off?" Veera asked.

"When was the last time we entertained anyone in our suite?" I asked.

"Let's see, Michael stopped in a couple of weeks ago…and Buddy dropped by twice in the past month."

"We'll make sure we are nowhere on Marshall's radar." I could handle him. "Leave him to me."

"You rigging the sprinklers in our suite so they go off if anyone walks in?"

"You underestimate my abilities. Although that's not a bad idea," I said. "We'll spread the word that we're meeting with a Santa Barbara investor interested in funding Lacy's next project." Marshall would never risk messing with potential money coming into the studio.

"And he'll spend the rest of the day trying to track down the investor," Veera said. "That should keep him busy."

"I'll check in with Lacy to tell her what's going on. Just in case they talk."

24

On second thought, that was about as likely as a herd of zebras running loose on my street. "Scratch that last part. Our priority is to persuade my mother to help with our investigation."

She'd been pretty cool-headed recently about my P.I. work, even though she'd been dead set against it in the past. Something about my safety and that I shouldn't follow in Dad's footsteps because look what happened to him. But she was singing a different tune these days. Go figure.

An hour later, Veera and I had packed a few necessities and snacks and were nearly ready to leave when my phone buzzed. It was Michael.

"Lucille Fay Nightingale," he whispered. "She goes by Lucy Fay."

Horns honked and voices shouted in the background. I recognized the hoopla. He was walking to campus. "Do I know her?"

"She was scheduled to arrive at Villa Sunset at six p.m. today."

"Was?" I liked the sound of that.

"She won't be coming."

That would have sounded ominous if it came from the likes of a Mafia boss, but from Michael? My insides glowed. He only doled out cheer and goodwill. Or at least news that offered the possibility of a happy ending. Whatever Michael did, he did legitimately. "How'd you do it?"

"I played around on the Villa Sunset website and accidentally got into… you know."

I would never force him to admit out loud a maneuver that may not necessarily be legal. The "h" word never crossed his lips, but he'd hacked into the Villa Sunset computer system.

"I remembered Aunt Charlotte paid in advance, but took her time moving into the Villa," Michael spoke quietly. "I looked for someone not moving in as scheduled."

"Genius." I put him on speaker, so Veera could listen.

"Three new arrivals were due to move-in today. Two confirmed, but one, Lucy Fay Nightingale, won't check-in for a week. She got a call twenty minutes ago from the interim Villa Sunset Director of Operations, played by yours truly, to confirm her later arrival. At first, I had to talk myself into calling, but it was easier than I thought. That's good, right?"

Good for me, but not so good for him. "If it means helping us to locate the missing senior faster, it's great news."

"I convinced myself that if Lucy Fay knew the truth, she'd throw in her support and not throw us under the bus."

His conscience was pricking him, thanks to me. How could I ease his guilt?

"She's giving us the opportunity," Veera said, "to evaluate the scene and make sure it'll be safe when she does check-in for real."

"Good one," I said. "I mean, we'll find the missing senior, clear up the little mystery and Lucy Fay can move in, in peace."

"She's doing us a huge favor by staying in Palm Desert with her grandkids until next week," Michael said. "Otherwise, we'd be in deep doodie."

"If we could've seen the sky through the Santa Barbara fog last night," Veera said. "We would've seen the stars aligned for us."

I said a little thank you to the Universe.

"Even so, I don't want to eat up *any* time with worry," Michael said. "And that's why I plan to fess up to the real Lucy Fay the moment you've wrapped up the case. Which, knowing Corrie, will happen long before Lucy Fay shows up."

That was the kind of pressure that started small fires that could burn down a whole forest. "Sure," was all I said. For his sake, I needed to be the first-rate version of myself. "We'll tell her together."

"One more thing: Lucy Fay's never actually visited the Villa," Michael said. "She chose it based on videos and a slide show. Some seniors do that."

I couldn't ask for more. "I'm about to implement Phase Two."

"Before you do, you might want to write this next part down," Michael said.

I grabbed my smartphone and scrolled to my notes page. "Ready."

"LFN twelve-twenty-three-forty."

"That's code for...?" Veera asked.

"Lucy Fay's initials and birthday. It's the secret password she'll need to get in."

That was news to me. The A-Team had nothing on my home-grown team.

26

"I'll send you background information on Lucy Fay," he said. "You'll need it."

* * *

Forty minutes later, we landed in Mom's kitchen.

"This kind of food should be prescribed medicine for anyone feeling down and out," Veera said. "Lifted me right up. I'm soaring in the wild blue yonder."

"She's right, Mom," I said.

"That's so sweet," Mom said. "I'm feeling hugs coming on."

She leaned over the kitchen counter and wrapped an arm around each of us.

Mom wore a big smile, big hair, and a crisp white apron over a floral print dress. She'd spent decades as a buyer for high-end fashion before she was laid off a few months ago, and she had the massive, hyper-organized, walk-in closet to show for it.

Veera polished off a hot pastrami on rye with a side of coleslaw and lemonade. I was still full from breakfast so I nibbled on half a sandwich. I swallowed my last bite and spit out my next words,

"Want to go for a drive?" I asked Mom.

She eyed me in a way that didn't require any words to turn up the heat. Her lips curved up in a small smile, but behind that narrowed stare, she was asking, "What's my only child up to now? Was P.I. work involved? Would this affect her lawyer job that she should be working right now? Why was she always wearing black sweats?

"Okay." She whirled around and faced the kitchen sink.

No one talked for a few beats.

"Don't you wanna know where we're going?" Veera said.

"I'm sure my daughter will inform me when the time is right." Mom turned and flashed a smile my way. "Won't you, honey?"

I'd never seen Mom so cooperative. "What's that humming noise?" It sounded like a Mary Poppins' tune.

"I hum when I'm happy." She stuffed the utensils into a basket in the dishwasher.

"Since when?" I asked.

"Since it's a lovely autumn day and I get to spend it doing who knows what with my daughter and her good friend who always appreciates my meals, knowing how much time and effort goes into each and every one." Mom took a breath. "What more can a mother ask for?"

I wasn't going to argue; we needed to get a move on. I stood. "Good, let's go. You may want to pack a few things." If I got her intrigued enough, she might really want to join us.

"How long will we be gone?" she asked.

Veera's eyes widened as she glanced from me to mom. "Uh, it'll be an overnighter."

Mom clapped her hands and turned toward us. "A slumber party?"

"You could say that," I said. "For more than one night."

A hand shot to Mom's hip and her tone dropped. "We're going to a hotel?"

"Sort of."

"How do you sort of go to a hotel?" Mom folded her arms over her chest and traded in her frown for a smile. "Oh, I get it. You want to surprise me. Better not be a cruise ship. You know I get seasick—"

"It's not your typical hotel," I said. "We're on a case and we need your assistance." I allowed that to sink in a few moments.

She lifted her chin and a brow. "Well, it's about time you brought your mother into the action."

Chapter Six

Come Together

Veera and I were speechless. Neither one of us expected Mom to be so agreeable, so quickly. Something was up. Or she was bored out of her mind.

"You saying you want to come with us?" Veera asked.

"On a case?" I was expecting the third degree, not instant agreement. Was it so she could keep a closer eye on me?

Mom flipped around to face us. "It's time I experienced your side of life."

I suddenly had a change of heart. This was like being in high school and under a microscope with your mother's eye examining your every move.

Mom wagged a finger. "Your father had help cracking his cases, you know."

"I liked helping Dad. That's where I learned the intricacies of P.I. work," I said.

"I'm talking about me." Mom wiped the counter with a dishcloth. "I gave him tips. Lots of them."

"You did?" Veera asked.

"I think she's referring to the vintage Perry Mason episodes she watched over and over," I said.

"Maybe I wasn't there in the flesh when Monty caught criminals, but I was there in spirit," Mom said. "There were cases he couldn't have solved without my know-how."

Veera turned to me. "You never mentioned your mom had P.I. game."

"That's because she doesn't." This was news to me.

"I've even got the fedora and matching trench coat," Mom said.

"We're off to a strong start," Veera said, beaming.

"This is for real, Mom."

"Of course it is, honey," she said.

Was she taking us seriously or not? "We'll be staying at a plush resort near the beach," I told her. "Up north a little."

"What'll I wear? Which resort? You want me to spy on someone?" She rubbed the palms of her hands together. "I can do that in my sleep."

"You'll be in disguise," I said.

Mom looked off to one side. "I'll wear a beret. A raspberry-colored beret." She headed toward the stairs. "And I'll need sunglasses. I've got a pair for each of us."

Veera and I scuttled after her.

"I dig butterfly sunglasses," Veera said. "The kind with a whole bunch of angles. It's flattering to the cheekbones."

Mom trotted up the stairs and into her bedroom. "Got just the pair."

"We brought the makeup you'll need," Veera said.

Mom put on the brakes and slowly turned. "Are we going to be on camera?"

"This type of makeup is special," I said.

"How special?"

"It'll make you look a little older," I said.

Veera had stopped by the movie studio makeup department and borrowed a few necessities.

"We'll have to play around with your hair some," Veera said.

"*Older?*" Mom headed inside a walk-in closet that looked like a condensed version of Neiman Marcus. "You're talking to a woman who works very hard at looking younger. Tell it to me straight or I'm out."

"You're going to be made up to look like Miss Trudy," I said.

Miss Trudy was Mom's pal and my landlady. She was somewhere between eighty and a hundred, wore her hair in a French twist, and considered the sky her second home. She was possibly the world's oldest flight attendant.

"You want me to look thirty years older?"

"Cicely Tyson was fifty when she played Miss Jane Pittman at age a hundred ten. She won an Emmy for that role," Veera said.

"But she was a talented actress," Mom said. "I'm…I don't even know what I am anymore."

Mom was suffering an identity crisis? At her age?

"You're a talented chef and a fashion icon," Veera said.

"And you've got tons of personality," I said. "It's for a good cause, Mom. You'll help us locate a missing senior citizen by impersonating a guest for a few days to get us into Villa Sunset." There. It was out.

"It's our first official private investigation case," Veera added. "We're going pro."

"Going what?" Mom said. "I know about your P.I. side jobs, but since when is that your main job? What are you not telling me?" Her gaze seared a hole between my eyes.

"Our office will be closed in thirty days." That was sort of true. Our office would be shut down sometime soon. We just didn't know when. "Lacy's production deal was axed." That was likely since Lacy skipped town.

Mom's hand flew to her chest. "First, I'm laid off, and now you? Oh, honey."

"No big deal," I said.

"We've been wanting to leave for a while, anyhow," Veera said. "All we do is shuffle paperwork around. We change the names and dates and do it all over again. We want satisfying work. There are people out there who need our help and we wanna give it to them. We're gathering seed money to get our business up and running."

Mom pressed her lips together. She'd changed her mind. She wasn't going for it, I could tell. I'd have to dress the part of the senior and impersonate Lucy Fay myself. I'd need a shawl, rubber-soled nursing shoes…

"Where is this place?" Mom asked.

"Santa Barbara," Veera replied.

Mom clasped her hands. "Why didn't you say so? I'll do it."

"You will?" Veera asked.

"You what?" Did I hear her right?

"When do we leave?" Mom grabbed a cashmere sweater and pushed past us. "You're not the only ones in a rut. Besides..." She straightened and looked me in the eye, "...who doesn't want to spend a few days in Santa Barbara with her only child and her sweet friend?"

"You'll be helping us while performing a public service," Veera said. "That's what we're all about. Public service. With you on our team, we're going to break this case wide open."

"Aww, sweetie." Mom patted Veera's curls. "What do I do first?"

"Change the way you look," I said. "Starting with your hair."

Mom's hand flew to big, thick waves that gave her plenty of height and bounce and ended just past her shoulders. Mom's hair was a hold-out from the eighties and added at least an inch to her height. Since she always wore heels, she topped out at nearly six feet. After a shower and in bare feet, she stood five feet five inches, an inch or two shorter than me.

"You'll need old lady hair," Veera said. "I picked out a silvery bob. Bangs'll look good on you. Glamorous like one of those old-time Hollywood stars."

"You'll rock the bob." I meant it. It would be the perfect sleek accompaniment to her high fashion outfits, which she'd need to tone down during her undercover stint.

"But I can still dress stylishly," Mom said.

"You'll have to ditch the fashionable for the practical. I see you in a long, flowy skirt and a high neck blouse," I said. "And you'll need sensible shoes. Heels could blow your cover."

We stared down at her four-inch heels.

"I can't pull off practical," she said. "It'll extinguish the spark in my life."

"It's temporary," I said. "You must have something practical."

"Even Jessica Fletcher wore heels," Mom said. "We'll compromise." She raised her chin. "We'll blow the roof off the Villa while looking like we belong on a Parisian runway. These people may have money, but we've got the best clothes money can buy. Let's get cracking, girls."

Chapter Seven

Suspicious Minds

Veera and I changed into duds befitting the granddaughters of Lucy Fay Nightingale of Palm Desert. Veera switched into a colorful, long-sleeved swing T-shirt over navy slacks, and I wore a watercolor print blouse tucked into a pleated skirt with a side slit. Mom insisted on wearing a classic leopard print coat over a matching dress. A little over the top, if you asked me. She was pushing boundaries that needed to stay in place.

"Seniors don't dress like that." We were in trouble already.

"This hipster senior does." She adjusted her coat in the hallway mirror.

I had to admit her silver bob and glossy pink lipstick amped up the glamour. I wouldn't have minded adding her emerald green handbag to my wardrobe.

"Private investigators lie low," I said. "We don't want to stand out."

"She's eye-catching," Veera said. "Which could either get her into big trouble or make her very popular with the right folks."

"See," Mom said to me.

Was she always so stubborn? Yep. She was also our passport into the Villa, and access to her wardrobe was a real deal-maker. Plus, with her silvery locks and dark shades, she was the bomb for our first stop: Ameripictures.

* * *

We parked as close as possible to the Otis building, not because walking a good distance in heels wasn't our style, but the prospect of bumping into Marshall gave me enough acid indigestion to burn a hole through my stomach, and I didn't have a fire extinguisher handy. Fortunately, we landed in front of the building unscathed.

"Hi, Buddy." I waltzed into the gleaming foyer. Mirror-backed cabinets hosted trophies including Academy Award statuettes. A white orchid sat on a circular reception desk. Buddy stood behind the desk.

He tipped his black security guard cap and grinned. "Afternoon, Miss Locke. Mr. Cooperman was here no more than fifteen minutes ago looking for you."

I breathed fire, but fortunately, Buddy turned to look over his shoulder right then and missed the sparks. What did Marshall want now? My smile returned when our stares met again.

"Told him you were in a client meeting off the lot," Buddy said.

"Why Buddy…" My mouth formed a perfect O. "How did you know?" I pointed outside at Veera and Mom. "She's a potential investor in Lacy's next project. We're driving to her mansion in Santa Barbara so we can talk specifics." I gave myself a mental back pat for telling a half-truth, instead of an outright lie. I was improving daily.

"No kidding?" Buddy stared past me at Mom. "Wait, isn't that…?"

"It's top-secret," I said. "Please don't tell anyone she was here. She and Lacy go way back."

Buddy gave a slow nod. "They'll have to use a crowbar to pry my lips open."

Marshall never left his office without his crowbar. I predicted he'd stop by again in an hour or so, crowbar in hand, and Buddy would spill the goods, telling him we were wrapped up with a VIP client. Poor Marshall would probably lose sleep tonight.

"Thanks, Buddy."

* * *

Nearly two hours later, the freeway narrowed into two lanes and the Pacific Ocean glimmered and winked on our left. Asphalt made way for concrete on the 101 while sturdy shrubs with small puffs of pale blue flowers dazzled us on our right. We left behind the aggressive L.A. vibe and embraced the tranquility known as Santa Barbara.

A gloriously green mountain range and glistening waves hugged a picturesque bubble of old-world charm, with enough wealth to fund every bank and then some in Southern California. We exited onto Coast Village Road and motored toward the ocean. Veera rode shotgun in my BMW, while Mom lounged in the back. I did a double-take at Mom through the rear-view mirror. She was fluffing her silver bob.

"I should've made you look older," Veera said to her.

"I am older, honey. I just look really good for my age," Mom said.

Truth was, Mom looked fantastic for her age. Her real age and her old age. But how good an actress was she? She needed to channel her inner Bette Davis to pull off this stunt. She didn't look a day over sixty, which was only five years older than her actual age.

"We were hired by Holly Lee to find her friend Dominic Rosetti," I said. "He's been missing for four days." I pulled into a residential side street crisscrossed by telephone and power lines. Older, elegant homes lounged behind white walls and gated driveways; homes best viewed from a helicopter. Even the greenery served as sentinels. Everything from wide-spreading banana trees to ancient oaks with outstretched arms to better guard the manors.

I cut a quick U-ey, parked, and rotated my body toward Mom. She didn't lie often, but I anticipated a whopping fib in answer to my next question. A face-to-face would help me to read her properly. "Holly called my cell phone last night. Said she was referred to me." I needed to pique Mom's curiosity enough to throw her off.

"No surprise there." She rummaged around in her purse. "You've been solving cases left and right."

"Guess where she got my number?" I asked.

Mom's chin snapped up. "You're not on Yelp, are you?"

"Not yet, but we will be," Veera said.

"Holly called Dad's old number and someone gave her my information." Mom didn't even blink, but her lips slightly parted and her brows dipped.

"Isn't that crazy? There is no answering service." I half-smiled to see if she'd do the same. She didn't. "Right?"

"Oh, honey," Mom said. "You know how your father felt about loose ends."

"He tied them in knots so there wouldn't be any," I said. "Because in the P.I. world, loose ends can come back and choke you."

"Leaving clients hanging was a loose end. His phone didn't stop ringing even after he was gone," Mom said.

"We need to reach out to those clients," Veera said. "That would be good for our start-up agency."

"Monty probably planned it so that if anything happened to him…" Mom looked away for a moment before recapturing my gaze, "…an answering service would take calls up to a certain time and find other P.I.s to help. He probably paid a year in advance."

"You knew about this?" I asked. What other secrets was she hiding?

"Not really," Mom said.

Translation: I didn't want to tempt you into taking on his cases.

"You should've told me," I said.

Translation: I would've taken on his cases.

"Your dad did what he wanted." Mom popped a mint into her mouth.

"You didn't explain how my number got on the list," I said.

"Are you sure Holly got your number from Dad's answering service?" Mom asked. "She probably read all about you on the Internet and decided to persuade you into helping her, by using your dad. And it worked. I'd do the same if I suspected criminal activity. I'd call and do whatever it took to convince you."

"Really?" I basked in the glow of Mom's first official endorsement.

"You wouldn't call the police first?" Veera asked Mom.

"Only after I talked things over with Corrie the lawyer and Corrie, the makeshift P.I."

"I'm not makeshift." Now my feelings were hurt.

"When your inexperience leads to mistakes that may end your chances of practicing law and land you in jail, you're makeshift." Mom leaned back into her seat.

Dad broke rules only when needed. So did I. P.I. work was a juggling act of solving crimes while eluding arrest. Mom didn't understand.

I pointed the car in the direction of the Villa and stepped on the gas. I'd have to call Holly and closely examine her mode of finding me. I was willing to bet Mom knew more than she was letting on.

Chapter Eight

Say A Little Prayer

C hannel Drive gently wound around a corner and brought us head-on into sun-soaked views of the teal blue ocean. Natives casually strolled the sidewalk looking like they'd stepped off a beachy Hollywood movie set. Even the canines belonged in a best-in-show competition. I rolled down my window to invite in the scents of jasmine, sage, and the salty breeze. We had a case to solve that could shoot us up to the next level. Life was sweet.

I hung a right onto a narrow road where towering trees linked branches to allow only snippets of sunbeams through. The Villa's self-parking lot squeezed itself between a couple of tennis courts and Channel Drive. I parked my BMW in an end slot and said a little prayer of thanks that my car didn't conk out. It was long overdue for an oil change, new tires, a tune-up—

"This person we're looking for," Mom said, "has been missing for four days. Did Holly call the police?"

"She filed a report," I said. "But since Dominic's not a health risk and free to come and go, he's not a priority."

"Sometimes guests leave the Villa for weeks at a time," Veera said.

"Then why do they need us?" Mom asked. "Maybe he took a little breather. I bet it gets stuffy in there."

"How would you feel if Corrie didn't answer your calls for four days?" Veera eyeballed Mom.

My mother tilted her torso forward and stuck her head between our seats. She pushed a strand away from my face. "I'd turn the place upside down until I had some answers. And that's what we're going to do." She leaned back. "Did Dominic have his own transportation?"

She was finally thinking like a P.I.

"He used the Villa's Town Car. Most residents don't have a vehicle. And we called around. No one fits his description in nearby hospitals." I extended my hand toward Mom. "I'll need your wallet."

"No, *I'll* need my wallet." Mom rummaged around her purse. "I forgot my cell phone, but I've got my driver's license, credit cards, and your baby pictures."

"Aww, you still carry those around?" Veera asked. "Let me see."

Mom's ear-to-ear smile lit up the backseat. "Here's one when she grew her first tooth."

"You sound like I'd planned it," I said.

Veera oohed and ahhed over the photos. "You haven't changed a bit. Even your hair's the same."

She showed me the photo. My toddler hair was dark, thick, and sticking out in all directions. Mom stood grinning behind me with a comb in her hand. Not much had changed.

"Mom, your I.D. and credit cards don't say Lucy Fay Nightingale. To make this work, you can't carry real I.D."

"Why? Am I going to be frisked? Who's going to know?"

"How about a compromise? I'll lock our wallets in my trunk." Dad had designed a fireproof mini safe to stow away valuables in my car. It resembled a big toolbox, only it wasn't. "We can bring everything but I.D. inside."

"That could be dangerous," Veera said. "What if one of us is captured and driven to an unknown destination where we break free and find ourselves in the middle of a world-shattering crime and can't prove who we are?"

"This is not a Jason Bourne film," I said. "We're hanging out in a retirement community for a few days. We'll find Dominic and go home."

"And add another successfully closed case to our portfolio," Veera said. "Don't forget that part."

"All I know is that no one better touch my purse." Mom hugged her handbag closer to her. "Or my person. Unless they're tall, single, and enjoy lobster and traveling."

"Is that part of your cover?" Veera said. "Or is that the real you? We don't want to take a chance on accidentally talking about our real-life selves."

"I'm rehearsing my part." Mom opened up her handbag and extracted her wallet. "I'll leave this in your car, but everything else goes with me. Goodbye, Victoria Locke, hello Lucy Fay Swallowtail..."

"Nightingale." We were off to a rocky start.

"Here you go." She handed me her wallet. "I'll need some cash." She grabbed her wallet again. "Got any bills on you?"

"For what?" I asked.

"You may need to tip someone to get information," Mom said.

"We didn't think of that," Veera said.

"We won't be tipping anyone," I said. "We won't be there long enough to tip."

"If you want Lucy Fay to be a cheapskate," Mom said, "fine by me. But money opens mouths and doors."

"I use my sneakers on doors. The right screwdriver and paperclips work, too."

"I didn't hear that, since you're the granddaughter of an upstanding resident." Mom took a few bills out of her wallet and stuck her hand in the pocket of her leopard coat. "I brought back-up." She fanned out enough bills to handsomely tip quite a few employees at Villa Sunset.

"Holy whoa!" Veera said. "You always carry around that much cash?"

"No," Mom said. "But it sure feels good. Are we ready?"

"Listen up, Mom. Lucy Fay lives in a spacious home in Palm Desert with a small staff. She wants a change so she's moving to Villa Sunset. She's also a widow who inherited her third husband's sporting goods business."

"Must be the outdoorsy type," Veera said.

"With an eye out for her next conquest," Mom said.

"Your job is to help us find Dominic," I said. Everything else that Lucy Fay may or may not do comes in a distant second."

"I'll have to get into her skin so that no one suspects I'm a..." Mom said.

"A substitute?" I asked.

"A spy," Mom said.

"She's got a point," Veera said. "We need her to be a believable Lucy Fay, if she wants to get anywhere."

"See?" Mom and Veera bumped fists. Mom turned to me. "There's nothing I won't do to help you solve this case."

"Thanks, Mom."

"But it doesn't mean we can't enjoy lounging in the lap of luxury while crime-solving," Mom said.

"Amen to that," Veera said.

* * *

Minutes later, we motored up a red brick driveway bordered by ornate gardens and enough palms and greenery to populate a small tropical island. I drove to the top where the bricks widened enough to fit three luxury vehicles, side-by-side. A circular, stone dolphin fountain rose up as the centerpiece. I'd pulled in front of a two-story Spanish colonial hacienda with ivory-colored adobe walls, red-tiled roof, and graceful archways.

Mom leaned her head toward the magnificent entry. "I heard this place was luxurious, but I was thinking of Four Seasons fancy, not Hearst Castle."

Last night, we couldn't see the Villa itself, but in the light of day, the historic masterpiece was the poster child for splendor, seaside serenity, and laid-back glamour. Wrought iron and small colorful tile squares added cheerful accents. And we hadn't even seen the interior yet.

"Mom," I said. "Write this down. It's your secret password. LFN, twelve-twenty-three-forty."

She pulled out a small notepad from her handbag and scribbled for nearly a minute.

"What are you doing?" I asked.

"Making my 'to do' list," she replied. "Visit the spa, check out the pool, ask about the buffet..." She looked up, "...seniors love buffets, which means the food here will be mind-blowing. Short-rib melt, shrimp and—"

"Focus, Mom. Lucy Fay's not going to be blown away by this luxury."

"You're right." She stuffed her notepad into her purse as the valet approached our car.

"What are we waiting for?" Mom asked.

Ten minutes later, a burly security guard waved us through to the entry. Lucille Fay Nightingale was on the arrival list. A tiled archway rose above our heads, leading into a lobby hosting handcrafted treasures. Tile floors gleamed while colorful wooden beams decorated the twelve-foot high ceiling. Mexican folk art adorned the tables. Large glazed pots housed robust palms and ficus. There was almost as much lush plant life inside as in the surrounding tropical gardens.

A short wall of windows framed the Ocean Vista, a dining hall boasting its own wine wall, massive stone fireplace, and mahogany and marble accents. A grand piano waited patiently in a corner of the lobby while another hallway led to more colorful gardens in the back. A pair of double-wide glass doors opened toward a stone terrace where residents scattered, drinking tea out of china cups. A table was laden with scones, cookies, and crumpets. The Queen of England would have felt right at home.

"Is that set-up for everyone?" Veera asked.

"Thumbprint cookies," Mom whispered. "Let's go."

I grabbed Mom's arm and pulled her back.

"Not a linoleum floor or fluorescent light in sight," Veera said. "We're going to be living the life."

Well dressed, smiling seniors dotted the surroundings. Tony Bennett crooned in the background. It was all casual chic and custom cocktails.

"May I help you?" A woman about the same age as Mom, her real age, that is, stepped up; her lipstick-free lips a straight line. Her hair was dyed a brassy brown, her slacks were gray and her sweater striped in muted colors. She looked like she didn't have a motherly bone in her body. A manila folder was tucked under one arm. Her name tag read Leticia Ospina.

"I'm Lucy Fay..." Mom's eyes darted to me.

"Nightingale," I said.

Mom's clasped hands fidgeted and her eyes rounded.

"I'm Lettie Ospina, director of the Villa. Is this your first visit?" Lettie asked her.

"No," Mom said.

"Yes," I said at the same time.

Mom and I exchanged glances.

"It's our first time, but Nana feels like she's been here before," I said. "She's watched the videos over and over."

Mom laughed. "They were mesmerizing."

"Today's her move-in day," Veera said.

Mom held out her hand, and after a short pause, Lettie extended her own and they shook briefly.

"Oh." Lettie pulled her hand away and turned her palm up. A small strip of yellow paper sat on it. Mom always carried sticky notes in her handbag.

"My secret password is written on there," Mom whispered. "In case you have any doubts it's me. LFN twelve something."

My elbow gently pushed into mom's ribs.

"Not that you would," Mom said, "doubt me because I'm who I say I am."

"Nana, stop joking around already," I said, laughing.

Veera joined me. So did Mom.

Lettie peered inside her folder. "We weren't expecting you until next week."

"Is that a problem?" Mom erased the smile off her face.

"Not at all." Lettie turned to Veera and I. "You are…?"

"My daughters were eager to come with me," Mom said.

"Granddaughters." I patted Mom's arm. "No need to lie here, Nana. This nice lady knows your real age."

Lettie peered at Mom. "You don't look a day over…"

"Thirty-nine?" Mom laughed and slapped Lettie's arm. "Me and Jack Benny."

"She keeps herself hydrated," I said.

"That's right," Veera said. "She's a mermaid when it comes to water."

Mom burst out laughing.

43

I cleared my throat and the laughter stopped.

"I have a few questions." Lettie's expression rivaled that of the Grinch.

Veera gulped. Mom stiffened.

"Are you a wallflower or a butterfly?" Lettie asked Mom.

"Nana likes to socialize," I said. "Where's the best place to start?"

Mom's shoulders relaxed.

"Afternoon tea is being served on the terrace. Happy hour starts at five. In the meantime, you're welcome to visit our aviary, day spa…"

Veera whispered to me, "This place is looking better by the minute."

"…our state-of-the-art fitness center, indoor saltwater pool or take a stroll on the beach," Lettie said.

"Can we spend the night?" Veera asked her.

"To make sure Nana gets settled in," I said.

"I'll request two rollaway beds," Lettie replied.

Mom's gaze scoured the room and its occupants. "In the meantime, we'll unwind and soak up the sights."

"Very well. That'll give me a chance to get your quarters in order." Lettie bowed her head and retired to the reception desk, while we huddled with Mom.

"Who says 'quarters'?" Mom leaned into me and whispered. "Why can't she say my small, but swanky one-bedroom apartment?"

"How do you know it's a one-bedroom?" I asked.

"I peeked at the dossier she had on the real Lucy Fay." Mom's warm brown gaze circled the room. "Lucy's in a second-floor apartment on the ocean side, which means the view will be spectacular, so it's bound to be swanky."

"You are good," Veera said. "We could use someone like you at the Locke Head Agency."

"The *what* agency?" Mom asked.

I squeezed my lips together and gave Veera a quick head shake.

"When we start our own private investigation agency," she said, "it'll be called Locke Head."

"Oh, great," I muttered.

Mom's gaze shot to the ceiling and back. "We could call it Locke Head &

Locke."

Okay, I was impressed that Mom could read upside down and actually retrieve information, but this was not the time to extend an offer. "This is a one-time job, Mom."

"And this is my on-the-job interview."

"What else did you see on the dossier?" I asked.

"Lucy Fay's hobbies are painting, knitting, and horse racing," Mom said.

"She bets on the horses?" Veera asked.

"And she loves sci-fi movies and martial arts," Mom said. "She just got her yellow belt in Tae Kwon Do."

I was impressed. Maybe Mom did learn a thing or two from Dad.

"I'm finding it hard to believe any criminal activity goes on here." Veera scanned the room. "These people don't seem like they'd threaten anybody. Look at all those smiling faces."

Sun hats, tans, martinis, and margaritas everywhere. They looked like they'd stepped off luxury yachts.

Mom grabbed Veera's hand. "It's Shangri-La. Where nothing bad ever happens."

A dish clattered and shattered onto the tile floor and someone screamed. A roundish older gent lay on his side, blood pooling near his head.

"What were you saying, Mom?" I hurried over to the man.

Chapter Nine

Heard It Through the Grapevine

Villa staff cleared the foyer as paramedics arrived minutes later. We'd barely made it onto the large stone terrace when Mom turned to an imposing woman hovering nearby, muttering and shaking her head.

"What happened?" Mom asked her.

"One minute he's strolling in from the garden and the next he's sprawled flat on the floor like a starfish."

The woman wore a pillbox hat with faux feather trim that matched her ivory silk blouse. Heavy gold jewelry and a diamond ring the size of a skating rink placed her squarely in the resident category.

"Peter fell with an awful thud. Probably because of his fathead." Her coral lipstick had faded and the tips of her fingers were smattered with powdered sugar.

I shifted my gaze back to the foyer. The man lay next to a square coffee table, groaning. He likely hit his head against the edge when he fell. I refocused on the lady.

"You were enjoying afternoon tea?" I asked.

"He was," she said. "I need something that puts fire in my lungs. I watched him stumble inside, looking even pastier than usual. I followed him to see what was up, and he crumpled right in front of me." She threw a hand his way. "He'll be alright."

"I'm sure he will, Miss?" I said.

"Esther Lilian Bain," she replied. "Also known as T.T.B.B. Tall, terrific, black and beautiful. Call me Lil."

"Nice to meet you, Lil. What's Peter's last name?" Might as well make a list of residents to run background checks.

"Cronkite. No relation to Walter."

Mom put an arm around Lil. "Let's go outside. This must've been a shock for you."

"More like an aftershock," Lil said. "Seems the ground beneath his feet is always shaking. This isn't the first time he's gone down. But I could use some fresh air."

Mom shot a glance my way and led Lil outside.

Veera leaned in to me. "Nana's fitting right in. What's our next move?"

My gaze roamed the room. Lettie stood near the paramedics. "We start our fact-finding mission. Locate Holly. Tell her we want to move our meeting up, and see what she knows about Peter Cronkite. Check Lil out too."

"I'll take the scenic route and grab a scone on the way." Veera zipped off.

In a few strides, I landed near Lettie, just as she followed the paramedics out the front archway. She turned and nearly bumped into me.

"What the devil...?"

"Do paramedics visit here often?" They'd arrived quickly. The nearest hospital was a solid fifteen minutes away. I'd checked. "They scare Nan."

"We have no need for paramedics," Lettie said. "This gentleman failed to take his blood pressure medication and we just witnessed the result. He does that. Now if you'll pardon me."

That was a convenient excuse for his fall. What if he was pushed? I slid aside and Lettie hurried over to a group of seniors huddled by reception. I strolled back through the lobby. Residents straightened themselves out and resumed the small talk and smiles. In minutes, it would look like nothing had ever happened. My gaze rested on a distinguished-looking fellow who'd folded his lean frame into a wingback chair near a corner. Had he been sitting there the whole time? No, I would've noticed him. Everything about him was unruffled from his slacks to the newspaper open in front of him. His gray hair rippled away from his forehead in thick waves; his cashmere cardigan whispered refinement. Possibly a fine art collector. A half-eaten coconut cream pie sat in front of him, filled with creamy coconut custard. I shook off my sugar craving. The man carried an air of confidence. He would know things. Where was Mom?

I hustled outside and discovered her in the garden next to the terrace, talking to a group of seniors by a turtle fountain. Little turtle statues spouted water out of their open mouths, while real turtles sunned themselves on large stones.

I waved Mom over and ushered her back inside. I discreetly pointed out the older gent. "Make friends with the guy reading the paper."

Her eyes widened. "Is he a suspect? Because I have pepper spray in my purse. I keep a bunch in all shapes and sizes. No one'll ever see me coming."

"Don't spray him. Just find out what he knows. I've been watching him. He's a dessert lover with an iron will..." I would've devoured the pie in thirty seconds, "...possibly collects fine art and dresses meticulously. How are your flirting skills?"

"Watch and learn." Mom sashayed over to the old guy in the chair.

Could she pull it off? When was the last time she flirted with anyone? Maybe we should've had a practice session first.

Mom stopped in front of the man, leaned her torso back and parted her lips. He lowered his newspaper and stared up at her, his face bland. I edged in closer.

"I like to cook, stroll on the beach, and listen to classical music," Mom told him in a low drawl. "I appreciate fine art and intelligent, well-dressed gentlemen."

The man rose, all six feet two of him, and broke into a silly grin. He offered Mom his arm, and they puttered through the glass doors onto the terrace.

"Well." That went smoother than I'd hoped. Someone seemed to know what she was doing.

Veera shot to my side. "Let's go," she whispered and headed toward the arched entry.

"I need to follow Mom."

"What for?" Veera asked.

"She's outside with a strange man." Mom and her new friend leaned over the wrought iron railing surrounding the terrace.

"That good-looking oldster? How's she going to get him to talk with you tagging along?"

Veera was right, but I was responsible for my mother. I'd dragged her into this, whatever this was. That guy looked too slick for Mom.

"I don't feel comfortable leaving her," I said.

"Don't think you need to worry," she said. "He's probably about a hundred years old. If your Mom's anything like you, she'll have him in a headlock if he gets fresh."

She was right again. Mom could take him if she needed to.

"We gotta find somewhere quiet to talk," Veera said. "Outside and around the corner, there's a place where the staff takes breaks. I noticed it from the terrace."

Minutes later, Veera and I lurked near flowerbeds hosting pansies and snapdragons. Veera reached into her blouse and pulled out a small, folded piece of paper. She handed it to me.

"Holly'll meet us out here in a few minutes," Veera said. "She was impressed with our cover."

"Thanks to Michael," I said.

"That's Peter's profile information and medical analysis." She pointed to the note.

I unfolded it and read, "Peter Cronkite, seventy-three years old, five-foot-five..." I skimmed the details. "Born in Budapest, owns radio stations in Nevada, was a theater actor. High blood pressure, heart murmur, diabetic, and prone to migraines and excessive drinking. Dry, sarcastic wit and very competitive." I looked up at Veera. "What kind of medical analysis is that?"

"I jotted down the last part after chatting with Holly. That's her take on him," Veera said. "Lettie assesses all residents before they move in."

Which made me think there were more detailed notes in Lettie's own file. She was the boss, after all.

Veera whipped her head around to make sure no one was nearby. "Seems like he should've collapsed earlier with all the issues he's got. Holly said he forgets to take his meds which spells trouble every time."

"What else?" I held out my hand. Veera pulled out another folded note. This one was filled with more scribbles.

"I took the rest of my notes in a real hurry while Holly talked. She was expecting Lettie."

I scrutinized the notes. "Three weeks ago, Peter collapsed by the pool?" I looked up at Veera.

She took out another, smaller piece of paper and handed it to me.

I unfolded it and read. "Lil's health is stable, but she's stubborn and mean? Needs a hefty dose of positive reinforcement." I looked at Veera. "They link personality assessments to health?"

"They assess the whole person here. Kind of like Montessori for seniors," Veera said.

Sounded good in theory. Finally getting to the reason for our visit, I skimmed Dominic's notes and read out loud, "Dominic's health issues are minimal. High cholesterol and skin rash on left buttock. Jokester who enjoys dancing and skinny dipping." I looked up at Veera. "Is that still Montessori?"

A woman, in her fifties or so, ran toward us on tippy toes. "I have to be quick. Are you Miss Locke? I'm Holly." She wore her black hair in a top knot with curly bangs. Her khaki outfit was bland; her dark eyes red-rimmed.

"Tell me what you know about Dominic Rosetti," I said.

"Six feet, hair soft as cotton and trim physique with significant muscle tone for a man his age."

"I mean about his disappearance." I wanted to see if it matched what she'd already said.

"He's never left the Villa without telling me first," she said. "I'm worried to death."

"He took off in the past?" I asked.

"Yes, but this time was different. Dominic didn't say when he'd be back." Holly's words ended in a sob. "I feel he's in danger and that his leaving wasn't voluntary."

"Just because he didn't tell you?" I asked.

She sniffled. "We met on the beach the night before he left. He was on the phone when I arrived. He sounded agitated and didn't see me behind him. Dominic's a happy, carefree soul who gets along with everyone. But he told the person on the phone he'd go to the police if needed. Then he disappeared the next morning."

"Did he tell you what was wrong?" Veera asked.

"He cut our meeting short. Said he wasn't well. You will find him?"

"We've gotta lot of legwork to do first," Veera said. "But we will."

I wasn't so sure. Maybe he wanted to disappear. Maybe this was his way of cooling things with Holly. Her emotional state and comments indicated she looked at him as more than just a friend. "How tight is security at the Villa?" Kyle was impossible to miss and I'd seen others hanging around. I'd read once that upscale retirement communities with fancy chandeliers and interior decor were steering prospective residents' attention away from old-fashioned brass keys, easy to break into locks, and sleepy security.

"Our team is tiny because we've had no security breaches. Our units have simple key entries, but we have exterior video cameras that are closely monitored." She dabbed at her eyes again. "I think someone at the Villa threatened Dominic. Why else would he leave?"

I was more worried about someone spying on me breaking into Dom's room in the near future. "We'll take a close look." Thank goodness they didn't have interior cameras. "Is there a photo of Dom you can text us?"

Holly pulled out her phone and scrolled. She softened when the photos turned up. "He's always dancing. Very light on his feet. I'll send this one to you both." She pressed a button and her chin snapped up. "There must be no publicity. Lettie takes the Villa's reputation very seriously, as we all do. We're in the top ten national retirement communities and we want to keep it that way."

"Everything we do and say is confidential with a capital 'C.'" Veera pulled out a piece of paper. "Soon as you sign next to the x, we'll be officially on the case and at your service." She turned around and slapped the paper over her shoulder and onto her back, pen between her fingers.

Holly took the pen and scanned the sheet. "This says I'm paying for legal services." She looked up at us.

"I am a lawyer as you know..." Now was not the time to tell her our P.I. agency was in simmer mode, "...who's conducting a private investigation for you. If you don't think I can do the job—"

Holly penned her name and reached inside her purse. She handed Veera a check. "I hope that's a sufficient deposit. I made it out to Ms. Locke."

Veera turned around, brows raised. "It'll do."

"How did you find my phone number?" I wanted her to tell me again about calling Dad's office.

"I contacted—"

"Don't you ever look at me like that!" A shout shook the cool ocean breeze.

"It came from the terrace." I shot off in that direction, Veera close behind.

Chapter Ten

It's Not Unusual

We arrived to find Lil stretched out on a sofa near the terrace. A napkin covered her face. The lower portion blew up as she muttered,

"Nobody's touching what's mine. No siree, Bob."

Mom stood on the terrace watching. She waved us over.

"I was drinking tea." Mom turned to me. "With Vincent Peabody." She hunched over, cupping a hand to the side of her mouth. "That's my target's name." She straightened. "Lil walked by, looked at Vincent, yelled, and ran inside, mad as can be."

"Maybe he hurt her feelings," Veera said, "by choosing you over her. He's got the looks of a heartbreaker. Could be they were nearly a couple before Lucy Fay showed up."

That was so far-fetched. They looked about as much like a couple as the Dalai Lama and Calamity Jane.

"Lil's feeling spurned," Veera continued. "I'll bet he used to be an actor."

Veera had quite the imagination.

"He wasn't an actor," Mom said.

"What's your new beau's business?" Veera asked.

"He's not her beau," I said.

"Honey," Mom whispered. "Isn't that what he's supposed to think? That I'm sweet on him?"

"You met him five minutes ago," I said.

"Enough time to gather intel," Mom said.

Now I was interested. "Like what?"

"He owns the Culver Cereal Company in Los Angeles. His grandpa Joe invented cream of wheat or shredded wheat or something wheaty. I told him the Villa seemed dull for a woman of my capabilities."

"What capabilities?" Who was this person?

"Bowling, golf, bingo...uh-uh. No can do. I need something more..."

"Exciting?" Veera asked.

"Anti-aging." She turned toward the Villa. "Vincent said he'd like to talk about my interests some more. We're meeting for dinner."

"You move in fast." Veera's eyes shone.

"What do you know about Lil?" I asked.

"She's temperamental. And if you're not on her good side, watch out." Mom reached in her purse and took out energy bars which she handed to us. "She's got a fabulous collection of church hats."

I opened the wrapper of my bar and took a bite of the chewy caramel. "What did Vincent say about her?"

"She's moody and has an aversion to losing," Mom said.

"That tells us a lot. I'll see what's up with her." Veera marched off toward Lil.

"Where did Vincent go?" His silvery locks were hard to miss.

"Told him I needed a breather." Mom stood and straightened her skirt. "A girl's gotta play hard to get. Makes her more appealing."

"That is so thirty years ago," I said.

"And that's why it works so splendidly here," Mom said.

* * *

We returned to the lobby. Veera joined us minutes later.

"Lil said she took one look at Vincent and saw her late husband, Bob, staring back at her. She said he was a looker, too."

"She created a distraction." Or did she? What was she up to? I didn't

54

put anything past these seniors. Not after seeing the movie props Ida Schlamberger managed to steal without anyone noticing for years.

"What do we do now?" Mom asked.

I scanned the lobby. A chipper older woman chatted up everyone near the elevator. Her curly, reddish-gold hair was the color of an apricot; her pale eyes twinkled, even at a distance. She was dressed to the nines in a sparkling gold tunic, black slacks, and matching bedazzled sneakers. She had hall-of-fame social skills, judging by everyone's reaction to her. I was willing to bet she could even charm Lettie.

"There's my target." I pitched my chin toward the curly-haired senior with the pert nose. "Find your own social butterfly, Veera. They get around the most."

She surveyed the room and rested her gaze on a guy with coffee brown hair and matching eyes. He sported a preppy look, with a crewneck sweater over a button-down shirt and tan slacks. Gripping a folder in one hand, he zipped past with a wave and a cheery smile.

"Target in range. Must be Lettie's assistant," Veera said. "Maybe his lips are looser than hers."

"He's the activities coordinator," I said.

"How do you know?"

I had the answer as soon as he'd walked past. "The gardening gloves sticking out of the back pants pocket and the paint stains on his hands. The 'Paint Like Picasso' class just ended. I noticed the schedule at the reception desk." I leaned my head toward hers. "Yet, he's not dressed for gardening or painting."

"I gotta sharpen my visual skills. Seniors probably say a whole lot while they're doing the three Ps. Painting, planting, and prattling."

Mom stepped past us. "Snack time. I heard they've got specialty Rice Krispie Treats. Pumpkin pie spice. Red velvet. Good thing I've got a large purse."

"Focus, Mom."

"I'm so focused," Mom said. "It's very possible I'll discover a clue while snacking."

"I'll come with." Veera joined Mom. "Two heads are better than one when checking out clues and snacks."

"Meet me back here in twenty minutes," I said.

* * *

"Love the shoes." I stared down at the octogenarian's sneakers. Traces of a grin played around lips surprisingly full for a senior.

"Your ensemble looks like something I would wear if I were a teensy bit younger," she said.

"Then we'd be twins," I said.

We giggled like kindergarteners sharing a secret.

She lifted her chin. "Take some advice. Keep your heels, your head, and your standards high. That's what I always say."

"Didn't Coco Chanel say that?" I had a weakness for quotes.

"Where do you think Coco got that from?" she said. "I modeled for her once. I'm older than you think." She placed a hand at the side of her mouth and whispered, "Eighty-five. Don't tell a soul."

That was a shocker. She looked almost as good as Mom. "I hope you'll share your beauty secrets with me."

"All in the attitude, my dear." Her slinky eyes gave me the once over. "Haven't seen you before. You're new."

She was charming and observant.

"My...nana...is moving in, today. She's touring the place."

"We love it here."

She was also the Villa spokesperson. "Does everyone feel that way?" I stared around. "How about the woman who yelled a few minutes ago?" Lil had disappeared. "She didn't seem happy."

"Lil's like a copper kettle," she said. "Light a candle under her and she'll simmer 'til she pops."

"Have you lived here long?"

"Nearly four months. Enough time for me to know everybody and for everybody to know me. Sofia Reyes. Call me Sofi."

"Corrie Loc... Nightingale." Nearly slipped over a banana peel with that one. There'd be more than just paramedics called to cart me away. One thing Veera and I neglected to discuss. Our new identities. Geez. "My gran is Lucy Fay Nightingale."

"Charmed. I look forward to meeting Lucy Fay."

I glanced over my shoulder. Veera and the activities director stared out a side window. He was pointing out something to her.

"He's available," Sofi said.

"What?"

"Trent, the activities coordinator."

I hit that nail on the head. "Oh? Is he good at his job?"

"Very," she said. "Unattached and fun. He lines up word games, charades, tide pool walks, you name it. If you like soft play. He knows better than to mess with our croquet matches. I've been on a winning streak since I moved in." Her gaze dodged past me and her smile vanished. I glanced over my shoulder. It was Vincent. Sofi didn't care for the man. Why?

"He rubs me the wrong way, too," I said.

"I don't know Vincent well enough to allow any kind of rubbing," she said. Nicely handled.

"He moved in a month ago." She turned to me. "Did you hear what else happened today?"

"You mean Peter?" I asked.

"Poor dear," she said. "He'll bounce back in no time. But his absence is going to impact our fun. We have a croquet game in less than an hour. Still need a replacement for Dominic, too."

It was all I could do to keep from begging to play.

"Why isn't Dominic playing?"

"He's off campus." Sofi stared at her nails. "Until he returns, we'll need a stand-in."

"Lucy Fay, my nan, plays."

"She any good?" Sofi asked.

"Let's just say, the lawn parts in the middle when she's using her...stick to get the ball under that...wire arch thing."

"Uh-huh. You mean when she uses the mallet? The hoop's called a wicket. You sure Lucy Fay knows how to play?"

"She's never without a mallet." Sort of true except Mom's mallet is used in the kitchen to pound a chicken breast to a pulp. "But she didn't bring her... croquet set."

"We have extra. Practice starts in forty-five minutes, on the north lawn, just past the terrace. Tell her to meet us there."

The elevator door pinged open.

"Toodaloo." Sofi stepped inside.

The door slid shut and I made a run for it. I needed to learn everything I could about croquet fast. And then give Mom a crash course.

No sign of Mom in the dining room. A cell phone would've come in handy. My heart beat a little faster. Would she answer a page for Lucy Fay Nightingale? If she was paying attention, she might. What if she got too close to someone who'd played a hand in Dom's disappearance? I bolted into the kitchen and stopped a server.

"Have you seen a new resident? She was in the dining room a few minutes ago, asking about...correction...eating Rice Krispie Treats. She's wearing a leopard print dress."

"How could I forget that outfit? She left a few minutes ago."

"Alone?" I asked.

"With Vincent."

"He seems nice," I said.

"To the right people." The server dashed away.

Vincent was a snob? The place was probably brimming with snobs. I needed to find out more about Dom, which stopped me in my tracks. I had twelve minutes before my meet-up with Mom and Veera. Just enough time to snoop around Dom's apartment.

Chapter Eleven

Something

Holly unlocked Dom's door for me, so I could take a speedy look. The lock wasn't only old school, it was practically antique. She used a brass key to open it. All I'd need to break in was a wrench and a sturdy piece of wire.

"Is the security office downstairs?" I asked her.

"Outside the lobby, past the beauty salon and into the main garden, on your right." Holly lowered her tone. "We've never had a break-in. Any problems are internal."

"Thanks." I slipped inside Dom's suite. "See you later." I closed the door and assessed the surroundings. The rich walnut flooring was bare except for Persian rugs with muted blue and tan kaleidoscope prints. A marble-backed wet bar and a brick fireplace anchored the room. Colorful mosaic tiles framed the fireplace while French doors led to a balcony large enough to entertain a half dozen guests. I strolled around the living room. A toffee-colored sofa faced the entrance and a mahogany writing desk rested on legs formed by carved lions. The front door clicked open behind me and I ducked behind the sofa.

"It's me," someone whispered. "Holly."

I shot up. "You came back?" What did she want?

"His wallet's in the desk drawer," she said. "Why would he leave it behind?"

"Didn't want any I.D. on him. Or he forgot to take it."

"What about his meds? Dominic needs those."

"We shouldn't be seen together," I said. She'd blow our cover and her job.

"You must find him."

"I will." I led her to the door.

"But don't you see—"

"I work better uninterrupted."

Holly wrung her hands. "What if something happened to him?"

"If someone sees you in here, how will you explain my presence?" Better yet, how would I explain if I got caught?

I closed the door behind her. Was there another reason she was looking for Dom?

I swept past a golden oak dining room table and entered a spacious kitchen, complete with a butler's pantry and more hand-painted tile work. I pulled out a latex glove from my purse, slipped it on, and opened the top portion of the stainless-steel refrigerator door. Shelves were stocked with gourmet food items, blocks of artisanal cheeses, and an egg carton featuring green eggs. Plenty of European beer and wines chilled on the top shelf. All high-end stuff except for three bottled waters on the lowest shelf. A low-end brand bottled by a major soda manufacturer. Didn't Dom care about the water he drank? I closed the fridge door. The top half of the exterior door featured a cold-water dispenser. The sink offered a separate water dispenser. Why the cheap bottled water?

I opened the door of the refrigerator again and examined the contents more closely. Artesian spring water bottles hid behind the cheap stuff. Nothing unusual except for an item in the way back: a contact lens case. I unscrewed one of the caps and stared at a blue lens. Who keeps contacts in the fridge? I texted Michael the question and replaced the case.

I checked the trash and recycle bins. Empty beer bottles but no water bottles. I dashed off to his bedroom and checked the wastepaper baskets. Empty. I'd have to ask Holly about the water. A plush black robe was tossed over a leather chair, slippers sat nearby and a throw pillow lay on the floor. Housekeeping hadn't made the rounds yet. I checked my watch and darted for the door. I had a croquet player to prepare.

* * *

Veera flagged me down in the lobby.

"Your mom was playing pool with some homies. She really cleaned up, sinking ball after ball into the holes. The stick never left her hands." Veera looked like a proud mother hen. "Who knew?"

"Not me," I mumbled. Dad was a formidable billiard player. Mom must've learned a thing or two from him. "How's that helping us solve the case?"

"If she gets in tight with the right residents, they'll become buds and share all kinds of information," Veera said. "And don't forget who made it easy for us to prance in here and look around."

"That would be Michael," I said.

"Anyone else?"

"Mom." Veera was right. I needed to lighten up.

"She's got what it takes, C. Your mom's gonna own this place by the time she's done. Someone else'll snap her up for their agency if we don't."

I was far from sold on adding Mom to our future employee roster. "The moment she hands us a big clue, I'll reconsider offering her a job."

"She's working hard on that. You'll see. You're going to want to hire her, too."

I appreciated Veera's optimism, but I needed results. "Get anything out of the activity director?"

Veera lowered her voice. "Seems some residents won't participate. They create their own fun and games."

"Renegades," I said. "Which seniors?"

"Couldn't pry it out of him."

"The day is young, even if no one else around here is. You'll convince him to talk."

Veera recalled her big smile. "You know I will."

"Ask if Vincent is one of the renegades."

"I'll throw out seeds and let Trent pour the water," Veera said.

"Meanwhile, where's Nana?" I asked.

I scoped out the stone terrace while Veera patrolled the dining hall and front entry. I peered down at exotic palms, agaves, and prickly cactus that popped out all over the perimeter. Plenty of silver-haired residents strolled the gardens, but no mom.

"Find Vincent, find Mom." He'd be easy to pick out. Not many male residents sported hair that belonged on a twenty-year-old supermodel. Maybe Vincent wasn't in his prime, but his gray tresses were.

"Your grandmother's a lovely woman."

A velvety baritone voice trickled over my shoulders and into my ears. I slowly turned. Vincent had moved in quietly as a panther. Another reason I didn't trust him. Besides his rakish good looks. At least I knew where Mom wasn't. I turned to face him. "She's smart, too."

He looked past me at the residents milling around the garden. "When your grandmother and I were chatting, your expression was…displeased."

"What?"

"You looked like you wanted to rip my head off."

He was the type of person who never wasted time with nonsense that cluttered up a life. Everything was calculated to move him forward.

"Oh," I said. "That's my normal expression, until I get to know a person better."

"You reserve affection for those you feel are deserving?"

"That's right." Especially while on a case where he was a suspect.

We locked stares like we were locking horns.

"I met Sofi by the elevator." I was going for it. "She mentioned you're missing a croquet player today."

"True. We'll have to play without Dominic."

"You're expecting him back soon?" Vincent knew something that I needed to know, I was certain. The man hosted a hotbed of secrets.

"Dominic is forever looking for a good time, and when he finds it, there's no telling how long he'll be at it." He turned serious. "Your opinion of me will change by the time you leave the Villa." He parted after a slow nod.

Vincent was wrong. My opinion of him had already changed, but not for the better. Maybe he was a really good actor, after all.

Chapter Twelve

I Saw Her Standing There

Fifteen minutes to croquet time and still no sign of Mom. I scoured the Villa and ended back in the lobby. The main building housed the lobby and the Ocean Vista dining hall, but it also had two legs kicking off to the sides to form an L-shape. Legs that housed the majority of residents. Bungalows scattered over the rest of the twelve-acre property. The main garden branched out into a putting green, croquet lawn, rose and meditation garden. At least that's what the grounds map behind the reception area wall told me. How was I supposed to find Mom? She could be anywhere.

"There you are," Mom whispered behind me.

I whipped around. "We've got work to do."

Lettie flitted by. "Your quarters are nearly ready," she told Mom.

"Super, thanks!" Mom gave her a finger wave.

"Seniors don't say super," I whispered.

"They don't?"

"Old folks are impatient, rough around the edges, and get straight to the point."

"Right," she said. "They speak their minds."

"Shouldn't be too much of a stretch," I mumbled.

She lowered her voice, "Why were you talking to Vincent?"

"You saw me?" Where was she?

"I'm always watching you."

That was kind of scary. Did she mean *always* like whenever I was with her? Or even when I wasn't? That could explain why I had this nagging sense of being followed.

"Leave Vincent to me, okay?" Mom straightened. "I've got his number." She glanced around while she talked. "He's a poet, a lover of old books, and a wine connoisseur, meaning he's got brains, which I'm busy picking to see what's hiding inside."

"You think he's hiding something?" I said.

"I didn't say that. But if he is, I'm going to find out what it is." She headed out the entry and onto the sunny lawn. I jogged after her.

She waved an arm toward the peacock blue sea. "This is the reason why I jumped at the chance to visit Santa Barbara."

"Not to help me?" I asked.

"Oh, sweetie, you're my main reason for everything, but Santa Barbara came in a close second. Who can resist the heady floral scents, the stunning sunsets, the healthy lifestyle?" She hugged me. "I'd gladly leave behind L.A.'s airports, high-rise buildings, and flashy billboards for this peaceful pearl in my California oyster."

I couldn't disagree. "Except that they roll up the sidewalks here after nine p.m."

"Just in time for my beauty sleep." She leaned her head toward mine. "Should we take a walk on the beach?"

"You have an appointment in ten minutes."

"What kind of appointment?" She patted her wig. "Because no one can touch my hair or the cat's out of the bag."

"What do you know about croquet?"

"Is that anything like croquettes? Because I make a zucchini croquette with sun-dried tomatoes to die for."

"Mom."

"I don't play old people's sports, because I'm not old."

Mom was cracking up. Maybe this was too much for her.

"Did you pack anything white?" White was the color to wear while playing

64

croquet. That much even I knew.

"I don't wear white," she said. "I need color and prints to give my fashion life meaning."

"Do you know anything about croquet?" I gritted my teeth.

"You use a mallet…"

At least she got that part right.

"…to hit a ball through the wicket. Every time you get the ball through, your playtime extends."

I'd underestimated her knowledge base. "How did you know that?"

"I had a client who dressed to win when she played. I selected her attire and watched her play to win every single time. It was no coincidence that she was the David Beckham of croquet. Wearing the right outfit gives a woman confidence." Mom gave a thumbs up. "By the way, the player who rolls the ball through six wickets in a row and again in reverse wins the match."

"Wow." I nearly reeled from amazement. It's like I never really knew the woman I called Mom.

"If you're really good," she said. "Your turn lasts a long time. Like billiards, which I'm also good at. And—"

"I get it. You're a power player. But playing isn't as important as cavorting with the *in* crowd," I said. "Dominic was one of their team members, and we need to know what they know about his disappearance."

"I'll charm their support socks off."

* * *

Mom, Veera, and I arrived just as the players were pulling out their mallets. Mom managed to slip into an extra pair of black sneakers I kept in the car, which matched her leopard print dress nicely.

Sofi bent over a shiny red ball and swung her mallet back and forth behind it.

"You'd think we were watching Tiger Woods at the Masters," Mom whispered.

Vincent strolled up, as did Peter Cronkite, the man carted away by paramedics a short time ago.

"I had a miraculous recovery," he explained with a high-pitched laugh that ended on a trembling note. "They shot a needle in my arm and I bolted upright." He patted his chest. "I feel twenty years younger."

"Was it a shot of tequila in your arm?" Sofi asked.

"Very funny." He walked away. "I forgot something important. I can't play without it."

"Probably his lucky shark's tooth." Sofi's gaze switched to me, then to Mom. "You're here. Lucy Fay, a pleasure to make your…" Her words got lost as she stared long and hard at Mom. "By golly, the wonders of plastic surgery are astonishing."

"I don't look a day past forty-five, right?" Mom smiled.

"I was going to say thirty-five."

Mom turned to me. "I'm going to love this woman." She refocused on Sofi. "You don't look so bad yourself."

Sofi took Mom and introduced her to the rest of the team.

After a few minutes, they joked around like old chums. Mom made friends instantly. Which made me question why she hadn't dated after Dad? Or had she? They'd divorced nearly fifteen years ago and he'd been gone a year.

My gaze drifted to Vincent. His piercing blue gaze was glued on Mom. The man was smitten. I strolled over to them, Veera at my side. Mom examined her mallet.

"See," Mom said. "No one's wearing white."

"If we did, we'd either be headed for the altar or an ice cream parlor." Lil showed up in another church hat, an ivory number with a tall, flared crown and black ribbon trim that matched her polka dot midi dress. Her leather shoes were white golf wear with black patent leather toe and heel caps. "I'll take ice cream over matrimony every time."

"You'd look lovely in any color," Vincent was telling Mom.

"Thank you." Mom batted her lashes and blushed.

"Oh brother," I muttered.

Veera leaned closer to me. "Be cool, now. I got something I need to do. Is it safe to leave you alone for a few minutes?"

"I'm beginning to think you have trust issues with me," I said.

"I only have trust issues with people who sneak around for no good reason." Veera eyed a guy hurrying along the perimeter of the lawn and shrubbery. It was Trent, the activities director. "He's ripe for questioning." Veera scooted off.

Trent had emerged from behind a snack shack serving mozzarella sticks, popcorn, and deviled eggs. The menu was printed outside on a portable whiteboard. Peter shuffled back, carrying a ceramic pitcher with both hands. I intercepted him before he reached the others.

"What'll everyone be drinking?" I asked.

He gave me a quick once-over. "A grown-up beverage for which you'd need to present an official identification before partaking."

I clicked my tongue. How rude. I looked every bit my twenty-six years. Probably been so long since he'd chatted with anyone my age, he'd forgotten what twenty-somethings looked like. Peter set the pitcher down on a glass-topped table and ambled toward the others. I slid to the table and sniffed the pitcher.

"There are twenty ounces of tequila in that margarita pitcher." Peter faced me. "Now go away so we can have some fun." He shooed me off like I was a fly trying to dip into his drink. I marched over to Mom.

"Nana."

Vincent was showing her his moves as he bent over a blue ball and aimed for a wicket.

"Nan," I said louder.

Vince's shot veered sideways and he tossed me an irritated glance.

"Honey, we're busy." Mom slid over to me. "Why don't you disappear into the lengthening shadows?" she whispered. "Reappear if something's amiss."

"What does that even mean?" I asked.

"Later, sweetie." She waved me off and cozied up to Vincent.

His ball had rolled down a gentle slope and landed about fifteen feet away. Peter scuttled over, dropped to his knees and tried to blow the shiny orb back up. Had he lost his marbles? The players erupted in laughter. I backed into a grove of lemon trees while the players clustered together. They'd barely started drinking and they were already going wild. I sank deeper into the grove and watched.

They returned to play as Vincent hacked the ball over a small log, where it landed on soggy grass. Then he pounded the side of the ball with his fist instead of the mallet. It landed close to the hoop.

"Cheating is not only encouraged." Peter sipped from a large glass. "It's mandatory."

They burst out in giggles. Lil kicked her ball through a wicket earning her a hearty round of applause. Sofi duffed her shot and almost hit a cat wandering the grounds.

"One shot penalty." Peter took another sip.

"What for?" Sofi stomped her foot.

"Nearly harming wildlife," Peter replied.

"That cat's domesticated," Sofi said.

And they went on like this for the next twenty minutes. Mom was the only one who actually seemed to make the target without acting ridiculous, although she did wield her mallet like a pool cue a couple of times. My cell phone rang. It was Michael.

"Did you find Dom yet?" he asked.

"No, but Nana's feeling right at home." I looked around for unwanted ears. "Talk to me. Why would Dom refrigerate contact lenses?"

"I can only think of one reason. That cool, refreshing, tingly feeling when he pops them into his tired old eyes first thing in the morning."

"Seriously?"

"No. Contacts actually do better at room temperature. Does he have a rare eye condition?"

"No idea." I texted Holly. "There has to be another reason." Which could be the key ingredient to solving his disappearance.

"I'll research some more," he said. "What's all that yelling?"

"They're playing croquet."

Peter was about to hit a pine cone through a wicket. Mom was chuckling right alongside the rest of them.

"Why don't they act their age?" I muttered. A twig snapped behind me. "Gotta go." I disconnected and whipped around, shuriken in hand.

"It's me, your able-bodied legal assistant and future business partner." Veera peered around a lemon tree.

"Don't ever—"

"I know." Veera scooted closer. "I wasn't thinking straight. I was all excited 'cause I got Trent to fess up."

"Which seniors refused to participate in the Villa games?" I asked.

"You're looking at nearly all of them right now. Sofi, Vincent, Dominic when he's around, Lil, Peter, and someone named William Merriweather. They call themselves the R.A.T. pack."

"How original," I said. "Which one's Dean?"

"Not that rat pack. This R.A.T. is an acronym," Veera said. "Retired and Tough. Trent said they're always trying to prove themselves."

Holly texted me back: *Dominic doesn't have an eye condition. He has beautiful eyes, the deep blue color of the ocean when it's calm.*

"Oh, brother."

A tall, slim senior with wintry gray hair and a high forehead screeched to a stop in a customized golf cart, nearly plowing down Lil. She cussed him out, slammed her mallet against the cart, and threw him the evil eye. The cart resembled a '57 Chevy complete with chrome rims, striped seat, and a fat pair of felt dice hanging from a windshield. He hopped out, mallet in hand. Thick, expressive brows matched his hair. He struck a shiny yellow ball so hard, it pounded against Peter's Gucci loafers. The ball bounced off the rubber sole and rolled away, stopping after Sofi smacked her white sneaker on top of it.

"Bulls-eye!" the tall man yelped.

"William, you could've hit me in a sensitive area and then I'd be very angry," Peter said. "You wouldn't like me to be angry."

"Poppycock," William said in a deep, creaky voice. "You play divinely when you're angry." He skipped over to Sofi and knelt to collect the ball lodged beneath her sneaker. He fingered the ball, but it remained firm.

"I thought this game was more subdued," I whispered.

"They're playing combat croquet," Veera whispered back. "My gran lives for mallet-to-mallet combat. She says it's a cheater's sport that's good for your health. A real stress reliever."

Sounded like something I should try. "Two things: first, croquet isn't a real sport. Second, it's not healthy when they're downing margarita after margarita. Mom will need a breathalyzer test when this is over."

"I've been watching our Nana, and she hasn't had anything to drink," Veera said. "She's on the job. I'm telling you we should hire her."

"We're not hiring anyone." Why was Mom bugging me more than usual? *Because you're afraid for her safety.*

Dad's voice drifted through my mind when I was stressed, like right now. Was I worried about Mom?

"Gran's team makes their own mallets out of PVC pipes. You lose a shot if you don't speak with a British accent. Worse accents you ever heard. They sure have fun."

I knew what the problem was. I wasn't having fun because I couldn't solve a case and Mom-sit at the same time. "I thought seniors sat around all day knitting and playing cards."

"Not these seniors."

Vincent's ball ricocheted off a nearby bench and missed Sofi's leg by a hair. She pulled back in the nick of time.

"I've had enough." I took a step forward just as Veera held me back.

"Wait for it…"

"Play it from there," Peter told Vincent. "Let's see how skilled you really are. Fraidy cat."

"I refuse to be goaded into playing poorly." Vincent hiccupped and hurried toward the main building.

"Cry baby," Peter said. "My turn." He picked up his mallet and continued playing.

"They'll be tuckered out soon," Veera whispered.

The game wound down as a narrow bank of clouds fanned out over the lingering sun.

"Let's go. Maybe Mom's room is ready." I'd drop off her luggage and pay

Dom's apartment a more leisurely visit without Holly hovering nearby. I had a strong hunch I'd find a clue in there.

Chapter Thirteen

(I Can't Get No) Satisfaction

"We're looking for Lettie," I told the receptionist.

He pointed us toward a short hallway off to one side of the reception desk. "Executive offices."

"That's where I found Holly after we first arrived," Veera whispered.

We knocked and when no one answered, I took the unlocked door as an open invitation. We welcomed ourselves inside.

"It's like stepping into a time machine," Veera said.

The office seemed as out of place as a rusty nail in a fine jewelry display case. Bare minimum furnishings were holdovers from the seventies. The window pointed toward the driveway. Personal effects, photos, and folders scattered across the desktops. The only other door was marked *Director, Leticia Ospina.*

"Maybe everyone's done for the day," Veera said.

"Everyone, but Lettie." The squeaking of desk chair wheels confirmed someone occupied her office. Someone who could step out any moment. I locked the entry and zipped next to Veera. "Get inside and keep Lettie busy. I need to search the filing cabinet." The tall metal cabinet rested between Lettie's office door and the window. "Close the door once you're inside."

"She'll be my prisoner until you give me a signal."

I gave her a thumbs up and hid behind the filing cabinet. Veera rapped on the door. Steps padded and it creaked open.

"What are you doing here?" Lettie asked.

"Door was unlocked so I thought I'd check in," Veera said. "Is Nana's room ready? She'll need to bathe after playing croquet, and change into her supper wear."

Veera tapped her inner trust fund child.

"Come in. I'll call housekeeping," Lettie said.

Footsteps pattered into Lettie's office and the door creaked, but before it closed, Lettie spoke,

"Leave it open."

"I've got something to say privately," Veera said. "Can't take a chance on anyone listening." The door clicked shut.

In seconds, I combed through the files, noting that Lil, Peter, and William were behind in rent a month or so. Were they going to be evicted? Sofi and Vincent were current, but they were newer arrivals. No trace of Dom's file. I closed the drawer and headed for Holly's desk. I rummaged through the trash receptacle until Lettie's voice drifted my way.

"Stand aside," she said.

"There's one more thing I gotta tell you," Veera said.

I rapped on the door and Veera opened it.

"I was just going to say you'd be here any minute," Veera said to me.

I entered a cluttered office with similar furnishings. Lettie's window was open and the blinds pulled all the way up. The scent of roses wafted in from the outside courtyard.

"I see no indication of your grandmother's health issues in her folder," Lettie told me. "She'll need a complete evaluation."

"Like I said." Veera turned to face her. "Nan's private when it comes to personal matters. How do we know one of your employees won't spread the word about her...problem?" Veera looked at me and whispered, "Told her Nana gets gassy if she eats too many Cheezee-Weezees. I requested an air purifier for her room."

"We have seniors with similar issues," Lettie said. "They use activated charcoal. I can send some up."

"That would be helpful, thank you," I said. "Also, Nana gets confused sometimes about payments. What happens if she misses a month's rent?"

"Why would you ask that?" Lettie opened a folder on her desk and removed a chart. "She's paid upfront for six months."

"Lordy," Veera mumbled and spoke louder. "She's on it."

"Is that how most residents pay?" I asked. "I don't want her to be taken advantage of."

Lettie's gaze nearly scorched my brows. "Residents have choices. She chose to pay upfront." Lettie stared at her cell phone. "Her room is ready. I'll contact the valet to take Lucy Fay's bags up."

"Oh, no need." I waved toward Veera. "My sister and I will get her luggage." Wait a minute. Would trust fund grandkids carry their own bags? No. But I didn't need eyes in my trunk with all I had stored inside. "We don't usually bring up our own bags, but..."

"Nan doesn't allow just anyone touching her personal belongings. She's only got a few pieces, anyhow," Veera said. "The rest arrive later."

"I'll take you up as soon as I'm free," Lettie said.

Most of the surface area was littered with papers so it looked like she was a permanent prisoner.

"Nan would like her room now," I said.

Lettie's steely gaze swung from Veera to me and she rose. "Wait outside."

We obliged and stepped out into the admin office, took another quick look, and moseyed out into the hallway, shutting the office door behind us.

I told Veera about the late rent and Dom's missing file.

"Maybe being behind is the norm around here," Veera said. "Lettie must have Dom's file 'cause he's M.I.A."

"I'll need to get into his apartment again." I updated her about my rushed tour. "But I won't tell Holly."

"Good thinkin'. That way she won't get into trouble."

And she wouldn't witness my search and seizure skills.

The door opened and we met Lettie's marbleized stare. "Holly's still occupied. One of our security guards will accompany you."

"Nana doesn't want anyone in her place, but us," I said. "She's a germaphobe."

Veera gave me a nod. "That's right."

"But *you* have her stamp of approval," I told Lettie. "You can escort us." I figured she wouldn't come, so we'd be on our own. These wealthy seniors had to be somewhat eccentric and demanding, so Lucy Fay's needs were probably reasonable.

Lettie's gaze narrowed. "Wait here." She retreated into the office and shut the door again.

"What do you think she's doing now?" Veera asked.

I stuck my ear to the door. "Talking to someone, but I can't make out the words."

Minutes ticked by while Veera and I leaned against the wall, facing the lobby. We watched seniors chit chat, play checkers, and trickle into the Ocean Vista for dinner. The office door opened and Lettie stuck out her head.

"Take the bags to the Golden Lotus Wing, second floor, room 220. Housekeeping will meet you by the elevator with a key."

We were finally getting somewhere.

* * *

We raced to the valet, hopped in the car, and motored to self-parking. I parked toward the back, popped open the trunk and we grabbed our bags. We hightailed it to the apartments, pausing only long enough to check on Mom. The R.A.T. pack dawdled on a bench under a shady tree, Mom included. Their elderly necks stretched toward the center, like turtles vying for a ray of sunlight. They spoke in low tones.

"What the heck are they talking about?" I asked.

"They're giving Lucy Fay the lowdown on staff and other residents," Veera said. "You know, like who to watch out for, who throws the best parties."

"How do you know?" Sounded logical to me.

"They may look like seniors, but down inside they're juvenile delinquents who've aged at high-speed thanks to turning civilized games into combat zones."

"And I served my mother to them on a silver tray."

Veera chuckled. "She's having as much fun as the rest of them." Veera's grin scattered my worries away. "Finding ways to have fun gives their lives a purpose."

Since when did Veera grow so wise? They did seem to be enjoying themselves. I picked up the luggage. "Let's go to Lucy Fay's apartment."

* * *

Veera and I hauled Mom's luggage and our own to the second floor of the Golden Lotus Wing. We dropped them near the doorway and waited for housekeeping in a wide corridor hosting pale yellow walls and carpeting with a burgundy swirl design. Hand-painted garlands topped the door frames. Jasmine scented the corridor, but something overpowered the gentle scent. Something green...as in the smell of money. Loads of it.

"Think we'll end up in a place like this?" Veera asked.

"Only if we can play combat bingo."

"We'd better start practicing." Veera looked around. "Seems like housekeeping should've been here by now."

I snapped my head toward Lucy Fay's front door. A faint tapping from inside the room demanded my attention.

"Maybe housekeeping's waiting inside." I knocked lightly. I'd barely finished the last tap when Holly cracked it open. She peered down the hall before waving us in. We scurried inside and she closed the door, securing the deadbolt.

"We're here with Nana's bags," Veera said. "Why the secrecy?"

"I'm genuinely impressed with how you managed to blend into the Villa without anyone knowing the real reason behind your visit." Holly's gaze seesawed between Veera and I. "I don't know how you did it, but I'm confident you'll find Dominic. Except, how did the older lady with you get on our list? She's been expected for months."

"That's confidential," I said.

"We've got everything under control." Veera's eyes widened and she turned her back to Holly. She whispered to me, "That can be our motto. We keep everything under control so you don't have to."

I gave her a thumbs up and she whirled back toward Holly.

"The Villa might wanna think about retaining us as legal investigators," Veera said. "We could assess your security needs."

"That would be wonderful. But there's something else." Holly's fingers fidgeted with the edges of her beige cardigan. "I may be in trouble."

"Trouble?" She was on edge about more than just Dom.

Her gaze darted around. "It's Kyle, night security." Her hands shot to her head. "Everywhere I go, he's there, watching. He might be the one behind Dominic's disappearance and he knows I suspect him."

"We'll look into it." Maybe Lettie had asked him to keep an eye on Holly, if she was acting extra fidgety lately.

"He's not tailing us." Veera turned to me. "Right?"

Kyle had been hovering near the stairs when we entered the elevator. Maybe I should take a closer look.

"Haven't seen him. But I'll be right back," I said. "I left Nan's favorite sweater in the car."

"I'll come too. I need some air," Veera said. "Do we get a key?"

Holly handed her two brass keys. "I know they're old-fashioned, but we pride ourselves on living simply."

"Why does Dom keep cheap bottled water in his fridge?" I asked.

"Maybe to drink?" She made no attempt to hide her eye roll.

"He has a water filter in his sink and on the fridge door," I said. "Some of the bottles in his fridge aren't water worth drinking for a man of such refinement."

"Probably his emergency supply."

Three bottles were hardly enough for an emergency.

"He stores canned goods for that reason, too." Holly turned toward the door.

"Why would he keep contact lenses in the fridge?" I asked.

"He doesn't wear them often." She turned the knob. "I suppose to keep bacteria away."

"Is that what Dom told you?" I asked.

"He didn't need to. I'm sure you'll have more questions in the morning." Holly trekked out the door.

"I'd call her a wannabe love interest who inserted herself into his life," Veera said. "She wants a relationship and he doesn't. And that explains his absence."

"Why, Veera...you've become quite the student of human nature."

"Got to in our line of work."

We slipped into cashmere sweaters, jeans and flats and hit the hallway. All was quiet except for the ding of the elevator door. An older man stepped out and shuffled in the opposite direction. The moment his apartment door shut we edged down the corridor.

I whispered to Veera, "Let's split up." We'd cover more ground that way. "Find Mom. Take her to her room and wait for me there."

"Where are you off to?" she whispered back.

"To pay Dom another visit."

"What about Kyle?"

"What are the odds he's following us? And if he is, I'll handle him."

"Which part of him are you going to handle? 'Cause he's like two short guys who melded together to form one big guy. He'll crush you with one of his four thumbs if he's mad enough."

"He's probably a gentle giant inside." He reminded me of a lion with a thorn in its paw. Remove the thorn and he'd be your pal for life. Did I want to get close enough to find the thorn? Nope.

"How about we find him together?" Veera said, "Then I'll distract him while you go about your business."

"Define distract," I said.

"I'll ask questions on behalf of Nan, like is there a curfew, are kids allowed upstairs, can she entertain gentleman friends in her room? Then I'll convince him to secure the place before I bring Nana up."

"Deal." Veera continued to impress me. We reached the end of the hall and I flipped a U-ey. "If he followed Holly, it means he's close by." I needed to explore all angles. "Where would he be right now?" I looked over my shoulder at a door marked housekeeping. It was slightly ajar. I inched closer.

"I'm glad Nana's living here," I said and yanked open the door.

A woman in a white housekeeping uniform folded hand towels. Her body jerked back when she saw me.

"Smells clean," I said. "Keep up the good work." I closed the door.

"At least we know where he's not," Veera said.

Moments later, we concluded a visual sweep of the hallways and all maintenance rooms. I headed to the adjacent building while Veera took off to fetch Mom. Time for my little detour.

Chapter Fourteen

Strangers In The Night

I quick-stepped behind the main Villa building. Residents had either retired for the night, were chomping down dinner or preparing to dine at a leisurely pace. And the R.A.T. pack? They were likely plotting on how to turn dinner into a food fight. Good thing Mom wore a wig.

Just past the maintenance room, a door cracked open enough for me to stick my head inside. Eight monitors displayed sections of the Villa in glorious black and white. A uniformed security guard reclined in a chair, gaze fixed on a different screen, the one on his smartphone. I rapped on the door and he jumped to his feet. I pushed the door open wider. His pale face was flushed, his brows bushy and his wispy hair slicked back.

"You lost?" he asked.

"I'm looking for the Silver Lining Wing. My grandma moved into the Golden Lotus Wing and I'd like to visit the other one. To make sure she made the right choice." I scanned the room. "I work while she has all the fun."

A small smile rocked his thin lips and his shoulders relaxed. I doubted whether anyone ever checked up on him.

"Follow the red brick path to the double doors, midway on your right. If you reach the beach, you went too far." He snickered at his cleverness.

I grinned. "Thanks."

He plopped back in the chair, leaning forward to watch the security monitors. That would last all of three minutes before he distracted himself again.

Minutes later, I hopped out of the second-floor elevator of the Silver Lining Wing. The lobby hosted minty green walls that cheered me down the hallway. As I rounded the corner, the elevator pinged and swished open. I picked up speed. Where to hide? Had to be fifty feet to the nearest stairwell. I slowed and casually walked back toward the elevator, sneaking a peek around the corner. Kyle loomed large, his back to me. So much for Veera keeping him busy. Had the other guard alerted him?

Kyle's head flicked to the right and I pulled back. He must have spotted me from his peripheral vision. His phone played a tune and I inched my head out as he pressed his cell phone to his ear.

"Yeah?" He went quiet for a beat. "Be right there."

He disappeared into the elevator. How could he have missed me? Maybe he saw me and didn't care.

I flipped around and flitted past closed doors back to Dom's room. If everything went according to plan, I'd buzz in and out without being seen. The lock looked a little different than the one in Lucy Fay's door. I dug around inside my shoulder bag and unzipped a pocket. I pulled out a small drawstring sack. I'd inherited Dad's tools, too, one of which was perfect for this job and should open up the door on the first try. I cradled an Allen wrench, a small L-shaped piece of metal, along with a sturdy piece of wire bent to a ninety-degree angle at one end. I inserted the wrench in the keyhole and wiggled it around. Where was the lever?

"Come on," I whispered.

The door behind me chirred open and I caught my breath. I pinned my knuckles to Dom's door and slipped the tools beneath my sweater. I glanced over my shoulder.

A woman in a purple chenille robe and old school curlers stood in the doorway across from Dom's. The rims of her eyeglasses matched the robe.

"Is he back?" My heart pounded.

"From where?" she asked.

I walked right into that one. "Dinner." That was the best I could do.

"I already ate." She threw her hand at me. "Spaghetti and meatballs. You hungry?"

"No, thank you." How to get rid of her?

"Good. Because I polished off all the leftovers." She retreated into her room and closed the door.

Was she spying on me out of her peephole? I ripped a piece of duct tape from the travel-size roll in my purse and taped it to her hole. I waited a minute before turning back to the doorknob.

Working the lock required both hands. I wiggled the wrench around, pushed up the lever, and held it in place while sticking the sturdy wire behind it. The two pieces of metal would act just like a skeleton key. Twisting the wire clockwise, the deadbolt clicked and slid back. I pushed open the door and tumbled inside. Sticking my purse between the door and the frame, I darted back to the room across from Dom's and tore off the tape. The coast was clear.

Chapter Fifteen

Catch A Falling Star

Veera texted me just as I slipped off my shoes and pulled on my gloves.

No sign of Kyle, but Nana and I are back in the apartment. You okay?

I texted her back:

I'm inside. See you in ten minutes.

I rested my back against the living room wall and admired the rich upholstery and the plush furnishings. This was one prime unit. Michael had said the waiting list to move into the Villa was long. What if someone got rid of Dom to get a suite like this one? Far-fetched, but if it was a senior who lived their life like they played croquet...

I made a beeline for the desk and pulled out my penlight. A diamond-shaped glass holding amber liquid tilted at a fifty-degree angle on the desktop. Designed to prevent spills, it was the perfect drinking glass for the individual who counted on getting tipsy. I rifled through the drawers. Holly was right. A leather wallet, complete with a driver's license, Triple-A membership, and credit cards were left behind. Why?

"Because he expected to be back soon." I drummed my fingers against the desktop. "Or didn't want to be caught with real I.D." That sounded familiar.

Faded newspapers populated the bottom drawer along with an old-school cocktail recipe book, but another stack was parked beneath. Overdue bills. Dom was in debt, like most of his pack. He didn't take the wallet because he was maxed out on his credit cards. How did he afford to live like a prince? Or at least a duke. Did Holly know? Did he skip out so he wouldn't have to pay?

I headed for the bathroom. You could tell a lot about a man by the items he kept in his bathroom.

"Oooh, la, la." I devoted a few moments to savor the heated floors in my bare feet before rummaging through drawers. I unearthed an old-school shaving kit and enough floss to maintain all the passengers aboard a cruise ship. A black cabinet shaped like a large pillar sat on his dresser. I pulled it open to view cigars with bright yellow and orange bands.

Padding back to the kitchen, I snooped around chef-quality appliances and paused by the pantry. It was packed with cans of soup and dried goods. His emergency supply included only the three water bottles. The bottles just didn't fit.

My hand was nearly on the front doorknob when I retraced my steps a few feet back. A powder room sat on my right and a closet door appeared to the left of the entry. Nothing worth mentioning in the bathroom, but the hall closet got me thinking. A black leather jacket hung inside. The supple Italian leather jacket hosted zip pockets inside and out. Translation: lots of hiding places. I searched the pockets, but all I found were old receipts and handkerchiefs.

Golf clubs leaned against the wall, but another item didn't fit. Why would a man who displayed luxury items everywhere store an old used vacuum in the closet? Especially when housekeeping took care of cleaning. The vintage, canister-style vacuum monopolized the floor space. Did it hold a fond memory? Maybe his mother had been a cleaning lady. I slipped into my shoes, shut the door behind me and wound my way back to Mom and Veera.

* * *

"Lil won the lottery, packed her bags, and moved to the Villa," Mom said.

Mom hung around the croquet crew long enough to get the financial and fashion run-down on each resident. Not a bad play. Sofi had plowed through four husbands in twenty-two years and preferred small boutique clothing. Peter favored tailored, monogrammed clothes, down to his skivvies. William owned a perfume factory on the west coast, and Vincent was quite the charmer, which was old news.

"What about Dom?" Veera asked. "Did he pop-up in conversation?"

"No one cares that he's gone," Mom said.

"Because everyone's expecting him to return," I said. "Including him." I pictured the drink on his desk and the fridge packed with goodies.

"Besides having one of the best buffets in possibly all of Southern California, the Villa serves fresh baked cookies and milk every night. How dreamy is that?" Mom pulled open the curtains and the window. A melodic baritone voice drifted in singing a romantic tune.

"Comfort food, that's what it is. Chocolate chip macadamia nut cookies dunked in milk equals pure comfort." Veera reached into a pocket and extracted a cookie wrapped inside a napkin. She handed it to me. "Soft and thick."

I bit into sugary sweetness. Glad there was only one, 'cause I could've polished off six or twenty.

"Little Ricky ran into Dominic every day, including the morning he left," Mom said. "Ricky's a morning server who stuck around tonight to serve the cookies."

"So he could eat them, too," Veera said.

Why didn't Holly mention Ricky? I swallowed the last of the cookie. "Did he confirm that Dom was headed for the Village?"

Mom leaned in closer. "Yes, to visit his favorite bar, the Villagers' Pub. The place serves old-fashioned cocktails, just the way Dominic likes them. Little Ricky said Dominic wasn't himself that morning."

"What does that mean?" I asked.

"Dominic was someone else."

"Did Little Ricky dip his cookies in a whisky glass?" I asked.

"It means Dominic wore a disguise. A hat and sunglasses," Mom said.

"He's hiding out," Veera said.

"Hardly a disguise. And even if it were, how did Ricky recognize Dom?" Was I ever going to get a solid clue?

"Little Ricky cracked a joke about men's shoes," Mom said. "And Dominic laughed."

"And how's that a giveaway?" My mental eye rolls were on spin cycle.

"Dominic's nose crinkles and his glasses nudge up his nose when he laughs," Mom said. "According to Little Ricky."

No wonder Holly didn't bother mentioning that. "We need something more."

"Listen to this. Ricky and Dominic chatted every morning, but on that day, Dominic sped past without a word. And he was carrying a bag."

"What kind of bag?" I asked.

"Recyclable cloth bag," Mom replied. "Like for grocery shopping, only it wasn't empty."

"Because it was filled with..." I might as well have tried to extract an eyelash from an ostrich.

"Bulky stuff," Mom said.

"You find anything?" Veera turned my way.

Like me, she was ready to move on. I told them about Dom's room and the ancient vacuum.

"It's a family heirloom," Mom said. "Or he's holding on to it because they don't make vacuums like they used to."

"Or it has another purpose," I said.

"Gran sucks up ants in the house using her vacuum. She empties the bag outside to set them free."

"No bugs in Dom's apartment." I paced the floor. "The canister can double as storage if the vacuum isn't operational." I mentally slapped myself. I should've considered that earlier.

"Don't tell me you're going back," Veera said.

"Okay, it'll be my little secret."

"We'll stand guard by the elevator," Mom said. "No one will get past us."

"Good thinking," Veera said.

Mom and Veera exchanged a fist bump.

"Let's dress for dinner first." We'd attract less attention and look like we had somewhere to be. "Then we'll take our detour."

"I'm meeting the gang at seven-thirty." Mom folded her arms against her chest. It was inquisition time. "How did you get into Dominic's apartment?"

"We met Holly there," Veera said.

"She let you in?" Mom asked. "She'll get in trouble if she's caught."

Not as much trouble as I'd get in if I was caught. I moved toward my duffel bag. "I'll handle her. Ten minutes to showtime."

* * *

Mom and Veera guarded the elevator while I darted back to Dom's room. Mom had slipped into a baby blue knitted midi dress with puffy feathered cuffs that looked like it belonged in *Downton Abbey.* Veera wore a sleek black sheath dress that hugged her curves, and I'd opted for a peach-hued wraparound dress. I paused by the suite next door to Dom's. Music seeped out beneath the door. Perry Como crooned, "Catch a Falling Star." My parents loved vintage movies, vintage tunes, and vintage furniture, so I knew my way around all three.

I slipped back into the suite, more quickly this time. Locking the door behind me, I reached for the closet and knelt on the floor. I slid my hands into a pair of vinyl gloves and rolled out the vacuum. The back popped open with a push of a button. Dust from the ages collected around the bag's exterior, but the inside told a different story. It was clean. I was about to replace it when a soft crackling near the bottom stopped me. I slit the bottom open with a penknife and wrapped my fingers around a squarish box. Stowed inside was a pack of playing cards. I turned the bag upside down and shook a pair of dice loose. I zipped open a pocket in my purse and deposited my discovery. Less than a minute later, I aimed toward the elevator. Voices drifted my way. Mom was talking to someone? Who?

Chapter Sixteen

Your Cheatin' Heart

"Y ou haven't properly explained what you're doing here. Or where you bought that impossibly simple yet impactful dress."

Sofi grilled Mom and Veera like they were hotdogs over an open fire pit. I hovered in the background debating my next move.

"What am *I* doing here?" Mom asked. "Right back at you, honey. My dress is from…"

Don't say Saks! Mom's the one who worked in retail for decades, not Lucy Fay. Don't say Saks!

"…a little boutique in Palm Desert. Didn't you say your suite was on this floor somewhere?"

"I didn't say," Sofi replied. "Residents don't take kindly to wanderers."

"Need I remind you that I am a resident?" Mom said.

"Didn't Dominic wander off?" Veera asked.

Not a bad move to include Dom in the conversation. Silence knocked us over the heads for a few beats.

"Are you referring to the fact that he didn't play with us today?" Sofi asked. "Because he'll probably join in the moment he returns."

"Where will that leave me?" Mom asked. "I had a blast playing today."

"Of course you did. After you beat us all so handily," Sofi said.

She did? That was news to me.

"I was just warming up." Mom rubbed her fingernails against her chest.

"A server said Dom wandered off and wouldn't be back for a while," Veera said.

Veera was on a roll. But the key to successful interrogation is to know when to switch tactics. Sofi wasn't interested in talking about Dom.

"Oh, he'll be back," Sofi said. "He's just cold-shouldering us because he's a sore loser."

My theories weren't holding water these days.

"Did Dom lose at croquet?" Mom asked.

"Not croquet. Dating. I rejected his advances and he vanished the next day," Sofi said.

Dom was a jilted suitor? That didn't match Holly's story. I stepped out into the foyer. "Hello. Thanks for letting Nana play today."

"Hello yourself," Sofi said. "What are you doing in this wing?"

I turned to Sofi. "We were out for a stroll and Nana heard a song..." I pitched my thumb over my shoulder and down the hallway, "...but she couldn't remember the name of the singer, so up we came, to get a better listen." I turned back to Mom. "Perry Como."

Mom placed a hand to her heart. "Well, the cat's out of the bag. I don't listen to music from my generation." Mom giggled and Sofi joined in half-heartedly, eyes narrowed.

"Can Nana play croquet or not?" Veera asked.

Sofi turned to Mom. "You'll play. We'll form teams and you'll be on mine. I don't like losing either."

"Stick with me, honey," Mom said. "You'll never lose."

I had to ask myself again, who was this woman? I turned to Sofi. "Is your apartment around here?"

"What if it is?"

Sofi ran hot and cold like a temperamental faucet. "I saw a mouse running loose near the stairwell. Thought you might want to know."

She held my gaze without blinking. Did anything faze her? Sofi refocused on Mom's blue dress.

"Aren't you warm in that?" she asked.

"I'm boiling over," Mom said.

"Let's get some air."

They strolled into the elevator. Mom looked at Veera and me. "Aren't you coming?"

"We're visiting the village tonight," I said.

The elevator door slid shut.

"Sofi's sly," Veera said. "She was trying to throw us off balance."

"Because she had her own plans for being here which you two must have interrupted."

"Think she was going to Dom's room?"

"I wouldn't put anything past the R.A.T pack."

"Are we really going to a village?" Veera asked.

"We'll poke around the lower Montecito village. The one Dominic was last seen walking toward. Maybe someone's seen him."

Montecito was a slice of Santa Barbara paradise off the beaten trail and a hideout for the very wealthy who lapped up the small-town feel.

"What about the vacuum?" Veera whispered. "Find anything?"

"I'll show you." I hurried toward the stairwell.

Minutes later, we sat in Lucy Fay's apartment. I examined the playing cards, while Veera rolled the black and white dice.

"Dom had a weakness for gambling and..." Veera said, "...the ladies."

"Maybe."

"Lots of seniors are hot for gambling. Gives them some excitement and busts up the loneliness. My gran used ice packs to relieve the pain and swelling from feeding the one-armed bandits in Vegas."

I grabbed the dice and rolled them. I held them up to a light. No sign of tampering. "The difference is your gran plays legitimately."

"You're saying Dominic's a cheater? That could get him into heaps of trouble."

"I need another pair of dice," I said.

"I'll make a call." Veera pushed buttons on her phone. "It's Monte Carlo Night every other Monday, according to Trent, which means the Villa should have what we need." She pressed the phone to her ear. "Veera Nightingale here. Can you send up a pack of playing cards and dice?" She punctuated the silence with a small grin that turned into a whopper of a smile. "Thanks! We'll be waiting." She disconnected. "This is better than a five-star hotel. Cards and dice are on their way."

The goods arrived before I'd finished shuffling Dom's cards. We pulled the curtains and dimmed the lights. I cradled Dom's pair of dice in one hand and the new arrivals in the other, while Veera examined the cards.

"What am I looking for?" she asked.

"Differences in the markings on the cards. Pay attention to patterns."

Veera shuffled through the cards, examined them front and back, and finally tossed them on the table. "I got nothing other than crossed eyes and the urge to yell, 'off with their heads.'"

I handed her the dice. "Are these different or the same?"

She cupped a pair in each hand and bounced them up and down. "The Dominic pair is heavier." She closed one eye and peered closely with the open eye. "But they're the same size."

"Dom baked his dice in the oven long enough to melt a small portion down to weigh them in his favor."

Veera sucked in her breath. "That legal?"

"If you're playing for fun, it is. Other players will get mad if they discover it, but that's a big if." Seniors wouldn't be paying close attention, so he probably got away with it. "Playing for money could get dicey, pardon the pun, if he got outted."

Veera passed the dice to me. "I figured weighing a little more or less wouldn't matter. See what you do? You make me think about stuff I'd never think about. You're making me productive. How come nobody figured out what Dom was doing?"

"He probably insisted on playing with his own lucky dice or he switched them when no one was looking."

"How about the card deck?" Veera asked.

We spent the next twenty minutes examining the details on the backs of the cards. I looked up at Veera. "These are cheater's cards."

Veera leaned toward me. "How do you know?"

"They have to be." If the dice weighed in his favor, odds favored marked cards. "We're assuming seniors at the Villa aren't sophisticated enough to suspect marked cards." An idea was bubbling in my head. "But if they played cards like they played croquet…"

"They're out for blood," Veera said. "Which explains why someone would want to trip up Dom's winning streak and threaten him enough to make him run off."

"We don't know who he's been playing with." Someone at the Villa or someone else? Chances are it's the R.A.T pack. But how to prove that? "We know he's in debt. I'd say he was on a losing streak."

"And he got his hands on a pack of trick cards and dice to turn that streak around."

I jumped to my feet. "The contact lenses." Not many older people wore them. Even Mom preferred glasses to contacts.

"What do contacts and trick cards have in common?" Veera asked.

"Marked cards need special glasses so only the cheater can decipher them." Sophisticated players are wise to special glasses. Contacts do the same thing and aren't as readily noticed." Especially by unsuspecting seniors. I grabbed Dom's cards and headed for the door. "Follow me."

Chapter Seventeen

I'm A Believer

Ten minutes later, an awestruck Veera steadied herself by gripping the back of a wingback chair in Dom's pad. I left her to oooh and awe over his digs while I rooted through his bedroom and bathroom for hidden compartments.

"Check out the heated floors," I said when she joined me.

Veera got on her hands and knees. "This is life-changing."

"No contact lens solution anywhere." Contacts needed saline solution. How did he keep them clean? "Come on." I hightailed it to the kitchen while I searched the internet on my smartphone. Veera trotted after me. I opened the refrigerator door, grabbed the lens case, and unscrewed the cap. Veera eyed the shelves.

"Everything gourmet and delicious," she said.

I lowered my nose to the open lens case and sniffed. "Does solution smell? Because this doesn't."

"Looks more like water." Veera peered closer.

I poured a few drops onto the back of my hand and licked it.

"Should you be doing that?" Veera wrinkled her nose. "No telling what it is."

"Since there's no lab handy, I'm doing my own chemical analysis," I said. "A fast one. It is water, which tells us a lot."

"My brain gets sluggish when I'm hungry," Veera said. "But even if I were full, you lost me."

"Notice the color of the lenses," I said.

"Blue like his eyes?" Veera said.

"They provide infrared vision to view the marked cards." I shut the fridge door. "Infrared lenses are stored in water." Tidbits from Dad's cases trickled into my head. "Let's see how they work."

I confiscated metal tweezers from Dom's bathroom and spread a couple of Dom's cards on his desk, face down. I picked up a lens with a tweezer, flattened it against a small dish on the table, then lifted it again.

"There's a penlight in my purse. Shine it through the lens and onto the card." I slowly moved the lens up, down, and across the card while Veera flashed the beam through the lens.

Veera puffed out a short stream of air. "Nine of… is that a diamond?"

I flipped the card around. "Bingo." I hovered the lens over a second card.

Veera shined the beam. "That cheater. Four of hearts. No wonder someone ran him off. People on the losing end aren't fans of people who cheat their way to a win."

I dropped the lens back in the case. "We have to find who he played with. That will tell us why he disappeared."

Veera rubbed her hands together. "Love the sweet smell of progress."

"I don't smell anything yet." I put the case back in the fridge and shifted gears. We headed for the entry. I held up my hand, opened the front door, and poked out my head. Nothing stirred the silence in the hallway. I shot out, Veera close behind. We didn't talk again until we hit the cool night air.

"The cheap-o bottled water was used to store the infrared contacts, right?" Veera said.

"Not unless my taste buds lied," I said, "The lenses were stored in high-end spring water."

"You tasted all that?" Veera asked.

"Of course I didn't." But my empty gut had plenty of room for hunches. "I've got a hunch the cheap water has some other purpose." Dom used a vacuum canister as a hidden compartment. What was up with the water?

CHAPTER SEVENTEEN

* * *

We took a detour to the trunk of my car where I'd stashed a burner cell phone. A not so smart, cheap, and disposable model, it provided a fourteen-day battery, which was ample time for Mom and us to wrap up this case. Since I was leaving the Villa for a while, I needed access to Mom.

She and her new pals lounged around the Ocean Vista dining hall feasting on grilled top sirloin with mashed potatoes and garlic butter. I pulled Mom aside and handed her the burner phone. "I don't like your being here without any means of communication. Only to be used in case of emergency. My number's programmed in there already. So is Veera's."

"It's about time. Now we can talk without you interrupting my delicate covert operations."

My stomach growled at the sight of all the delicious food.

"We picked the wrong end of undercover investigations," Veera said. "The meatloaf looks fit for a queen."

We dragged ourselves out of the dining hall and aimed for my car.

"Did I say I was hungry?" Veera asked. "'Cause now I'm feeling hollow inside."

"Your cheeks do look a little sunken in," I said. "Let's investigate the food situation in the Village." Specifically, the Villagers' Pub; the bar Little Ricky had mentioned as a regular hangout for Dom. Maybe somebody there could point us in the right direction.

Chapter Eighteen

Bad Moon Rising

The nearly mile-long stretch of Coast Village Road hosted a well-appointed downtown flanked by eucalyptus trees, upscale retail shops, and inviting eateries. The whole block smelled deliciously of fresh-cut flowers, baked bread, and coffee.

"What kind of villagers live here?" Veera asked.

"The well-heeled refugee from city life who refused to leave behind their taste for gourmet food and bespoke clothing."

"Does this mean we're gonna split dinner?" Veera asked. "Because I can't go halfsies tonight."

"That makes two of us. Don't worry, I checked out the menu at the Villagers' Pub. The prices are reasonable." For Santa Barbara pricing, anyway.

"Now we're talking." Veera settled back in her seat.

Ten minutes later, we'd angled behind a bar of another white stucco building in a Spanish Colonial style, and a popular watering hole in the posh enclave.

The bar ran in a half-circle, with patrons facing an open kitchen. Three booths hugged the walls of the compact space. Nimble servers in vests and ties maneuvered effortlessly in tight quarters. It was all shareable snacks and a laid-back vibe, as we ordered burgers and fries. A large flat-screen TV tilted downward and blared out the latest in local news.

The chef popped in and out of the kitchen to make sure every plate reflected perfection. When we polished off the burgers and devoured the crispy fries, I waved the bartender over.

"This was one of the best burgers ever," I said.

"One of the best? We'll have to try harder next time." She filled our water glasses.

"An old friend recommended this place," Veera said. "By old, I'm talking eighty years young and goin' strong."

"He's a big fan of old-school cocktails," I added. "He's got all the right dance moves, too."

"We have a few customers in that age bracket and class. But only one real dancer. Is he tall, slim, and smiley?" she asked. "Lives over at Villa Sunset?"

That was quick. Almost too good to be true. I nodded. Veera's beaming smile warmed our section of the pub.

"Dominic's one of our best customers," the bartender said.

Veera's eyes widened. "He is?"

"We thought he'd be here tonight." How could I encourage her tongue to wag some more?

"He was," she said. "Comes in like clockwork."

Veera and I locked gazes.

"We must've just missed him," I said.

"He's usually a day patron. We get him the Bloody Mary Kicker every morning."

"Maybe he went back to the Villa," Veera said.

The bartender leaned in. "Between you and me, I'm a little worried about him."

I leaned in, too. "So are we."

"Can you help him?" she asked.

"With his...problem?" I had to insert the right word or we'd fall flat.

"He's going to lose the shirt off his back one of these days." She picked up a pitcher.

"We were just talking about finding him help." Was she confirming that he had a gambling habit?

"Better hurry. He left over an hour ago for the casino. Hope you can get him out of there. He's a good guy." She slid away to refill a customer's martini glass.

"Now we know he's alive and drinkin'," Veera said. "And gambling, too."

"He probably spreads his gambling wings far and wide," I said.With what money was he gambling?

"Where's this casino?" Veera asked.

I searched the Internet on my smartphone. "There's a Valley Casino near Solvang about forty minutes north of here."

"That's why he hasn't returned to the Villa," Veera said. "These wild and wooly seniors are like out-of-control teenagers."

Would Mom get into trouble because of them?

"Good thing your mother can fend for herself," Veera said. "Should we head for the casino?"

I slapped two twenties on the counter and stood.

"Wait a minute." Veera grabbed my arm and pointed to the TV. Someone turned up the volume.

"Police didn't disclose the amount taken from Village Bank of Montecito, but Channel Two News has learned the robbery took place shortly before one p.m. today." The coiffed reporter gripped a mic while she stood in front of yet another white stucco, Spanish colonial-style building.

"That bank's just down the street," someone said.

"The bandit handed the teller a note and threatened her before fleeing on foot," the reporter continued. "Police searched the surrounding area, but the lone robber remains at large. He was described as a tall, bearded white male with brown hair in a ponytail. Last seen in dark sunglasses, wearing a jacket in camouflage print, khaki pants, and a Panama hat. It will take a village to find him and bring him to justice. Be on the lookout. Erin Miles for Channel Two News."

"Sounds like the dude wanted to be remembered." Veera stood next to me.

A theory floated through my head. A theory about why Dom carried a bag. I waved an arm toward the bartender. She hustled over moments later.

"What can I do for you?"

"We need a place to crash tonight that's walking distance and inexpensive," I said. "We don't want our boyfriends to find us. Know of any?"

"Heart of the Village Inn. Economical, clean, and off the beaten trail. It's across the street, tucked behind some shops, about half a block north." She scooted away.

Veera leaned back. "Is everything around here called Village something?"

"I've got a feeling we may find Dom at the Heart of the Village."

"The hotel next door would be more his style. Old school, luxurious and classy. Let's check that out, too."

"Too high profile. He flies under the radar." I could relate. That was my favorite mode of travel.

"What are you thinkin'?" Veera asked when we stepped outside the bar. A few people mulled around an outside table. A black cat crouched beneath a bench.

"That the bank robber and Dom may be one and the same."

Veera's gasp sent the cat scurrying up the street.

Chapter Nineteen

After The Thin Man

"**I**f he's anything like the other Villa residents," Veera said. "He's not hiding out in a cheap motel. Why wouldn't he just come back to his apartment?"

"For some reason, he can't." She made a good point. Criminals didn't usually lie low so close to the scene of a crime. They crossed several towns to rob a bank. But was Dom a criminal? Or acting out of need? Maybe he figured no one would look for him at the Heart of the Village Inn. Especially if he'd checked-in days before as the dapper gent he really was.

"If he's a thrill-seeker, he may find it exciting to be a fugitive."

She made another good point. "You're on a hot streak, Veera."

We hustled along the sidewalk beneath rows of elegant trees with striped bark; branches expertly pruned to reflect the surrounding refinement. We slowed to walk up the asphalt driveway of the Inn, a quaint motel ripe for a facelift, if the faded eaves and trim meant anything. Potholes punched out bits of the asphalt. The Inn had probably been around long before the rest of the other businesses had dropped anchor.

"You think Dom's hiding out here?" Veera asked.

"That's the burning question." How to find out without peeking into every room? If he'd checked in as himself and he'd been here before, the staff wouldn't regard him as a suspect. I needed to think this through. "Let's move on to the bank first."

"What about the casino?"

"He'll be there for a while," I said. "Seniors don't do anything quickly. Especially gambling."

"True story," Veera said.

The Village Bank of Montecito popped up near the end of the block. A parking lot hugged three sides of the small building and a miniature hill reigned behind it, dotted by mature trees and shrubs. Hedges bordered the hilltop. We took a self-guided tour of the exterior.

"The layout is perfect." No wonder the robber escaped.

"Can an eighty-year-old haul butt fast enough to elude the police?" Veera asked. "Somebody must've seen him climbing the hill, assuming that's where he went."

"Dom entered the bank and hid in the bathroom long enough for everyone to forget he came in. The bathroom's probably out of sight. Tellers' eyes are glued to the front or back entry. Robbers go straight for the money." I let my imagination run wild. "When he finally emerged, he's disguised. Dom kept his head down and targeted an open teller. He demanded cash and threatened to use a weapon."

We made our way to the back of the bank.

"Think he was carrying a gun?" Veera asked.

"No, but the threat's enough to make any teller quake. Dom grabbed the money and disappeared out the back."

"Where he climbed on top of a car hood, crossed onto the hill, and hid in the shrubs and trees above the parking spaces."

Veera was getting into the groove, too.

"I just thought of something. We could start a side biz checking out security holes in banks. I'm going to write this bank a letter." She pulled out her phone and tapped in a message.

I faced the small building. "No windows out this way. Dom discarded the disguise in a bag he left at the hilltop." Or dumped it somewhere else. Would he carry it off? I eyed the nearby businesses and settled my gaze on a liquor store. "I have an idea. Follow me."

I ran across the street toward a large neon sign for *Ye Olde Village Shop*

Liquors. The bones of a former gas station had withstood the transformation into a small liquor store. Like the bank, parking was abundant. Dom was a Village regular. He knew his way around, and the shops that he frequented knew him, just like the Villagers' Pub. This really was a small town.

"Let's take another look at Dom's photo."

Veera scrolled through her phone and showed me a shot of a pleasant-looking older gent smiling broadly. Feathery gray brows arched over twinkly blue eyes; his snow-white hair was thick and his complexion ruddy.

"Maybe the robbery had nothing to do with Dominic."

"It's our only lead and we're chasing it down." I paused at the shop's entrance.

"Then again, maybe this is how he affords living at the Villa. We may have a professional bank robber on our hands."

Veera was back into the criminal profiling groove.

We stopped in front of an entrance flanked by an ice machine and wine barrels. There were even cords of firewood. A life-size metal statue of a faceless man stood guard, hands outstretched in welcome mode. The place had all the fixings for an impromptu party.

Inside the shop was a maze of wall-to-wall, floor-to-ceiling liquor bottles. A cash register peeked out behind a whiskey display on my left. An middle-aged man slumped on a stool behind the register, slowly pounding keys on his cell phone with the enthusiasm of a bear in hibernation. His tight curls were dark, his cheeks full enough to store a fair share of nuts, if he'd been an oversized chipmunk.

"May I use the restroom?" I asked.

"Only for customers," he spoke with a heavy accent and didn't bother looking up.

I couldn't place the accent. Russian? Middle Eastern? I grabbed a candy bar and slapped it on the counter.

"Six dollars." His eyes were still fixed on the phone screen.

"That's unfreakingbelievable." Veera faced me. "Isn't that price gouging?"

"It's taking advantage of two young females who need to use the facilities."

He rolled his eyes and continued scrolling on his phone. "Buy one get one free."

"I'll go for that." Veera grabbed a Snickers bar.

"Bathroom over there." He pointed a finger down the bottle-heavy row.

"What happens if there's an earthquake?" Veera's gaze scoured the place.

"Reporters come and we get free press."

"Meaning you get a lot of pity purchases," Veera said.

"Good for business."

I dropped my elbows on the counter. "Dominic Rosetti used your bathroom." It was another shot in the dark, but my batting average was decent these days.

The man kept his chin down, but his eyes flicked to mine. "Don't know him."

"Oh, you know him alright." I straightened. "He was here earlier today."

"He's a good friend of our nana," Veera said. "And we need to find him. Make sure he's safe."

The man put down his phone. He finally focused on us. "Prove it."

That was progress. He went from not knowing Dom to asking for proof of our identity. Now we were getting somewhere.

I pointed to Veera's phone and she flashed the photo of Dom smiling brightly over his shoulder. "We know he's your loyal customer."

"What's my name?" he asked.

Behind his head, a piece of official-looking paper was pinned to the wall. I felt sure his name was on the paper. But his stare was glued on me, so I didn't dare look. I opened my mouth, "That's easy. It's—"

"Hiya." A man with sun-bleached blond hair waltzed in. He disappeared inside the bottle maze. The moment the cashier's gaze wavered, my stare pushed past to the paper on the wall behind him. I found what I needed.

"Look, Aram." I leaned in closer. Dom mixed with the wrong crowd, and Nana doesn't want him to get into trouble."

"Our job is to watch over him." Veera shot him her better-do-as-we-say look.

Aram gave a slow nod. "Dominic is one of my best customers. When he comes in, I ask no questions."

"He's been missing from Villa Sunset the past few days. And he's been staying in the Village." I made sure that didn't sound like a question.

He gave another slow nod.

"He left his bag with you?" I asked.

"He left nothing with me."

Was Aram lying? Dom wouldn't risk taking his disguise or the money with him. If he were caught, he'd be hauled in for the bank robbery, especially if he left DNA behind. I needed Aram to talk some more.

"Talk to us," I said.

"We'll make it worth your while," Veera added. "We've got a lot of pull at the Villa."

"What do you pull at the Villa?" he asked. "Carts? Or you pull old people around in wheelchairs?"

"She means since they respect us there, we can help promote your..." I waved a hand toward the shop shelves, "...goods."

Aram's Adam's apple bobbed in his throat. I'd say he was about to spit out the truth or something close to it.

"Dominic comes in, goes straight to the toilet room. He doesn't look so good. Comes out wearing something else and leaves. It happens fast. No big deal." Aram waved a hand. "We're buddies."

Dom likely removed the wig before rushing inside and was in a hurry to unload the robbery get-up. Once he did he took the bag with him because he didn't trust Aram. Or because there were items in the bag Dom needed.

"Was that so hard for you to share?" I laid a ten on the counter. "Thanks."

We scurried out the entrance, back onto the sidewalk, and fast-walked away.

"Do you believe him?" Veera asked.

"I do."

"Something's bothering me," Veera said. "Don't banks mark their bills so they can't be spent?"

We slowed by the entrance to the Inn.

"Don't they keep track of the serial numbers?" Veera asked.

"Only in the movies. Wait." And some old school banks. Maybe new school banks did something more. My feet dragged while my mind raced. "That's why he went to the casino."

"To give them the marked bills?"

My brain snapped to attention. "Yes and no." I hurried along. "He'll trade the money for chips. Spend a few, cash them in and poof! The money's clean."

Veera pulled out her phone and started jotting notes. "Would've taken me weeks or longer to figure that out. I bet if you were a criminal, you'd never get caught."

"Criminals always make mistakes because they don't know when to stop. That's where we come in."

"To catch them when they stumble, and haul them to the law," Veera said. "Next stop, Valley Casino?"

"Yep." I jogged up Coast Village Road. "Who knows? We may run into Dom tonight."

Chapter Twenty

Ramblin' Gamblin' Man

We decided not to poke around the Inn. A couple of squad cars and unmarked vehicles changed our minds.

"Must be the investigative division, SBPD." I hurried past. "Chances are they've got a warrant to conduct a search for a suspect."

"Someone ratted on Dom?" Veera asked.

"Or he got sloppy." That would be my guess. I also guessed he was well known enough to be tipped off by a pal like Aram and wouldn't be coming back to the Village tonight.

We sprinted away, not slowing 'til we got into the car.

"I'd say we were on the right track." I motored onto the 101 freeway.

"Maybe the police at the Inn had nothing to do with Dom," Veera said.

"Want to lag behind and find out?"

"What I want is to be fast asleep on the extra firm mattress of my rollaway bed," Veera said, "with a goose-down pillow under my head. After we're done investigating the casino, of course."

I punched the accelerator to pass a big wheeler and Veera shifted in her seat.

"Think the police will catch Dom before we do?" Veera asked.

"Not a chance." Not if he was anything like the combat croquet players. These seniors were craftier than they looked. We'd show them we were the craftiest of all.

* * *

We whisked our way up a winding mountain road with only headlights to light the path past dry brush and charred silhouettes of fire-ravaged trees. The mountain range gave way to rolling hills and fewer curves. Once the terrain and the road straightened, hints of civilization emerged. A rustic wooden sign announced the appearance of a western-style town the size of a circus tent. Quite a contrast to the looming structure ahead. A bustling contemporary building emitted enough light to blot out the stars. The earth tone walls of the entrance blended in with hills rising behind the three-story casino. I hung a left and motored by the grand entrance so slowly, horns blared behind me. Why were gamblers so eager to tempt luck? That was a question for Dom.

I swung the car into the valet section and waited. Veera stuck her neck out the window.

"Sure are a lot of old people out," she said.

"Time stops inside those walls." Another reason why Dom would still be here.

"There he is." Veera pointed to a slim senior toddling toward a ride for hire.

"Too short. Dom's around six feet."

"How about that guy?" She pointed to another man with silvery hair, tinted aviator glasses and an asymmetrical hairline.

"If we were looking for a Stan Lee type, I'd say yes. Think Dick Van Dyke. More hair and a full-fledged smile."

A valet scampered to my side.

I rolled down my window. "We're here to pick up our gramps. He's in the casino. Maybe you saw him?"

Veera flashed the phone photo.

The valet stuck his head closer. "Nope, not familiar. Wanna hand me the phone and I'll ask around?"

"Hold up." Veera pulled out a plastic bag from her purse, dropped her phone in, and zipped it up. She passed the bag to him. "No funny business, you hear? I'll be expecting my phone back in equal, if not better, condition."

He nodded and rushed off.

"I've seen one too many movies where these valets mess with other people's personal belongings," Veera said.

"Keep your eyes on him," I said. "And I'll keep watch for Dom."

"I can do both."

Fifteen minutes ticked by. Veera's phone was returned with a message that no Dom sightings were reported. I pulled away from the curb and parked in a lot behind the place. We floated around the main entry until Veera knew most of the security guards on a first-name basis. Still no sign of Dom.

"We aren't prepared for a stakeout," Veera said. "We've got snacks, but I need to use the ladies' room."

"Good idea," I said. "Take a look around while you're inside. I'll bring the car upfront."

Veera disappeared through a dramatic glass entry leading to gleaming escalators beneath a sunburst chandelier. Meanwhile, I parked my BMW in the half-circle out front. The same valet rushed over to me.

"My boss wants you to leave if we can't park your car."

"My sister's in the casino, and she's disabled, so I have to wait here for her."

"Didn't look disabled to me," he said. "Where's your handicap placard?"

"In her purse," I said. "She took it with her in case she needed it inside. And not all disabilities are visible to the naked eye. Don't you forget that."

"I'll have to check." The valet took off.

It was times like these that I was grateful to be such a skilled liar. My nose never grew, my pants never caught on fire and I usually got what I wanted. But a liar's got to know her limitations. Otherwise, she'd fall into the pathological category.

After my leg fell asleep for the third time, I hobbled out of the car and strolled the front until the blood flowed again. I paused and craned my neck toward the entry. I blinked a few times. Was it possible?

An older woman emerged out of the casino, gripping the handles of an oversized purse with gnarly hands. She wore a camera-ready smile and a shapeless floral midi dress, muumuu style. Granny glasses perched on the bridge of her large nose. Oversized sneakers reflected her height. I hurried over as she boogied toward a red Toyota Camry. The driver waved and stood next to the back door. He opened it. What had Little Ricky said about Dom's nose when he laughed?

I slid between the woman and the car. "That is a lovely dress."

The lady giggled, crinkling her prominent nose as her glasses crept up and away from her nostrils. She finger-waved goodbye, elbowed past me, and lowered her head to scoot into the Camry.

"Dominic," I said.

The lady stiffened and froze briefly before slumping inside. I slid to the open door, but before I could grab the handle, the driver bumped me aside, slammed the door, and locked it. The lady gazed up at me through the window and wiggled another finger wave. It was Dom alright.

I ran to the driver's side, grabbing the handle before he could close it.

"Hey! I'm a licensed, hired driver. You'd better move or I'll call security."

"No, *I'll* call security if you don't let me speak to your passenger right now."

The driver slammed his door, nearly crushing my fingers in the process. The Camry tore off.

I texted Veera that I'd be back and sprinted for my car. In less than a minute, I'd pulled up to a red light leading to the highway. Where'd the Camry go?

There were two ways back to Santa Barbara. The mostly one-lane, curvy mountainous route that got me here, or the 101-highway, which took longer, but was a straight shot. I cut a sharp right for the faster route. Two miles later, with no sign of the getaway car, I flipped a U-ey. I slammed my hands against the wheel. Why'd I let him escape?

I hung a left toward the casino and spotted Veera at the corner. I pulled over and she dove inside.

"You found him, right?

"Right. But that was before I lost him." I gave her the rundown.

"Dom's one slippery eel."

"Even eels get caught." They thrashed back and forth to escape, but they turned quiet at night. That's when the hunting got easy. "We'll find him. And when we do, he won't escape."

Chapter Twenty-One

Devil in Disguise

Veera typed into her phone. "A smart criminal will have a getaway vehicle ready and will switch genders when disguised. "Where would you go if you were a tired old man, with a ton of loot, who needed to hide out?"

"I'd find a dark hole and disappear," I said. "Or blend into my surroundings."

"One thing's for sure," Veera said, "he's not going back to the Inn."

My little voice agreed. "I was so close."

"How much do you figure he escaped with?"

"Anywhere from one to twenty thousand."

"Sounds like chump change for a wealthy man."

"With his debts, he might settle for anything."

Nearly an hour later, we motored into the Villa's self-parking lot beneath a towering tree whose branches spread over Channel Drive. We hopped out and watched Kyle roaming around the entry; his gaze stuck on us until we slipped inside the grounds.

"That man's eyeballs are on the wrong people," Veera said.

"He could be an information source," I said, "if we can get him to talk." We still didn't know who Dom's gambling partners were. "Let's find Mom. I have another assignment for her."

We stood at the entrance to the spacious dining hall. It was way past senior bedtime, but night owls were plentiful. I scanned the talking heads and spied Mom laughing up a storm with Vincent near the bar. I headed for them, but they slipped through the French doors before I got close.

"Hold up." Veera pulled me back. "Should we be interrupting her while she's on duty?"

I plunged forward into the dim terrace. "She needs to be briefed on what to ask. Mom's our ticket to finding the serious gamblers at the Villa."

Mom and Vincent lounged by the railing of the stone terrace overlooking the moonlit ocean.

"Excuse us." I sauntered up. Veera lay low behind me. "May I have a word, Nana?"

Mom's hand shot to her waist. She smiled, but her eyes glittered. "Back in a jiffy," her words spilled out through smiling lips. We fast-walked away from the railing and into a dark corner of the terrace.

"What do you think you're doing besides ruining a perfectly smooth undercover operation?" she whispered. "I was just getting to the good stuff."

Veera chatted up Vincent. "The food's mighty exceptional here," she was saying. "What did you eat for dinner?"

"We found Dom," I whispered. "But he slipped through our fingers." I nutshelled our little excursion from the sleepy village to the bustling casino.

She tossed a glance toward Vincent. "Our job's not over yet, is it? I've barely tapped into my inner Miss Marple."

The downturned corners of her lips registered disappointment. "The fun's only just starting. Dom's using disguises to his advantage. I wasn't expecting that."

"Oh, honey." Mom stroked my head. "You know a good P.I. expects anything and everything. Never underestimate your client or your criminal."

She was right. Which meant Holly could know more than she was telling and Dom probably had enough tricks to fill both his sleeves. "There's a gambling operation at the Villa that may have gotten Dominic into trouble."

"Trouble like he's in hot water with the other residents or like the FBI's got his number?" Mom asked.

The bank robbery popped into my head. "Could be either. That's where

112

you come in. Find out if they're playing more than bingo with more than play money."

"Isn't that a little extreme?" Mom asked.

"Did you see how they play croquet?" My gaze drifted over her shoulder to Vincent. "Why are you spending so much time with Vincent? He's too new here to know much. You should be circulating."

"Because he's a handsome, wealthy, devil of a charmer with a keen eye for reading people, which is useful in figuring out who's who around here. Did you know Lettie used to be a dealer in Vegas?"

"What if he reads right through you? And no, I didn't."

Mom's ruby-tinted lips parted. "I didn't think of that." She chewed on her fingernail. "Okay, I'll hobnob with someone else. After the book club."

"What book club?"

"That's where we're headed in a few minutes. They meet twice a week to discuss books. Vincent invited me. He said it's livelier than I'd think."

Which meant they probably managed to stay awake during the discussion. We stared at each other a few beats.

"Mom, I'm glad you're here."

She moved a loose strand from my eyes. "Me, too. You know, wishes do come true. I've been hoping we'd spend more quality time together and now we are."

"Thanks," I said, "for jumping in and helping."

"That's what Moms do." She tossed a glance over her shoulder. "I'd better get going before Veera sends him over the edge. He's such a gentleman."

"And about twenty-five years older than the real you. Remember what you said about underestimating?"

She stuck a hand on her hip. "Can't a girl have some fun when working undercover?"

"No."

"There's no law that says I can't enjoy a delicious meal, smart conversation, and a game of croquet." She waved to a resident. "Even if I am impersonating someone else, which I can't think about or I'll come clean."

At some point, the real Lucy Fay would be told. At some point, we could be arrested. I shook off that thought and turned back to Mom. "We were hired by a high-level employee of the Villa to find a missing resident. Don't lose your focus."

"Where are you headed?" She took a few steps toward Vincent.

"I'm not leaving the Villa, but I may not be in your unit tonight."

"Where are you going to be?"

"In someone else's bedroom."

Chapter Twenty-Two

With A Little Help From My Friends

"Dom's been hiding out. We know that much." Veera sipped hot chocolate.

We'd changed into our surveillance clothes, aka black hoodies and joggers, and reclined on Mom's bed.

"Hope we never go back to our legal jobs."

"Until we find Dom, we're not leaving the Villa." I polished off my hot chocolate. "Unless it takes longer than anticipated and the real Lucy Fay shows up to claim her spot. Only then will we vacate."

"Because we'd have no choice." Veera took a long final sip. "Think we'll be arrested?"

"Not if we solve the case. The Villa will be so happy with our results..."

"They'll forgive us our trespasses," Veera said. That's what I keep tellin' myself. I've blocked out other possibilities."

"We'll comb the village again tomorrow for traces of Dom." I jumped to my feet. "Meanwhile, I've been pining to take an evening stroll with my sister."

"I had the same pining, only we ended up in the spa for a foot massage and some mini sliders with extra cheese."

Ten minutes later, Veera and I padded along the brick walkway amid a gentle breeze, large potted flowers, and swaying palms. Teams of gardeners were the only insurance against the abundant greenery overtaking the property. It was like we'd retreated to a tropical paradise where the plant life grew twice as fast and hardy. Pools of soft golden light cast by tall gas lamps lit our way; teak benches scattered every twenty feet so that we could rest our weary bones if we were octogenarians who really did live here.

"Do you hear something?" Veera asked.

"Mermaids and mermen beckoning us to the sea." I really did feel like I was living a fantasy life.

"I hear humans partying."

I shook myself out of my fantasy trance and listened. Voices trickled out of one of the dwellings. Which one? Bungalows dotted the grounds, hidden behind screens of bamboo and hedgerows.

"I don't get why these seniors aren't sleeping," Veera clicked her tongue. "Don't they get tired from all the mischief they get themselves into?"

"Maybe they're energized by all their naps," I said. And maybe they thrived on spending time doing things more enticing than sleep.

We hustled toward the voices and took a breather in front of a well-lit bungalow concealed behind a stucco wall and tall shrubs. Just past a metal gate, a fountain showered streams of water. A sign hung in the window.

"Book Club," I read.

"This isn't your average book club by the sound of things," Veera said.

Loud voices, laughter, and shrill hooting made me agree.

I strolled to the gate, unlatched it, and trekked along a gravel path. An in-ground hot tub bubbled patiently off to one side. The bungalow shutters were closed, but the interior glowed through the slats.

"Do you hear what I hear?" Veera whispered.

The noise had diminished to a cough and quiet voices.

"Somebody pressed mute," Veera said. "Maybe the book club just started."

Or they saw us coming. I rapped on the wooden entry. Peter Cronkite cracked open the door; one bulging eye stared through the slit. His blue flannel shirt was neatly tucked into black jeans buckled with a cowboy-style belt.

"Yes?" His bug-eyed gaze shifted from me to Veera.

"We're looking for Nana," I said.

He tried to stare me down, but I held fast.

"Shouldn't you girls be fast asleep in your cribs?" he asked.

"Did he just insult us?" Veera whispered to me.

"He did." I turned to Peter. "We're awaiting our bedtime story."

He stepped back, opening the door wider. A group of seniors lazed around on a pale green sofa and matching chairs. The same book sat on each lap, *Unique Destinations.* No sign of Mom, but Vincent was settled in an easy chair, surveying us with a trace of a smile. Sofi reclined on the couch, looking as relaxed as a lioness after devouring a hearty meal. Another senior gripped her book in both hands. The man sitting next to her stared at the walnut floors. The furnishings were antique. The paisley-patterned oriental rug was hand-knotted.

"Whose bungalow is this?" Veera asked.

"Mine," the book gripper replied.

"We were discussing the lower Zambezi National Park in South Africa," Peter said. "I visited there as a child."

"What was it like?" I strolled around the room while he rattled off the highlights. I admired the artwork, a carved limestone fireplace, and scoped out hiding places. There was enough tension in the room to wipe out a swarm of bees.

"Lucy Fay left already." Sofi interrupted Peter's musings.

"Run along now. Your nana must be looking for you." Peter ushered me to the door and practically pushed me outside. Veera stumbled out behind me and Peter shut the door.

Veera and I waited a full minute before stepping away.

"Think they're smoking or sniffing something?" Veera asked.

"Whatever they're up to doesn't involve books."

We stepped out the gate and back on the brick path. I listened for sounds of laughter and didn't hear anything.

"Most older people need glasses to read," Veera said.

She knew her seniors. "They were hiding something." What didn't they want us to know?

"I wouldn't be surprised if they're cooking up some dangerous scheme,"

Veera said. "Maybe they're all bank robbers. They look disruptive even when they're sitting quietly."

I couldn't disagree with that. Time to see what Mom had uncovered. "Let's find Nana."

* * *

Michael called just before we entered the main building.

"You go ahead," I told Veera. "I'll meet you upstairs."

"We could use another pair of eyes if he wants to drive up," Veera said before heading toward the Golden Lotus Wing.

"Can you talk?" Michael asked when I answered.

I sauntered toward a garden bench. "With you, always."

"I hope you'll still feel that way," he said, "afterward."

"After what?" I couldn't imagine feeling differently about him.

"I have a confession to make about Lucy Fay."

A dozen thoughts streaked through my head. Was she arriving at the Villa sooner? Did he make her up and put her into the Villa system? Were we in trouble?

"I told her the truth."

I opened my mouth to speak, but a frisky breeze wrapped its fingers around my throat, whisking the words away. The truth could strap a ball and chain around my ankle.

"When I first called Lucy Fay," Michael said. "I blurted out my phony identity and then, I couldn't go through with it." His voice rose to a higher pitch when his nerves were rattled. "I confessed. And asked for her blessing."

"You stopped me at 'blurted'." What kind of trouble were we in?

"I told her about the missing resident. About you, your famous P.I. dad, your nearly started-up investigation business."

"You played the sympathy card?" That wasn't like him.

"I wasn't playing anything. I painted an honest picture of who you really are and why we need her support to help find the missing senior. We are an awesome team of security and investigation experts and with her help, we'd make the Villa a better place to live for all, including her when she moves in."

The worst part? Veera and Mom would be tangled up in my mess. I sank onto the bench. It wasn't all that long ago that I would've lashed out at him for confessing. But he'd shown me that being virtuous helped me sleep better at night, when I wasn't case-cracking, that is. "Is Lucy Fay pressing charges?"

"Of course not. At least I don't think so."

I slapped my hand to my forehead.

"I expect her to give us the green light any moment." Michael's voice returned to normal pitch. "I really do."

"You mean..."

"I expect her to throw in her support."

"We're so close to finding hard evidence." I felt rudderless in a brewing storm. Maybe Michael was right. Why hadn't she turned us in? "I need time to digest this. Let me know when you hear from her."

"Are you...?"

"I'm not mad, Michael. Talk soon." I disconnected and headed for Mom's room. How could I be angry with him? I was the one perpetually jeopardizing the safety of the people around me. Isn't that what Dad did? And look what happened to him. What do I say to Mom and Veera?

Veera opened the door when I arrived. "You're gonna want to hear this."

Chapter Twenty-Three

Ain't No Mountain High Enough

The lights were off when I slipped into Lucy Fay's suite. Mom's silhouette appeared by the open window. The chilly wind didn't stand a chance of ruffling her hair. Her real hair, that is. There was enough hairspray to ward off a tornado. She whirled around when I called her name.

"Oh, honey." She hugged me tight.

"What happened, Mom?"

"They wouldn't let me into the book club." She hung her head. "I feel so rejected."

"First of all, this is all pretend, remember? They're not rejecting you. They're rejecting who they think you are."

"Then I feel doubly rejected. Wait." Her gaze darted upward. "Did I do the math right?"

"She went to the book club, but they sent her somewhere else," Veera said. I turned to Mom. "Details."

"Peter wouldn't let me inside. He said the book club was for members only. I needed to pass a test before I could join."

"He must be the gang leader," Veera said.

"What test?" I asked.

Turned out when Mom arrived at the book club with Vincent, they were instantly separated. Vincent stayed put while Mom was escorted to Lil's bungalow. She quizzed Mom before sending her home.

"Lil said the book club was for serious readers and I had to prove myself first by answering questions."

"They're like the pigs in *Animal Farm* rebelling against the establishment," Veera said.

"What kinds of questions?" I closed the shutters and turned on a small lamp.

"Did I prefer knitting or bowling, oatmeal or eggs benedict, driving or flying?"

"How'd you answer?" I asked.

"I don't knit or bowl, eggs Florentine and sailing on my two-hundred-foot yacht." Her grin flashed in the darkness.

"You are good." Veera and Mom bumped fists. "They're checking you out to see if you should be a member of the R.A.T. pack."

"You painted Lucy Fay as a rebel." How far would that get Mom? Seemed like rebels were what they were after.

"Then she asked about my favorite guilty pleasure, what item I always carry in my purse and if a lipstick was named after me, what would it be called?"

"Risqué questions for a bunch of old folks," Veera said.

"They've got money and time that could run out at any moment. The time part, I mean. A dangerous combination that could turn an ordinary senior into a daredevil," I said. If I were living here, I might exhibit risky behavior just for fun, too. Not that I didn't already. Why wait to have fun?

Mom sank onto a brown leather sofa.

"Can't blame them for preferring unconventional fun and games to playing horseshoes and painting by numbers." That was my best guess. "How did you answer, Mom?"

"I didn't say a word. Lucy Fay did all the talking."

Was Mom losing her marbles? Maybe this was taking a toll on her.

"I channeled how I pictured the wealthy, unmarried and fashionable philanthropist, as played by me," Mom said. "Younger men are Lucy Fay's guilty pleasure. She keeps her phone, breath mints, and a healthy stash of cash in her purse. And maybe a little something for her boy toy."

"Mom!"

"She likes younger men, okay?" Mom said. "I had to make it interesting so they'd let me in the club. You know that's not the real me."

I really did need to spend more time with my mother. I hardly knew her. "Then what?" I asked.

"They sent me away." Mom fluffed up her hair. "Just when I was getting started."

"What's your lipstick's name?" Veera asked.

"*Come to Mama.*"

"Oooh, baby," Veera said. "You are up and running so fast, you'll be leading the R.A.T. pack soon."

"Why are you trying to be a swinging senior?" I asked Mom.

"I'm creating someone they'll want to let into their silly little club." Mom took out a nail file from her handbag and filed her thumbnail. "They need to view me as unpredictable and exciting."

"It's a power play," I said. Just like in high school. Someone's leader of the clique and the rest have to follow or suffer the lonely consequences. "You're right, Mom. You can't be an outcast. Good work." I was truly impressed.

"Which brings me to my next point. This place is fabulous." She swung her arms around the room and dropped them. "Except I can't sleep here, pretending to be someone else. I won't take advantage of an innocent, but very wealthy senior who should be here in my place."

Why was everyone upstanding, but me? Was the Universe sending me a message? "Good news, Mom." I told them about Michael's call and Lucy Fay's blessing, even though we didn't officially have it.

"You're not lying to me, sweetie, are you?" She gave me a hard, long look. "Because I would be deeply hurt if you were."

I held up my phone. "Call Michael." I pushed his number.

She grabbed my phone and held it to her ear.

"Don't you trust me? Don't answer that." We had quite the history where I hadn't earned her trust, but I found her kind of sketchy, too.

After Michael reassured her, Mom disconnected. She even hung a few of her dresses in the closet. "I hope I meet Lucy Fay someday. I'm going to pay her back somehow."

"She sounds like our guardian angel," Veera said.

I guessed Michael left out the final blessing part. I said a little prayer that Lucy Fay wouldn't be too hard on us.

The apartment phone rang. Mom's eyes widened. "What do I do?"

"Answer it." Didn't anyone ever sleep around here? I picked up the receiver and handed it to her.

"Hello?" Her dark eyes darted from me to Veera. "Lil?" Her brows shot up and lowered as she grinned. "I'm happy to be part of the book club."

Seems like the only doubter was me.

"I'm telling you," Veera whispered to me, "we should make her a job offer."

"Yay!" Mom said. "When do I start?"

Was she talking to us or Lil?

* * *

Mom slept in the bedroom on top of the bedspread while Veera and I laid down in our surprisingly comfy rollaway beds. Veera had pulled hers into a small office adjoining the living room, but I slept in my favorite position; facing the front door...for a whole fifteen minutes. I figured Veera's rousing snore would wake me up. I figured right.

Since I still wore my black hoodie and joggers, I was ready to take off. I eased my way out the front door. Silence sprouted like mushrooms in the empty hallway.

I wound my way downstairs and out to Dom's building. Before I got to his apartment, I paused by the elevator. A TV blared from the end of the hallway. But other residents' rooms were silent. I operated from a shaky set of facts, but even so, my gut told me to break into Dom's room again tonight. There was something I needed to find there.

Chapter Twenty-Four

In My Life

S topping in front of Dom's apartment door, I pressed my ear to the wood. Not a peep. Just before I turned away, a low rumbling vibrated the hallway. My heartbeat quickened. Did the rumble come from Dom's suite?

While I worked the lock, the elevator door pinged. I stumbled inside, closing the door behind me; my heart beat at hummingbird tempo. The rumble had come from the elevator. Had I been spotted? I listened for a few moments. Hearing nothing, I pulled out a penlight and scanned the surroundings. Dom had clearly not returned. I trekked forward and froze. Something scratched at the front door.

I sprang toward the master bedroom and practically somersaulted into the bathroom. A night light radiated a soft red glow. On my right sat two pedestal sinks. An enormous bathtub jazzed up the left side; I plowed ahead on tippy toes to a smaller room housing the shower and toilet.

"Oh no." The frameless glass door meant no hiding places for yours truly.

The front door clicked shut as my creative juices started to flow. A chrome towel bar doubled as the handle pull on the shower door. Flinging open a cabinet between the sinks, I grabbed a large bath towel. I slung it over the towel bar, stepped inside the shower, and crouched behind the towel on the cold tile floor. There was a chance he wouldn't notice the fresh towel or me sitting behind it in the shower, assuming it was Dom returning home. Was it him?

The closet door in the hallway creaked open and shut. Moments later, kitchen cabinets swished open. Everything happened quickly, which meant it wasn't Dom. It was an intruder looking for...what?

I had two choices: continue hiding or confront the interloper. Then what? If it was another senior and I played a little rough...the prison sentence would be a long one for assault, and breaking and entering. Longer for fraud. I had one choice. Wait it out and formulate a plan to take control of a sticky situation. I texted Veera:

Hurry up to Dom's room, knock on the door and run like the wind.

Veera was a sound sleeper. If her phone wasn't on, I was out of luck. Even if it were on, chances were she'd sleep through my texting. We were on the job, so I prayed she slept with one ear open. I stiffened.

A soft shoe shuffled closer and stepped onto the bathroom tile. The sole was rubber, the step slow and calculated. A dim beam lit up the area. A cabinet opened. Did they have a key to Dom's apartment? Or was it a well-oiled breaker and enterer like me?

Footsteps pranced closer and I stopped breathing. I snuck my phone beneath my thigh to muffle any sound or light. Wake up, Veera. Wake up!

The steps stopped, but the beam of light grew brighter. If the intruder peered over the towel bar, I'd be cooked. I crouched lower trying to roll myself into a ball like a pill bug, except without the coat of armor, which would've been very helpful right now. Brittle tumbleweeds rolled around in my throat.

The beam grew dimmer and the shuffling faded. I sniffed the air for the scent of cologne or something to give the prowler away. I jumped at a small buzz under my leg. Pulling out my phone, I stared at the screen.

On my way.

It would take Veera a few minutes to reach the apartment. I leaned toward the shower door and barely pushed. It swished open. Drawers groaned in the living room and I slowly exhaled. The intruder was too busy snooping to notice me. I lifted my bottom, jetted to the bedroom entry, and stuck my head out.

"Cripes," a voice whispered.

Male or female? I couldn't tell. I slowly planted my shoe outside the bedroom. Then the other one. Long, slow strides brought me to the end of the short hallway. Leaning my torso forward, I peered around the corner. A dark silhouette wearing a suit jacket and pants leaned over Dom's desk, a fedora on his head. But it wasn't Dom. The intruder seemed slight and petite in stature. Was it Peter? A tiny flashlight lit up the inside of a drawer. Gloves covered the intruder's hands. If I moved quietly enough, I could creep up and—

A pounding rattled the front door. I jerked away, pressing my back against the wall.

Silence filled every corner. My gaze stayed glued on the path leading to the entry. The prowler would have to pass by me to escape.

Minutes ticked by without any footfall. Was he hiding? I straightened and waited some more. My phone buzzed. It was Veera.

What's my next move, C?

The intruder was no scaredy-cat. Which meant he was either still here or had escaped another way. The balcony! I texted back:

. *Could someone exit out the balcony, down to the ground?*

She texted back in moments:

Shimmy down a palm tree or jump onto a hedge. Thick enough to break your fall.

She thought I was the one escaping. I sidestepped into the living room. No sign of the prowler, but the French doors leading to the balcony gaped open.

Chapter Twenty-Five

In the Still of the Night

I gripped the wrought iron railing bordering the top of the balcony wall. Batches of hearty ferns with sturdy fronds waiting below promised to break my fall. One large frond drooped close to the mossy ground, injured from the intruder's landing. Lighting was scarce, and I strained my eyes and ears searching for a runner.

To spare the ferns below, I climbed over the railing. A stocky palm was close enough for me to grab hold. I leapt toward it, gripping the rough trunk with both hands, wrapping my feet around until I found grooves to guide my climb downward. I jumped onto the grass, landing on all fours. My penlight shined around the soft dirt by my feet. The Villa grounds were green for a reason. The soil was perpetually damp, which kept the dirt wet enough for me to pick out a fresh set of prints a few feet away. I got on my knees and examined them.

Smallish for a man. I put my sneaker next to them. Smallish for a female, as well, if my size eights meant anything. I'd peg the shoe size as a size five or six. The heels were tiny, round, and separated from the top third of the shoe, like on a boot. Where had I seen boots like that before? I picked up a fern frond laying on the dirt and crawled to where I'd landed. Brushing away my sneaker prints, I leveled the dirt using the frond. I strode to a patch of moss that resembled a welcome mat and wiped my sneakers to remove excess mud. I swept the lingering mud away with the frond.

After scanning the immediate surroundings, I hurried away.

"Freeze."

I recognized the deep-as-an-oil-well voice. I flipped around.

"Hi, Kyle," I said. The full moon behind him outlined his enormous silhouette. I couldn't make out his face, but I imagined a grimace twisted his mouth.

The security guard stepped closer, the fingertips of one hand touched the taser at his belt. He tilted his head and pivoted slightly so he viewed me from his left side.

"You're loitering." He shifted from one boot to the other.

If that was all he thought I was doing, I was good. "I'm not loitering. I'm admiring the abundance of plant life at the Villa. I'm an amateur botanist."

"Oh, yeah?"

"That over there..." I pointed, "...is called a bird's nest fern." Had I read that somewhere? Sounded legit to me.

"What are you doing?"

"I thought I saw something in these bushes so I came over for a closer look." I took a few seconds to rethink that last part. If the break-in in Dom's room was discovered, would I be a suspect for hanging around here? I decided to switch tactics. "Can I be straight with you?" I stepped closer and tilted my head farther back. "I'm worried about leaving my grandmother here. These seniors...they're..."

"Evil old folk that hide Tommy guns under their recliners."

I swallowed my words. That was unexpected. What made him think they were evil? Or was he joking? "I was going to say they're party animals. Party turtles, really."

"They're plotting ways to rule the world," Kyle said.

"The whole world or the Villa world?"

"Villa." He slightly bent toward me. "What are you looking for?"

He was a persistent fellow. "Not what. Who? I saw someone run out of these bushes."

"Run or hobble?" He sauntered past me and stopped in front of the shrubs and palms. He lit a police-grade flashlight over the dirt until the high beam

128

rested on the boot prints.

"It wasn't a hobble." The person I viewed moved lightly on their feet. Not like an older senior. I knelt next to Kyle. "Male or female prints?"

"Small, dainty," he said. "I smell a female."

I waited for the "Fee, fie, fo, fum," but it never came. He sounded like the Giant who sniffed out Jack. He straightened to his nearly seven feet hulk. His face continued to turn to the left as he gazed downward. He switched his stare to my shoes. My sneakers clearly didn't make that print.

"Go back to your apartment." He trudged away toward the main entrance.

I'd say that somewhat friendly encounter indicated progress in our professional relationship. What was it about the way he turned his head to look around? I switched on my penlight and continued hunting for boot tracks. He or she had jumped onto wet dirt, which meant the boots trekked mud…that could've been wiped on grass before hopping back onto the brick path, just like I did. Why did my investigation keep stalling?

Footsteps pounded the bricks behind me. I whirled around.

"I saw you talking to that overgrown security guard." Veera panted. "You okay?"

"Kyle and I bonded over a shoe print." I brought her up to speed and shared his comments.

"Sounds like we have geriatric delinquents on our hands," she said. "What would someone be looking for in Dom's room?"

"I must've missed something of value hidden in there," I said. Could it be the playing cards? Someone trying to prove he cheated?

"Only two places the thief could've gone. Back to the Villa or out to the street." Veera turned toward the Villa entry. "I'll have a talk with the valet and security guard on duty. See if they saw anything."

"I'll look around the Villa some more." I hopped onto the brick path and wound my way toward the back of the main building.

Wasn't long before fast steps padded behind me. Veera caught up.

"Only one valet was on duty and his eyes were on his phone, but the security guard and I had a nice chat."

We slowed our steps and moved off the path into the dimmer recesses of the garden.

"He didn't see anyone running, but after I told him I was worried about Nan, he opened up some." Veera craned her neck around to make sure we were alone. "He said police are called only if security can't handle a situation. He wouldn't disclose any names, but he said there've been incidents."

"Between seniors?"

"Uh-huh," Veera said. "One senior punched out another for singing off-key during karaoke night."

"Sure are a lot of short fuses running loose here."

"Told him I heard a senior was missing. He said they come and go as they please. You suppose it was Dom coming back to his apartment after his crime spree?"

"A spree implies more than one crime," I said. "We're not even sure if Dom robbed the bank." I was sure, but I needed proof. "His disguised appearance at the casino may've been a coincidence or maybe he likes wearing dresses now and then."

"Did you forget who you're talking to?" she asked.

"I'm playing Devil's Advocate. No one except Holly seems worried about the absentee. They're expecting him back any moment. We need another meeting with Holly."

We rounded the corner toward the back of Mom's building. Veera pulled me behind a large palm tree sticking out of a hedge of bushes.

She pointed to the brick path running parallel to the building. A tall man with a shock of silvery hair danced along at a brisk speed.

"Didn't Holly say Dom likes to dance?" Veera asked. "That's a happy dance and he's good at it, too."

"Of course, he's happy. He stole money, cleaned it up, and made it home without getting caught. Let's welcome Dom home."

Chapter Twenty-Six

Dance to the Music

This time I entered Dom's suite in a more civilized manner. I knocked and when he answered, I shoved my way inside, Veera marching behind me.

"Who are you?" Dom asked. "Why are you visiting me this time of night? Wait a minute." His mouth hung open as he stooped to get a better look at me.

Up close, his lips were a straight line, his pearly whites nearly perfect, and his brows sparse.

"I've seen you before," he said to me.

"That wasn't your twin sister at the casino?" I asked.

"Are you always this funny?"

"Only when I'm given good material."

He wrinkled his nose and looked at Veera. "Who's your cohort?"

"We ask the questions," she said. "Troublemaker."

"Who me?"

I opened the closet door and pointed to the vacuum. "Hiding a little something in the canister?"

Dom's brows shot to the moon and his mouth invited flies inside. "You're a cop," he whispered.

"We should discuss the bank robbery," I said.

"It's like you were handcuffed to me today." He snickered. "That's a joke by the way."

Veera sidled behind Dom, so he was practically surrounded. We moved in a slow circle around him. His suede slippers moved in a smaller circle while he tossed glances between us. Beads of sweat glistened around his hairline.

"You're not arresting me?" He lumbered off toward the hallway and Veera jumped in front of him. He was nearly her height, but not as solidly built.

"Do you mind?" He planted his hands on his hips.

She moved aside and he stumbled toward his bedroom.

"What do you want? Money?" Dom asked. "I have plenty."

"Your desk drawer tells a different story," I said.

"You're with the FBI, aren't you? No, you're with the IRS. Oh, please not the IRS. Wait, you've been in my place before? Who gave you permission?"

"We're the S.W.P.," Veera said.

"What's that, a utility company?" His breathing turned heavy. He removed a hanky and wiped it against his damp face.

"Senior Watch Patrol." Veera beamed proudly at her impromptu acronym.

"We work for a private party who hired us to find out what's going on beneath the glossy veneer of the Villa," I said.

"I have nothing to say without my lawyer." He walked in reverse until he nearly tripped over his Persian rug. He caught himself and fumbled back onto his bed, wiping his palms on his slacks.

The room temperature was comfortable, but he was sweating enough to fill a bucket.

"Who *are* you?" he asked. "You're not with any agency. You would've flashed a badge or something. Did Sid send you?"

"Who?" Veera asked.

"Water." He coughed.

"Water bottles are in the fridge," I told Veera.

"You searched my refrigerator?" He sputtered between coughs.

Veera zipped out.

"Tell us everything and we'll protect you," I said.

Dom wheezed out a deep cough just as Veera returned and handed him a bottle. He eyed the bottle, shook it gently from side to side, then guzzled and slurped, dribbling over his jacket. "Can you make me a martini?" he asked after a deep inhale. "Stirred, not shaken." He played it straight. "Get it? Like Bond, only not." His laughter turned into a hacking cough.

"Cut the sass," Veera said, "before we haul your sorry butt into the police station. Why'd you leave the Villa?"

He turned serious and cradled the bottle in his palm. He spoke quietly, "I left because I had business to handle." He hooked a finger into his collar and rolled his head around.

"What kind of business?" He looked worse by the second.

"A do or die assignment." He took another sip. "I need to see I.D."

"You're not in a position to make requests," Veera said.

"Is that so? You just brought me water after I requested it, didn't you?"

What a pain. "Let's take him in." I reached for his arm and he pulled back.

"Look, I've had a rough day, a rough week, actually, and I came back to lay low and get some R and R. I'll...I'll cooperate." His eyes rolled back and he gasped for air. "Can't breathe." His eyelids shut and his head slumped to one side.

"Is he for real?" Veera asked.

I wasn't sure. I gently slapped his cheeks. No response. I lifted his arm and it fell limply. "Call 9-1-1." I bent over him and attempted hand-to-chest CPR. His eyes flickered open and he stared at me.

"Watch," he muttered.

"What watch?" I lowered my ear to his lips.

"Water. Safe." His chin dropped and his eyes closed. I couldn't rouse him and neither could the paramedics when they arrived ten minutes later.

I'd nabbed the water bottle and sniffed it. Sweet, somewhat fruity, if the fruit were on fire. I stared at the label. No added flavor. I swished it around and shined my penlight on the bottom. No residue. What has an ether-like smell and dissolves in liquid? "Poison." The very mention sank me to the bottom of a rocky abyss. My father's last cup of coffee was laced with ricin.

"Did you say poison?" Veera asked. "Glad we didn't give him a heart attack. I was seriously considering quitting our P.I. business when he keeled over. Is he going to be okay?"

"Hope so."

As the paramedics carted him away, I handed one the water bottle. "He was drinking this."

Veera and I trailed them down the hallway. Lettie came running. I told her the same story I told the paramedics.

"My sister and I couldn't sleep so we went for a walk and met Dom downstairs. He invited us up to show off his cigar collection, then he complained he couldn't breathe."

"Do not mention this incident to anyone," Lettie said. "We don't want to frighten residents unnecessarily. Once I make sure he's okay, I'll circulate a statement."

Veera and I nodded and headed toward Lucy Fay's apartment.

"Our missing person case just turned into attempted murder." I stopped outside the Golden Lotus Wing and whispered, "How many water bottles were in the fridge?"

"I should know that, being a part-time night law school student and P.I. trainee." She squeezed shut her eyes. "I've been working on my memory and recognition skills. Let's see. I opened the fridge. I reached inside for a water bottle sitting on the bottom shelf. I grabbed it and ran back to you and Dominic."

"How many bottles were on the shelf, in the front?" It seemed vital to know the exact number. It would confirm that the intruder tampered with the water.

Veera exhaled slowly and flicked open her eyes. "A half carton of eggs, an unopened quart of whole milk, a block of cheddar cheese, three small strawberry yogurts...the bottle sat on the lowest shelf. Above the crisper drawers."

"Bottle? As in one?"

"Only one. Maybe more in the door. I didn't check there."

I'd counted three bottles on my visit to Dom's pad, all on the lowest shelf. Were the others moved? Did Dom move them? I'd bet on someone else. "Someone wanted to make sure he drank out of that bottle." Was it the prowler who'd been in his room tonight?

Chapter Twenty-Seven

Stand By Me

Was I a light sleeper? Let's just say a floating feather would wake me once it fluttered to the floor. But it wasn't a feather in the wee hours of the morning. It was a scritch-scratch creeping along the hardwood like a beetle walking on the claws of its feet. I lifted my head to shoo away the noisy bug when I saw Mom, tiptoeing toward the front door. Tiny pebbles must've gotten stuck in her rubber-soled wedges.

I sat up. "Going for a sunrise stroll?"

"Shhhh." She spun around, her index finger pasted against her lips. "Veera's sleeping." She pointed toward Veera's silhouette near the French doors.

I hopped out of bed, fully clothed. I didn't even pack P.J.s since my job was 24-7. I slipped into my sneakers and flitted toward Mom.

"Where to?" I said.

"I got a text to meet beneath the giant fig tree in the main garden."

"You shared your burner phone number? That's only for us."

"Listen, honey." Mom hooked her gaze on mine and held up her phone. "Lucy Fay shared her number with her new friends so invitations would flow in. How else is she going to get anywhere?"

"May I see that?" I took her phone, snapped a screenshot of the R.A.T. pack phone numbers, and texted the photo to me. I handed it back to her. "That's a desolate hangout. You're not going," I whispered. Unless I went, too. The overgrown fig tree lay between the corner of the two residential buildings. "Who are you meeting?"

"Someone named Sid."

A chill scattered down my spine. "You gave Sid your number?"

"I haven't met anyone by that name. Someone else must've shared it."

I grabbed my purse and phone. "Dom mentioned Sid and asked if we work for him." Or her. I brought Mom up to speed about the intrusion into Dom's place, the intruder's getaway, and the fate of Dom later. "Any idea of who Sid is?"

"None. Why would anyone want to kill Dominic?" she said. "If you weren't there—"

"We need to find out who texted you." I opened the door. "Let's go."

We scurried outside. I was surprised and grateful that she didn't argue with me...until we reached the elevator.

"Sid's expecting me. If he sees you, he won't show and we'll be standing high and dry," she said.

Mom didn't believe in quiet parenting when I was growing up. She needed to be upfront, holding the lantern high, with me firmly behind her overflowing pioneer skirts.

"What are you packing?" she asked.

"About four different weapons on my person and three in my handbag."

"That's my girl. But don't use any unless you have to, and watch your aim. It's dark outside. I should've worn white."

"Mom!"

She straightened her burgundy cashmere midi skirt, matching sweater and patted her silvery wig. "How do I look?"

"Like you always do. Fabulous." Truth was, my mother was an important component of my life that made it complete, even if she didn't have all the right skills and know-how. I felt oddly secure with her around.

The elevator door slid open. I moseyed next to Mom. She pushed the button for the lobby.

"Once we get into the open, keep your distance," she said.

"Don't you think I know what I'm doing?"

"If you did, you wouldn't keep interrupting me during important conversations."

"Don't make a move without me." I sounded just like Mom.

She stopped. "I'm a little nervous."

"I thought you helped Dad solve cases."

"I helped in theory, without actually being present. I packed him lunch and stuck little notes inside his bag. We talked about the cases afterward."

"So far, you've infiltrated Villa Sunset incognito, made all the right friends, and displayed skills I didn't know you had. You are a go-getter and you know what you're doing."

"Are you just saying that to make me feel better?" She reached for my hand. "Don't answer that."

"I never just say anything." That was another lie. I said whatever got me ahead, but not this time. Not with my mother. Not today.

The elevator landed in the lobby.

"Go ahead, Mom. I'll follow about twenty feet back."

She pranced into the lobby.

"Wait." I dug into my purse and pulled out a pepper spray bottle shaped like lipstick.

"It may be my first investigation," she said. "But I'm never empty-handed." She held up a small white key chain in the shape of a cuddly teddy bear.

"Cute," I said.

"Not when it spits bear mace in your face. Otherwise, it's adorable." She planted a kiss on my cheek. "We're going to bring these felonious seniors to their knee replacements." Mom stepped out, swinging her purse by her side.

I waited near the elevator for a few moments, running my gaze back and forth in the wide hallway, finger pressed against the button to keep the door open. Four oversized wingback chairs were scattered around the lobby. All empty. Mom turned the corner into a corridor leading to the main garden, and I stepped onto the tile floor. I patted my belt buckle housing my five-pointed throwing star. The sharp points and cold steel were a big confidence booster.

I rounded the corner seconds later. Mom strolled ahead, like a model on the runway, knees slightly raised with each step, wedges kicking forward, one in front of the other. My head pivoted in all directions, surveying the scene for someone hiding in the shadows. Two men manned the reception desk; the gift shops lining the hallway were closed and a few bussers milled about the restaurant. No one paid us any attention. I cut the next corner behind her and watched her stomp along the brick pathway outside the building. She looked like she didn't have a care in the world.

My fingers dove into the side pocket of my purse and I pulled out a small mirror. I held it up to my face, tilting it to view activity behind me. I passed the mirror over two wing chairs. I froze. Was that my imagination or did a head jerk back? Who was sitting in the seat? Sid? Should I double back and find out? That would take Mom out of my line of sight. She was my priority.

I shoved the mirror back in my purse as quick steps thumped along behind me. I glanced over my shoulder. Veera was closing in, also dressed in last night's black sweats.

"Wait up," she whispered.

I waved my hand. Slowing down was not an option. I'd lose sight of Mom once she passed through the archway.

Veera jogged over. "I woke up and no one was home so I headed down here as fast as I could. Didn't even brush my hair." She gave me a quick once over. "We're two peas in a pod."

Our black joggers and sneakers matched. But my unbrushed hair looked a lot more frazzled than her elbow-length, indestructible curls. Meanwhile, my hair was pulled back in a wild, hop-along ponytail, with loose strands springing around my face like baby weeds.

"There are four wing chairs by the Ocean Vista," I whispered. "One's occupied. Find the occupant."

Veera shot off before I finished talking.

I jogged through the next archway and put on the brakes. I whirled around. "Oh, oh." No sign of Mom. My heart pounded. Where was she?

Chapter Twenty-Eight

The Twist

I darted around the giant fig tree and along the patios of the rooms stretching behind it. Most shutters to the apartments were closed. My peering inside a couple of windows didn't go over too well with the occupants. Where was Mom?

I retraced my steps and stood beneath tree branches spreading more than a hundred feet above me. A sturdy old tree didn't grow strong and hearty by doing nothing. I marched toward the building and stopped. A yellow strip of paper unfurled on the grass near the sprawling roots; a sticky note strip about half an inch long. I plucked up the blank strip, eyes darting back and forth. Was mom leaving me a paper trail?

A train rumbled on the tracks behind the Villa; the blare diminished in seconds so as not to rile the residents. I'd skipped along about twenty paces and there it was: another sticky note, fluttering to the side of the bricks. I snatched it up without slowing. Twenty more paces flew by. The path continued toward two bungalows, but it also branched out to the right, leading to a staircase and second-floor rooms of the Silver Lining Wing. An exterior light spotlighted another sticky note laying near a bottom stair.

My phone vibrated. A text from Veera rolled in.

Nobody's sitting in any chairs or sofas, but Sofi's wandering around. Seems like she's in a real hurry. I'm on her tail.

I sent her a thumbs-up emoji and scooped up the note. Climbing to the top of the stairs, I tugged open the door. The hallway was eerily quiet. My gaze was pinned to the carpeted floor, but I reached the end of the block of rooms with no sticky notes in sight. I waited in the elevator lobby.

I swung around toward a flapping noise down the hallway. Around a corner, at the opposite end, a man walked behind a lady dressed in a burgundy sweater and skirt. Even from the back, the man was dapper with wintry gray hair.

"William," I whispered. Or should I say Sid?

Mom pushed open the stairwell door and they disappeared outside.

I raced down the hall after them and cracked open the door.

"I won't drink tequila that's aged more than four years." Mom was saying as she stomped down the staircase.

Was she making small talk? Buying time? Or speaking in code hoping I'd be listening?

The voices grew faint and I bolted downward. The brick path was empty. For people with achy joints, these seniors hustled. I rocketed across the grass in time to view them cutting the corner into the main building. Where was he taking Mom?

My phone vibrated. It was Veera.

Sofi's sitting in the restaurant with her homies. The Ocean Vista's serving a buffet today. Wait until you see the dessert spread.

I texted back:

Meet me by the wingback chairs. Mom's headed that way.

Minutes later, Veera and I hovered outside the dining hall. A glass wall bordered the large wooden archway leading into the Ocean Vista.

"Sofi hauls butt," Veera said. "She crossed the road over to the beach. Then she pulled out a phone. I followed and hid behind a palm tree. She spoke real low so I couldn't hear, but she called somebody 'boss.'"

Why did she need to go outside to talk? Who did she work for?

"When she headed back to the Villa, I made it look like I bumped into her by accident. We walked back together, but she didn't say much. That would've been a prime opportunity to switch phones, if I'd thought of it and if a prison sentence wasn't waiting in the wings."

"Let's go."

"Where?"

"To find the nearest cheese blintz."

* * *

Mom hobnobbed with the usual gang: Peter, Sofi, Vincent, Lil, and William. They'd snagged a table next to the floor-to-ceiling, ocean-view windows. Veera and I squeezed into a booth toward a back corner and gobbled up our cheese blintzes, French toast, and spinach frittatas. The distant vantage point gave me a chance to view the interplay among the residents. Envious glances and whispers were aimed at Mom's table. The table hosting the popular kids. Most residents were well dressed, but those at the VIP table were exceptionally well outfitted in suits and glitzy, toned-down dresses. Laughter erupted often from their seats. Mom looked like she was having a ball.

"We should've put a wire on her," I said.

"You have one?" Veera asked.

"No," I said. "Put that on the list of supplies to stash in my trunk."

"I've been thinking. Got any idea of what Dom's last words meant?" Veera asked. "Last words before he was hospitalized, I mean. 'Cause I've got some ideas."

"Watch. Water. Safe," I whispered. The words floated through my mind, but I couldn't make sense of them.

"He was asking us to watch a safe near the water. Probably near the swimming pool. I'll scout around for it."

I pushed my chair back. "I'll be back."

"Where're you off to?"

"To crash a party." I made a beeline for Mom's table. I needed to be where the action was. "May I join you?" I stood behind Mom's chair.

"My lap is free," William purred, patting his thighs.

"Do you know how inappropriate that is?" I asked him.

"She's right," Sofi said. "You could get hauled into court for that."

141

"Fiddlesticks. I'm O.G. which means Old Gentleman, which means I have a free pass to be inappropriate any time I damn well please." He took a long slurp from his Bloody Mary. "Want a sip?" He held up his glass.

"He doesn't know what he's saying," Lil said. "That's his third Bloody Mary and he hasn't even had breakfast yet."

"What she means is that you caught me while I'm still sober," William said. "I don't really get started 'til at least the fourth or fifth one. Stick around for some fun."

I borrowed a chair from a nearby table and squeezed it between Mom and Vincent. He scraped his chair away and gave me a squinty eye.

Sofi placed her cellphone in front of her. A timer was displayed. "You have exactly one minute to tell us all about yourself. Then we'll decide if you can stay or we'll banish you."

"Maybe forever," Peter said.

"Don't be silly," Sofi said. "Nothing is forever. Except for Twinkies and Spam."

Why did I feel I was down the rabbit hole with a pack of talking playing cards?

"She means Spam made from pork, not the kind in your email," Lil said. "Go ahead, we're listening."

Talking about myself wasn't my thing. Making up a story about someone else wasn't so bad. "I was born in Pittsburgh. Mom and Dad ran a Christmas Tree farm and that's where I spent most of my time when I wasn't writing songs and taking acting lessons." I took a deep breath.

Mom's lips slightly parted.

"Next thing you know I'm running a flower and lei shop in Hawaii. Thanks, Nan."

"I'm so proud of her." Mom patted my head.

The table went silent for a moment.

Sofi turned her gaze to me. "Now tell us why you're really here."

"Okay." I turned to William. "I wanted to thank you for asking Nana to meet you this morning so you could escort her to the dining room."

Vincent's brows dropped over his deep-set eyes.

"Asking who what?" William stuck his neck out. "I saw Lucy Fay wandering around and asked if she knew how to sew on a button."

"Which I did in thirty seconds," Mom added with a grin.

"Without breaking a sweat," William said. "The button popped off my lucky jacket. I have to wear it when we play—" He cleared his throat and stopped.

"Play what?" I looked around the table.

He straightened the lapels of a two-button sport jacket in a houndstooth pattern.

"Croquet," Sofi said. "Makes him look downright smart."

"Otherwise he looks downright stupid." Lil slurped her coffee.

"We're in the middle of eating, sweetie," Mom said. "Why don't you and Veera go shopping? Use my credit card. It's in my office desk." Her eyes rounded and she lowered her voice and slowed the words when she said "office" and "desk," neither of which she had upstairs.

"Run along." Peter waved me off. "There's nothing here for you."

All eyes stuck to me as I rose. I strolled back to Veera.

Veera tossed her napkin on the table. "As soon as you left, they started whispering again."

"They're hiding something." I told her about the conversation.

"What was your mom talking about? The Villa office?"

"It's the only office around."

* * *

"Staff won't be back for an hour," Veera spoke low, reading the sign on the administration office door. "They're in a meeting."

"Excellent timing," I said.

Veera and I had swapped our black op clothes for casual wear. Veera turned heads in a red floral print blouse over black pants and I opted for a V-neck mixed-print tee over jeans.

"Why would your mom send us to the office?" Veera said.

"Must be something in the desk we need to see." Maybe I could find more about Sid's identity, too.

* * *

Veera positioned herself at the reception area so she faced me, and grilled the two employees about the activities. Unless they had eyes in the backs of their heads, I was good to go.

"Nan wants to know all about the history of the Villa," she was saying. "What was here before, how did it become a retirement community, who decides the menu..."

I rushed down the short hallway and whipped out my key, except I didn't need it. The doorknob turned and I scooted inside. If anyone entered the admin office, I'd dive out the open window.

Nothing new showed up in the desks, so I scuttled toward Lettie's office. I pressed my ear to the door. Not a sound. I gripped the handle. Locked. That meant there had to be something worth seeing in there. I scooped up two paper clips off a desktop, straightened them out, and jiggled them around in the lock until a friendly click invited me inside. I shut the door behind me, locked it, and aimed for her filing cabinet. Two folders on Lettie's chair tripped me halfway.

"Hello, Dom." The top sheet in his folder was an accounting of outstanding payments. He was in the hole nearly twenty thousand dollars. Two months' rent. Why did they permit him to stay? The second file was thin and unmarked. I'd barely thumbed through it when I lingered over a typed note to Lettie.

One word from you and the place will go up in smoke. I'll make sure you're in it.

Sid

"Blackmail." What did Sid hold over Lettie? And over Dom? What did he want with Mom, aka Lucy Fay? I peered closer. A typewriter was used. I could tell by the slightly misaligned letters and the off-spacing. Also, the typed y's were thick, meaning the key stuck. Who at the Villa used a typewriter?

CHAPTER TWENTY-EIGHT

My phone vibrated. It was Veera.

Someone snuck past when I wasn't looking. The door to the office just closed.

I dropped the folders onto the chair and dashed toward the window just as the floor creaked in the staff office. A desk drawer squealed open. I unlatched the window and lifted it gingerly. It faced a little alcove where I wouldn't be seen unless someone walked by. I braced a sneaker against the ledge and was about to hop over when loud voices interrupted me. I ducked back inside. A gaggle of ladies strolled by.

"Holly, you left my window open," Lettie's monotone voice drifted through the window.

"I haven't been in your office today," Holly replied.

"Then you left it open yesterday."

I'd have company in a few minutes. Meanwhile, who was prowling next door?

In three quick moves, I landed on my rubber soles on the pavement outside and slinked away toward the nearest corner. I peered around the edge in time to view the admin staff hang a right to the front entry. I was home free.

"Corrie! Help!"

I flipped around to view a leg dangling out the window from the admin office.

Chapter Twenty-Nine

All Shook Up

Mom sat on the ledge of the window in the admin office, tugging on something inside. I inched closer. Her skirt was hiked up around her thighs; she clenched the fabric in her fists and tugged in short jerks. The hem was stuck.

"What are you doing?" I asked. Her legs dangled over the ledge. She'd sent me to the office. Why would she follow?

"I've always wanted to ride sidesaddle and thought this would be good practice. What do you think I'm doing? I've been snagged," she said, half whispering, half shouting.

I pulled myself up next to her, lay on my stomach, and leaned over the ledge. I grabbed hold of her rogue hem. It was stuck on an old nail head.

"Why would you break in and risk arrest?" I asked.

"It was truth or dare. I couldn't tell the truth so I took the dare."

Since when did Mom not lie?

"They dared me to come into the office. I thought it would be a cinch. You'd be inside and help me. Thanks, by the way, for leaving the door open."

"I... never mind." I ripped her skirt to unhook it and grabbed the torn piece of fabric stuck on the nail. I scooted backward and jumped down. Mom landed next to me seconds before the front door creaked. We hotfooted away, the torn piece of Mom's skirt trailing behind her. I scooped up the renegade strip and scuttled by her side.

"Didn't anyone at the cool kids' table wonder if you'd passed me some sort of clue when you mentioned a desk and the office?"

"Why would they? This isn't an Agatha Christie novel." Mom slowed so we walked side-by-side. "These are people who dare each other to push the envelope. I snuck past Veera, by the way, when she wasn't looking." She did a mini fist pump.

"They set you up," I said. Or did they just want to see if she fit in their pack? "What if I wasn't there and you were still stuck on the sill?"

"Oh, sweetie. One of those nice valets would've helped me."

We slowed as the valets turned toward us.

"Good morning, gentlemen." Mom tossed them a big smile and a wave, and they reciprocated.

"Lettie would've walked in before help arrived. Then what?" I switched direction and led her away from the Villa. "Don't you wonder why the R.A.T. pack really sent you there?"

"They sent me on a hunt to find one item. A photo of Holly and Dominic."

There'd been a framed picture in Holly's desk drawer that I didn't bother with. Just another photo of her with Dom. Why would they want that? "Did you find it?"

Mom pointed to her handbag. "Stuffed in my purse."

Maybe I wasn't just a chip off my father's block, but my mother's, too. Can you be a chip off of two different blocks? "Let's go to my car and get you out of that skirt."

"What am I supposed to wear? A tire?" Mom trotted next to me.

"There's an extra pair of sweats with your name on it."

"What you're really saying is that I flubbed things up." She dragged her feet and stuck out her lower lip.

I didn't like seeing Mom downcast. This was senior citizen hazing. I put an arm around her shoulders and she patted my hand. "They'll be totally impressed when you show them the photo, after I take a look at it. Besides, using the sticky notes as breadcrumbs was sheer genius."

"It was either that or toothpicks, which I also carry in my purse."

"After you show them Holly's photo, what happens?" I asked.

"I'll be initiated into the pack." Mom's face lit up like she held it over a lantern.

"Is William's codename Sid?"

"I questioned him, but all I got was a recipe for a banana tequila daiquiri and a lecture on why cigars promote good health," Mom said. "When he asked if I'd help with his button, I couldn't resist those goofy Basset Hound eyes."

"The man's a high-functioning alcoholic, that's why his eyes are so heavy-lidded." Since when was Mom such a sucker?

"When I said I was waiting for Sid…" Her eyes grew round, "…he told me they all were."

"What does that mean?"

"Beats me. He changed the subject after that."

We stopped by my trunk and I popped open the lid. I needed to cut Mom some slack. Couldn't be easy hangin' with old folks. I handed her the sweatpants. "I make mistakes, too."

"Dumber than getting stuck on a nail?"

"Much dumber."

"I just thought of something." Mom settled in the backseat, made the switcheroo, and dumped the skirt inside my trunk. "What would Sid want with Lucy Fay?"

"She's the new old kid at the Villa," I said. "And she's got money."

Mom unzipped her purse. "Here."

It was the photo of Holly and Dom together, grinning.

"What's it say on his shirt?" Mom asked.

Dom's oversized black T-shirt displayed bold white letters. I peered closer.

"Tennis anyone?" I read. Dom was the athletic type. Probably played tennis. A green tennis ball loomed above cascading playing cards. What did tennis have to do with card games? Below that, I read "Tricky play." Those two words hovered above a row of three wine bottles. I took a picture of the photo with my phone. Was the shirt a result of a quirky sense of humor or a message?

"Dominic's a man with a funny bone who likes to drink and play games,"

CHAPTER TWENTY-NINE

Mom said. "That's what that shirt's telling me. And he likes custom T-shirts."

"Dom's last words," I said, "before he lost consciousness were, 'Watch, water, safe.'"

"Keep his watch water-safe?" she asked.

"More likely there's a watch in a safe," I said. "But where does water fit in?"

"A floating safe! Out in the ocean somewhere. These seniors are constantly on the lookout for some action." Mom stuffed the photo back in her purse as a security guard scooted by in a golf cart. I took Mom's arm and we strolled toward the exit.

"Why would the R.A.T. pack want that particular photo?" I steered her to the brick path leading to the main building.

Mom snapped her fingers. "Either to get back at Holly for something or they want shirts just like Dominic's."

I sort of agreed with the last part. It had to do with the shirt. "Next time they dare you to pull a stunt like that, don't. If you'd been caught, you'd have been thrown out of the Villa. And where would we be?"

Mom stopped and faced me. "William said they don't throw anyone out."

"Seriously?" Maybe he was right. Being behind on rent didn't make waves.

"The stakes get higher after initiation into the book club," Mom said.

"Did William say that, too?" I asked.

"No." She looked around again. "It's something Vincent said." She turned to me, doing a mini, silent handclap. "Oh, honey. I'm getting good at putting pieces together. I can see why you and Veera love covert investigations."

"Keep it together, Mom. What did Vincent say?"

"That he wasn't going to prison if the game became too…risky. I read between the lines."

Dom risked a jail sentence by robbing the bank. Did the R.A.T pack assign daring stunts for fun? I yanked Mom behind the trunk of a sycamore tree. Peter scurried past us like a man on a mission. I debated following. Where was he off to?

"Go back to your room, Mom. I'll meet you there." I switched direction.

"Why can't I come?"

"Because Lucy Fay's friends shouldn't catch her in those sweatpants."

Mom looked down at her pants. "You're right."

I took a few steps.

"Where are you going?" Mom asked.

"To find Holly." I texted Veera to make that happen. "Time we chatted again."

Chapter Thirty

Move It

I aimed in Peter's direction, but he'd disappeared off the face of the Villa. Was he headed for the Village? Before I could conduct a search, Veera texted back:

Meet me in the staff parking lot.

I flipped around and jogged past William, perched on the edge of the turtle fountain, eyes closed, face tilted toward the sun. He didn't budge when I passed by. I slow jogged until I finally reached the north end of the Villa. Veera waved me over to a bench across a chunk of lawn on the opposite side.

"Over there." She pitched her chin to a patch of shade where Holly paced back and forth. She stared down at her cell phone.

"Did she mention Dom?" I asked.

"Not a word," Veera said. "Said she'd talk when you arrived."

We marched over and I grabbed the phone out of Holly's hand. "Mind if I take a look?"

Holly gasped. "That's so rude."

I glanced at the phone screen. She was texting Kyle. Why text the security guard? "Thought you didn't like Kyle."

"Are you throwin' us curve balls?" Veera asked.

"Follow me," she whispered out of the corner of her mouth.

Holly slunk toward the edge of a bushy border, opened a metal gate, and

151

waved us through. We landed in a narrow alley behind the Villa. High stucco walls held back a condo complex about twenty yards away. A black and white cat trotted past, tail pointing to the sky.

"My cell phone?" Holly held out her palm.

I passed her the phone. "What did Kyle say?"

She leaned forward. "Someone was sneaking around Dominic's room last night."

"Did Kyle happen to mention who pointed out that small detail to him?"

"You?" Holly's brows shot to the tree branch jutting out above her. "I should've known."

"Did you talk with Dom last night?" Veera asked.

"You knew he returned?" she asked.

"We ran into him," I said.

Holly's face fell. "I didn't see Dominic."

My gaze dropped to Holly's feet. They weren't on the dainty side. It wasn't her sneaking around last night.

"Paramedics hauled him away," Veera said.

"Lettie said he arrived back in his apartment, felt unwell, and paramedics were called." Holly's eyes welled up. "Is he alright?"

"He'll be fine." I hoped.

She sniffled. "Dominic could've called me, but he didn't." Her gaze wavered between Veera and I.

"It was late. Had a lot on his mind." I gave her the edited version, omitting the bank robbery, the casino, and the potential poisoning. I told her he spent a few nights in the Village. For all I knew, Holly was playing us. Maybe she wanted us to bring Dom back so she could get revenge for something she blamed on him. Maybe she already had.

"Was he alone?" she asked.

"Yes," I said. If I didn't know it already, here it was again. She clearly had the hots for him.

"Is that all the information you have?" Veera asked her.

Holly massaged her temples. "Yes. I'm so worried. Maybe the bullies got to him."

"What bullies?" Had to be the R.A.T. pack.

"I don't know who they are…just that they're the ones who empty purses and threaten harm when nobody's looking. You know how easy it is to say that an accident put a senior in the hospital?"

Veera and I traded glances.

"Is Sid one of the bullies?" I asked.

"There's no 'Sid' at the Villa," Holly said.

"Our job here's done. We found Dom last night. We'll send you our bill." I turned on my heel and left with Veera at my side.

"Wait." Holly trotted after us.

"Why didn't you tell us Dom owed so much back rent?" I asked.

She wrung her hands. "I hired you to find a missing person because I feared for his safety. There'd been attempts on his life. He was nearly run down at the beach crossing. I told you he felt threatened."

"Why didn't he report any of this?" I asked.

"He didn't want police involvement. Dominic said his friends were joking." Holly rubbed a hand across her forehead. "He said he'd be current on his rent soon and Lettie accepted that."

Why wouldn't he want cops involved? Either he had a record already or didn't want them to know about an illegal operation going on at the Villa. That was my hunch of the day. "Did any former residents end up in jail?"

Holly caught her breath and nodded. "Only one. Claude Devoro. He tried to rob a liquor store on State Street and was caught escaping in a taxi. He only spent a day in jail since he took nothing from the store."

"Is Claude still at the Villa?" Veera asked.

"He moved out right after."

"Who were his friends?" I asked.

"Dom?" Veera asked.

"Yes."

"And Peter, Lil…"

"They're a close-knit group," Holly said.

"That like to play rowdy games," I said. "Like combat croquet."

"I thought if you could catch one of them in the act," Holly said, "Dominic

153

would be free from them."

"You should have called the police about the bullying," Veera said.

"I called you instead."

"That was a good call." Veera gave her a thumbs up.

"It wasn't always like this," Holly said. "She's the cause of the problems."

Veera's gaze locked on mine. "Who?"

"Sofia Reyes. She stirs up trouble." Holly's black leather clog practically pawed the ground.

"She hasn't been at the Villa all that long, but she came between you and Dom." Jumping to conclusions seemed to get answers.

"Is that why he didn't tell me he was back? Was she with him?" Holly asked.

It really was high school all over again. Bullies, jealousy, and all the alcohol you could drink without supervision.

"You weren't a topic of conversation," I said. "Sid was."

"How many times do I have to tell you?" Holly fidgeted with her fingers. "There is no Sid."

"What is going on here?" A woman's deep, husky voice cut into our conversation. Lettie stood outside the gate, clipboard pressed to her chest, pen dangling from her fingers, ever ready to jot down incriminating notes.

"Holly's giving us pointers on how to make Nan's stay more comfortable," I said.

"What pointers?" Lettie asked.

"Make sure Nana's surrounded by kind, loving friends, visit her often..." I turned to Veera.

"And talk to the chef about Nan's favorite foods," Veera said. "Especially fruit pies. They're packed with antioxidants."

Holly put a hand to her head. "Excuse me. I have work to do." She scurried down the alley, while Lettie gave us the evil eye.

"What brings you to this seldom traveled corner of the Villa?" I asked Lettie.

"Where's your grandmother?"

"At the beach," Veera said. "Sunbathing. Or was it seashell hunting?"

The squeal of tires interrupted our chatter. We turned in time to view Holly crumpled by the side of the alley, and a golf cart speeding away. A customized cart; black matte with matching rims. The driver wore a tan bucket hat. I dashed off with Veera close behind. Lettie hurried behind us.

Holly lay half-hidden beneath a batch of bougainvillea bordering the Villa. I knelt next to her. Her cheek was scratched. Her hair was dotted with leaves and brittle twigs.

"You alright?" I helped her to her feet.

She gulped and blinked back tears. "I was walking—"

"Did you see the driver?" The souped-up cart was probably going forty or so miles an hour.

"He wore sunglasses and a hat." She wiped the leaves off of her pants.

"How do you know it was a he?" Veera asked as Lettie joined us.

"I'm not sure," Holly said.

"It was an accident," Lettie said. "The driver didn't see her around the bend."

He must have driven toward Holly, flipped a U, and raced away, trying to run her down in the process. "Call the police, Lettie."

Lettie stepped up to Holly. "Did the cart hit you?"

"No, I got out of the way," Holly said.

"I don't see anything beyond cuts and scratches." Lettie turned to me. "Holly wasn't paying attention and walked in the center of the road, risking injury. Since she wasn't hurt, there's no need for police. They wouldn't come anyway."

"Who's the golf cart owner?" I asked. "He shouldn't be driving so fast and—"

"I make decisions here." Lettie turned to Holly. "Follow me. We'll get you cleaned up. You're a mess."

Holly limped away after her.

"Wait." I ran after Lettie. I'd nearly forgotten about Mom. "You were looking for Nan. Why?"

"She was reported leaving Dominic's apartment last night, just before the paramedics arrived."

"That's not possible. She was with us, in her bedroom, sleeping. I would've known if she left." Kyle saw me. Who would report Mom?

"I saw you two last night. After the paramedics left," Lettie said. "Didn't look like you were in your grandmother's quarters."

"When we left her, she was sound asleep and had been for a while," I said.

"How's Dominic?" Veera asked.

"Conscious," Lettie said. "His blood pressure is high and he's nauseated, but he'll be fine. I want to speak to Lucy Fay immediately."

"We'll let her know," Veera said.

Lettie turned her back and stormed off with Holly.

I called Mom. No answer. "The police will be all over this once it's discovered the water was tampered with."

"Which means we gotta make sure your Mom's in the clear."

Why wasn't she answering the phone?

Chapter Thirty-One

California Girls

Why didn't Mom follow directions? She wasn't in Lucy Fay's apartment.

"She left a note," Veera shouted from the bedroom. She barreled around the corner and passed me a sticky note.

"In the garden with Vincent. Do not disturb," I read out loud. "Let's go."

* * *

Mom's arm was linked with Vincent's as they strolled among the abundant plant life. I zipped over to them.

"Nana, you weren't in your apartment," I said.

"Vincent invited me for a walk." She'd switched into a floral print chiffon dress with lace trim. She widened her eyes and lowered her head so that only Veera and I could see her expression; a wave of her bob shielded her face from Vincent. She rolled her eyes to one side, giving me her best "get lost" look.

"Have you two been strolling long?" I asked. "Say fifteen minutes or so?"

"Uh-huh." Mom's lips were partly smiling, part bunched up.

Vincent wasn't the golf cart driver. "See you," I said.

Veera and I marched out the entry. I paused by a valet.

"Can I help you, Miss?" A big, goofy grin sprang up on the bottom half

157

of his face. His eyes matched his blue polo shirt, and his damp, beachy hair was combed back with a little help from hair gel. The Villa logo sat over his left chest beneath a badge that read, "Eddie". He batted his eyelashes at us.

"Did Sofi Reyes come out this way? My nana's looking for her," I said sweetly.

"Yes." He pointed toward the sparkling ocean. "She and William crossed over a few minutes ago."

We scrambled away and Veera whispered,

"Why did he say, 'crossed over'? Sounds like they're a couple of cocker spaniels heading over the Rainbow Bridge. Eddie rubbed me the wrong way."

"We'll overlook that if we find Sofi."

Butterfly Beach was a narrow stretch of sandy shoreline buffered by a stone sea wall. Two sets of concrete steps at each end dipped toward the white sand. Locals body-surfed and jogged along the edge of the frothy sea; happy kiddos splashed in the tail ends of rippling mini-waves, while kelp dried their branches on the beach. No sign of Sofi or William.

"I don't see any restrooms," Veera said. "Which means they didn't go far. Senior bladders don't hold up long."

"Impressive." I wouldn't have figured that one out on my own.

"Life skills learned from living with Gran."

"Where would your Gran go if she wanted to enjoy a private chat on this beach?" I spoke over the rumbling of the waves.

Veera assessed the landscape. "She doesn't like sand in her Mary Janes. And you know old folks don't go barefoot." She pointed to a group of large rocks. "Gran would take over one of those boulders. Soaking up the sights away from the beachcombers."

"Excellent deduction."

We trekked closer, scanning the boulders for signs of silvery hair or pale, reddish curls. The crown of a straw hat popped up moments later behind a large boulder. A few more steps revealed a curly-haired woman underneath the hat.

"Follow me." I flipped around and jogged up the short concrete staircase back to the sidewalk.

"Wait." Veera hustled behind me. "Aren't we going to interrogate those two?"

"We are." I cut a sharp left and hot-footed toward Sofi and William. "But we don't want them to know what we're up to."

I crouched and Veera mimicked me, with only our eyes peeping above the wall. As we inched closer, William came in full view, sitting cross-legged on a squat boulder below Sofi. He gazed up at her with a silly smile, like he'd fallen into a vat of bubbly champagne. I crouched lower on the sidewalk, my back pressed against the short wall separating us from the shoreline.

"I can't hear them over the crashing of the waves," Veera said.

"We need to get closer."

"Want me to distract them so you can do that?" Veera asked.

I shifted my gaze from Sofi to Veera. A pinch of longing in her voice caught me off-guard. "You take the lead on this one. I'll distract them while you slide in, position yourself behind Sofi's boulder and listen."

Veera's face shone brighter than the sun. Good thing I wore my darkest shades. "I'll memorize every word."

I gave her two thumbs up. "I'll backtrack and stroll by. Take those stairs…" I pointed to the shorter set of steps a few yards away, "…and make your way down once I'm in place. Ready?"

"It'll be like I'm wearing an invisibility cloak."

Chapter Thirty-Two

Everybody Loves Somebody

I hit the sidewalk at a brisk jog. The wind scattered my hair while sand grits peppered my cheeks. I hopped down the stairs, slowing to a casual stroll once I neared the batch of boulders. Thankfully neither senior had budged, but William had slid closer to Sofi, perching on the corner of her boulder. He looked just as comfortable on the beach in his two-piece suit as he would in bathing trunks. They huddled beneath a smattering of shade to protect their aging skins from the searching rays of the sun. Sofi's pink cotton dress covered her bare legs. William whispered to her and Sofi's mouth tightened, but I had a strong feeling the tightening was more in response to my interruption than his sweet nothings.

"Hi there," I said.

William rotated his head, hawk-like, to stare at me, and flapped his hand my way. "Go away, little bird. Can't you see we're in the middle of a deep, dark adult discussion?"

"Been sunbathing long?" I asked.

"Since breakfast," Sofi said. "Why?"

That was a lie. I saw William no more than thirty minutes ago by the turtle fountain. "How about you?" I asked him.

"Where she goes, I'm never far behind." William practically swooned next to Sofi.

"What do you want?" she snapped.

"Advice." My eyes were fixed on them, but, from my peripheral vision, I spied Veera scooting down the stairs and diving behind the boulders.

"Use at least an SPF 50 sunscreen and your skin will be as radiant as mine if you're lucky enough to live as long as I have," Sofi said.

The top few buttons of her high-necked dress were undone. She caught my stare and reached her manicured hand to fasten it. Her straw hat was pulled down low enough to nearly cover her brows. What was it my father always said?

A good disguise is like an onion with many layers. Watch out for what lies below.

I fastened my gaze on the opening. Her neck was remarkably smooth for a woman in her eighties.

"You're wasting our time." Now she sounded cross.

Making an exit wasn't a problem since Veera was in position, but I wasn't ready yet. "I don't trust Vincent. He's spending too much time with Nana."

"Is she complaining?" Sofi asked as William stroked her hand.

"Well—"

"Let her enjoy herself in peace. Go on, leave us alone." William's chin was raised and he regarded me with the disdain reserved for a virgin eggnog.

"Have you seen Peter?" I asked.

"Headed for the tennis court about twenty minutes ago," William said. "I'm sure he'll be thrilled to see you."

Peter had my vote for most likely to be the rogue golf cart driver. I'd spotted him near that end of the Villa a short time before, just like William said. I dropped my head and shoulders and dragged my feet away, tossing a peek over my shoulder. Sofi eyed me while William caressed her hand. Veera crouched behind the boulder wearing aviator shades and her signature smile. Why did I have the feeling Sofi knew that Mom, Veera, and I were phonies? Maybe because I suspected Sofi of being the same.

I hurried up the Villa driveway. What about Lil? Hadn't seen her in a while. I called Holly. She didn't pick up, but she texted me a minute later.

I'm in the office. Can't talk. Lettie's door is open and she can hear everything I say.

"Hey, you."

I looked up to find Eddie the valet blocking my path with a grin.

"Have you seen Peter or Lil?"

"No. Want to grab some food?"

"Can't. Do you know where Lil lives?"

"Bungalow seven."

"Thanks." I walked past him and stopped. He could be more useful. "Eddie, my Nan wants a custom golf cart. Know where she can get one?"

Eddie clasped his hands behind him and grinned some more. "We've got a bunch. All designs and colors. I'll show you around."

"Great."

"Meet me here in half an hour." He zipped away toward a Mercedes pulling up.

I moseyed over to Lil's bungalow and knocked. No answer, but music drifted through her door. I knocked again. I circled around to the back, but no sign of her being at home. Just when I'd given up, her back door groaned open. I couldn't see over the walled yard, but shoes stomped outside. I scurried closer to the wall, hopped onto a large rock, and peered over. The edges of Lil's lavender cardigan blew behind her, as did the hem of a wildly patterned shift dress. Her low-heeled suede pumps pointed toward the back gate. Where was she off to? I jumped down.

"Hi, Lil." I met her as she stormed out. "Got a minute?"

"I'm late for class." She hurried away and I kept up.

"Which class?"

"'Getting Your TikTok On'. I'm gonna be dancing up a storm. More like a tsunami, and it's gonna be all over the Internet. My last video had over sixty-five hundred views."

I could see her cutting loose to the beat. "This is important."

She waved me away. "So's my class."

"I know what you're doing," I said.

"Can't hear you." She picked up speed.

I hurried in front to block her path, which wasn't easy since she was sturdier than a tugboat. She switched direction and headed back to her bungalow.

"Don't fool with me or you'll be sorry." She swung her purse at my head.

I ducked in the nick of time. These seniors were mean machines. Did her mean streak start when she moved to the Ritz Carlton of retirement communities and fell in with a bad crowd? Or was she always like this?

"I wanted to talk because I don't want what happened to Dom to happen to you." I turned on my heel.

"Don't you turn your back on me, young lady."

I whirled around. Lil strode toward me, stopping inches from my face, hands on hips.

"Dominic had a heart attack. That's what I was told." She spat out the words like she dared me to contradict them.

How could I prove I knew more without giving away my cover? The clock was ticking and someone else could get hurt. "He was poisoned."

She straightened, eyes rounded. "That's an egregious accusation. How would you know anything? You and your glamour granny just got here."

"Can't reveal my source," I said.

She squinted at me so long and hard, I nearly fossilized. "You've got my attention."

"Someone broke into Dom's room before he returned. They were after something, but he wouldn't say what."

Her quick nod turned into a headshake. "I've fought off shingles, Diabetes types one and two, and arthritis in both my knees. No one's going to make me do anything I'm opposed to." She headed back to her place. "I told Dominic to stay away from them."

"From who?" I trotted beside her.

"From people trying to get him to do things he shouldn't do just because they know things they shouldn't."

"Give me a name."

"I'm not rattin' out anyone." She circled around to the front of her bungalow.

"What if someone else gets hurt?" I hoped to appeal to her sympathy button. "My Nan…"

"No one's getting hurt as long as I have a breath left in my lungs." She pulled out her key and stuck it in her doorknob. "Tell Lucy Fay to lock herself in her room and don't come out 'til this blows over."

"Two questions." I stuck my foot in her door. "Where've you been the past hour?"

"None of your business, but I'll tell you anyway. I've been practicing for my video."

I spied a pair of tap-dancing shoes and a fan on her coffee table through the crack in her door. "What's the book club?"

Lil practically spit at me. "A club that has nothing to do with reading books." She slammed the door shut behind her.

I retraced my steps back to the front of the Villa when Veera showed up.

"Sofi's a bull who thrives on locking horns," she said.

"Did you get anything useful?"

Veera grabbed my arm and pulled me to a corner of the lobby. "Turns out William's an ex-Marine who hosts Happier Hour in his suite. That's after the public happy hour in the Villa bar is over. His favorite weapon is an antique dagger named dirk."

"A dirk is long, skinny and sharp, kind of like a knife." Dad was a weapons collector, antique and modern, so I knew a little something. "A personal weapon of naval officers back in the day."

"William said Dom's a sap that never should have been allowed to play the game."

"Card game?" This could be the answer we'd been looking for.

"Don't know. Sofi called William a sore loser," Veera said. "And said she planned to win the next round."

The wheels in my head spun at breakneck speed. "The book club is a cover for a high-stakes game where the winner takes all, and losers lose big-time," I said. "Good work, Veera."

"Old people," Veera said, "aren't scared of getting arrested."

"Maybe they consider it a badge of honor." It was my turn to pull Veera aside. I led her to an empty corner of the restaurant. I waved aside a server and waited until he was out of earshot to speak, "How old would you say

CHAPTER THIRTY-TWO

Sofi is?"

"Seventy, tops. Hardly any wrinkles, dresses with style and has a spark about her. Like a firecracker that's lit."

"She said she was eighty-five when we first met, but her neck is wrinkle-free."

"Maybe she got herself a neck lift," Veera said.

"What about her hands? Those can't be lifted."

"You're saying she's one of us?"

"I'm saying she's here under some pretense. She's after something, too. We have to get that something first." I told her about Lil. "How do we get her to talk?"

"If she gets spooked, she'll talk," Veera said. "Lil's nerves rattle easily. I still say she's got a crush on Vincent. I've seen how she looks at him."

I stared out the window and spied Eddie surveying the lobby. I jumped up. "Come on. We've got a golf cart to trace."

Chapter Thirty-Three

Smoke Gets In Your Eyes

"Sorry, I'm late," Eddie said and nodded to Veera. "Follow me."

We trailed him out the front and across a carpet of lawn where any patch of grass rebellious enough to turn brown was instantly fertilized and watered into fast compliance. We exited through a metal gate that locked behind us, and marched across Channel Drive. A gravel path pulsed between a private beach club and a condo complex. Squeezed near the end was a medium-sized structure topped with a red-tiled roof. Tall maples provided sun-dappled shade. Veera and I flanked Eddie, making small talk about the Villa, until I upped the conversation a notch.

"Anyone at the Villa been arrested lately?" I wanted to see if his story matched Holly's.

"Why? Did you hear something?" Eddie darted his eyes from side to side, like he was buying time to figure out what to say.

"Villa activity is on police radar," Veera said. "And arrests are public record."

She had no problem jumping in and backing me up.

"That was a while ago, and it was a case of mistaken identity. You know, that's when two guys have the same name."

Meaning the resident had a sharp lawyer.

"What makes you think we don't understand what mistaken identity is?" Veera's shoulders shot back.

I knew what she was thinking. Eddie was about our age, but he regarded himself as a man of the world, and regarded Veera and me as females with fluff for brains. Didn't matter what he thought. What did matter was getting the information we needed.

"Lettie keeps the staff well informed, doesn't she?" I nudged my way between the two.

"She updates us every Monday morning."

Lettie doubled as the Villa spin doctor leaking out only necessary news to the staff. Wasn't hard to do since cops never made the whole arrest story public, anyway. We strolled up to the structure.

"You hear about last night?" Eddie's eyes lit up at the prospect of impressing us some more.

"Why don't you enlighten us?" Veera said.

"A resident had a heart attack. Should be okay though." Eddie slowed. A wide, roll-up door dominated the front. Eddie held up a ring of keys. "A couple of senior attendants have keys to the cart house, in case a resident wants to borrow one."

"Borrow?" Veera asked. "You mean they belong to the Villa?"

"A lending library of golf carts," I mumbled.

"That's right," Eddie said.

The squeal of a siren scattered away a flock of pigeons snoozing on the limbs of an old maple. Shouldn't be hard to figure out who'd borrowed the cart that nearly flattened Holly.

Eddie unlocked a side entrance. We followed him into a dim space that smelled damp and chemical fresh at the same time. He flicked on a light switch and pushed a button. The roll-up door made way for natural light which shone on a dozen or more shiny carts slant parked inside, with a center aisle between them. Each was customized to fit a different personality. From zebra stripes to a yellow Ford Mustang.

"We're looking for a matte black ride with matching rims and interior," Veera said.

"With tinted windshields?" Eddie asked. "That's super cool."

"Where is it?" I didn't see it.

"Out for repairs." Eddie stuffed his hands in his pockets and strode around. "Get a load of this." He pointed to a powder blue cart with a white top. "Goes up to thirty-five miles per hour. Wanna take it for a spin?"

"Back up," I said. "The matte black one. What kind of repairs?"

"Dunno. A dent or a battery change, maybe."

"Our Nana's gonna want to check these out," Veera said.

"She should reserve in advance to get the one she wants. Street legal ones are the first to go."

"Who reserved the matte black one yesterday?" Geez, you'd think we would've gotten an answer already. What kind of customer service was this? "Our nan liked *that* one."

"It'll be back in a week or so."

"Now, Eddie," I said in my I-might-kill-you-if-you-don't-answer-me voice. "Who reserved the black one yesterday?"

"Let's find out." He sauntered over to the side entry and stopped by a podium with a clipboard and a pen on top. Eddie blinked and dunked his head closer. "They fill out this form."

I pulled out my penlight. A magnifying glass materialized in Veera's hand and we inspected the sheet. The signature was barely legible. Either it was a senior with shaky fingers or someone who didn't use his dominant hand to scribble the name. I'd go with the latter.

"You always carry a magnifier around?" Eddie grinned.

"I carry a lot of surprises in my purse," Veera said.

"Cart check-outs are on the honor system," I said. "They sign in and out on their own." I examined the writing from different angles, turning the clipboard sideways and upside down. "Did the borrower say the cart needed repairs?"

"They never do. They take it for a spin, knock over trash cans, plow down a fence and think it's no big deal." Eddie bent down and examined the hood on a leopard print cart. "The groundskeeper does a final check nightly. He noticed the black one needed repair during cart count. Residents aren't great at communicating with us."

"Looks like it says Lid Liner." Veera examined the writing closely.

Using Veera's magnifier, I gave it another go. "Pied Piper. That's what it says," I whispered.

Veera's eyes widened and she narrowed her scrutiny. "You're right."

Maybe the resident thought of himself as a rat catcher like the Pied Piper of Hamelin. Were the R.A.T. pack the targets? Maybe Holly was asking too many questions.

"I get off at seven tonight." Eddie winked at me.

My cell phone chimed. A text from Mom:

S.O.S. in lobby now!

"We could take a cart into the Village," Eddie was saying. "Grab some food."

"Not tonight, we've got plans." I showed Veera the text.

"We'll take a raincheck," Veera said.

"Thanks for showing us around." I hustled out with Veera by my side.

"What's up?" she asked.

A funnel of thick gray smoke rose ahead of us, blemishing the greenery and blue sky.

"Hopefully not my car." Please. What were the odds? Stacked against me, that's what.

Chapter Thirty-Four

Go Boom

A slow-moving mob of seniors mulled around the side of the Villa closest to the self-parking lot. A narrow road and police officers were all that kept the old-timers from plunging forward into the smoky fray. Residents packed together in different states of dress from bathrobes to smoking jackets, wrinkly faces lifted toward the dark gray funnel whirling skyward. A fire truck thundered up, grinding to a stop and blocking the view. I couldn't tell whether the grumbling hum was from the engine or the seniors.

Mom spotted us and wriggled her way to the front of the crowd, waving hands over her head. We hurried over.

"What happened?" I asked.

Her hand shot to her cheek. "Something exploded in the parking lot."

"I didn't hear anything," Veera said.

"Me neither," Mom said. "But that's the story."

"I'll be back." I needed to get close to the action, whatever action that was.

"I'm coming with you," Mom said.

"You're a resident here, remember?" I said. "You need to act like one."

Mom's lips bunched, but she turned and bustled away.

"Fact-finding mission time," I told Veera.

"We'll compare notes when you get back." Veera angled her way to Mom.

I raced through the tropical gardens toward the road. I stood a better chance of making headway far from the mob. Vines twisted around an arbor and lilies bloomed on the outskirts of the lawn. I eased up when I neared the edge of the greenery. The air smelled like a rubber tire had been thrown onto a grill.Lettie tottered at the parking lot entry, chatting with a uniformed police officer.

I hid behind a lofty palm, peering through the neighboring bushes. Firefighters gathered at the far end of the lot, dousing a black coupe. I caught my breath. Was that my car?

"You shouldn't be here," a loud voice boomed behind me.

I flipped around and lifted my chin. Kyle, the ever-present security guard, cocked his large head.

"Lettie told me to come." I sincerely believed there was a slim possibility she would've called me or Mom, if she thought our car was involved. "I'm trying to gather my senses before I go out there. It's scary."

"You don't look scared," he said.

I switched topics. "Looks like Nana's car was damaged." Here was my chance to find out.

Kyle's deep-set gaze raked over the cars. One of his eyes squinted more than the other. What was it about the way he held his head? The answer sailed into my mind.

"Your secret's safe with me," I whispered.

He whipped his gaze down to mine. If he blew enough air out of his mouth, he could probably knock me off my feet.

"Secret?" he asked.

"Your right eye. The vision's impaired." It was a half guess, half certainty. His head seemed perpetually tilted and his eyelid slightly drooped. That eye wasn't working properly.

He lowered his voice, "Why do you say that?"

My observation skills were sharper than a prickly pear spine, thanks to my P.I. father's training. But that's not what made me notice. "I have a cousin who's impaired in one eye. You remind me of him." That was actually true, if my cousin were a foot taller and as wide as a telephone booth.

"I got this job because I'm good at security."

He got the job because he looked like he could take down every single valet that worked here while drinking a cup of coffee without spilling a drop. He'd spotted Veera and me sneaking around that first night. "You do your job well." I meant that.

He stared at me for a few beats. "Follow me."

Did I have a choice? Was he going to turn me in? It could be my car that exploded. Kyle led me to Lettie. She flashed a look that would have petrified a jellyfish.

"Can't you see I'm busy?" She spoke through gritted teeth.

Kyle pointed at me. "Her car blew up."

"I knew I should've valet parked." I peered between the vehicles and the law enforcement personnel. I couldn't see my BMW. Bomb squad members, slumped with helmets off, formed a relaxed circle. Whatever had happened wasn't life-threatening.

"Sorry to hear that." Lettie crossed her arms over her chest.

She sounded about as sorry as a black widow spider sucking the life out of her victim.

"There'll be a full investigation. Isn't that right, Officer Yamamoto?" Lettie nodded toward the uniform next to her.

Officer Yamamoto didn't reply while she scrutinized me. Her shiny dark hair was pulled back in a bun, a furrow of concern etched a thin line between her brows. "You say it's your vehicle?"

"Yes, pretty sure it's my grandma's car." My heartbeat quickened. Did any of the R.A.T. pack keep cars in the lot? "May I confirm?"

"Follow me." The officer turned on her boot and I hightailed it after her, matching her step for step. Kyle tramped behind us.

I'd parked at the back end and that's where we were headed. Who'd mess with my car?

"Do you know the make and model of the vehicle?" I asked.

Officer Yamamoto pulled out her cell phone. She tapped the screen and read, "Black two-door…"

That would be me.

"CTS Coupe."

"A Cadillac?" My insides did a little tap dance that would've made Fred Astaire proud. We were still in business.

"The engine's damaged, as is the front windshield. Minor damage to the interior." She stopped in front of the charred remains.

"That's not Nan's," I said.

"You sure?" she asked.

I padded around the front and peered under what used to be the hood. Tangled bits and pieces of metal heaped together. "Pipe bomb. Homemade. How was it detonated?"

"Remotely, approximately twenty-five minutes ago."

"Placed beneath the engine?" Oh-oh. I'd better keep my P.I. questions to myself.

"That's right," Officer Yamamoto replied, moving closer. "How did you know?"

"I saw it on an episode of *Columbo*." When I watch TV, it's an oldie, but a goodie.

"Any idea of why this car would be targeted?" she asked. "Did you learn that on TV?"

"No idea." I had a million possibilities. What if she asked my name or wanted to see my I.D.? Excuses raced through my head.

"Please return to the premises." The officer turned her back to me.

I trekked back, Kyle by my side.

"Which one is your grandmother's car?" Kyle's steely gaze bore into mine.

Thankfully, Mom's Mustang was safe at home. "A black BMW, circa 2010."

"The front desk will need your information," Kyle said. "It should've been collected earlier. Any cars that don't belong will be towed."

He probably spouted out those words all day long. "Any idea of who owns the Cadillac?" I asked.

"Vincent Peabody," Kyle said.

I stared up at him. "Did Vincent do something to make someone mad?"

"That car hasn't left the lot in six days."

Doubtful that would raise anyone's ire. There were plenty of slots and this wasn't New York City.

"Vincent makes plenty of people mad," he added.

"I don't like him hanging out with Nan."

"Why were you snooping around last night?" he asked.

Not again. "Like I said, Nan's new here, and I don't know much about this place. I need to ensure she'll be safe."

I waited for a comment from Kyle, but he didn't say another word.

We walked over to the rest of the group. I turned to Kyle. "Thanks for walking me back."

His face cracked into an awkward grin that probably appeared once every full moon. He pushed past to the front of the crowd. I scoured the faces for Mom and found her with Veera near the dining hall. Veera was on the phone.

"Did you know—" Mom said.

"Vincent's car was bombed," I said.

"What? I was going to say they're serving afternoon tea soon." Her eyes popped. "Who would plant a bomb?"

"That's what the cops are working on," I said.

"Villa Sunset," Mom said, "is becoming Violent Sunset."

"Excuse me, we need some privacy." Veera motioned some seniors away and grabbed Mom's arm, pulling her away from the throng.

I sidestepped after them to a corner where an older man leaned on a cane, dozing.

Veera tapped him on the shoulder. "You're missing all the action." She flicked her thumb behind her.

He mumbled something and shuffled away.

"Holly called the hospital," Veera said. "Her friend's a nurse who gave her an update."

"Isn't that a violation of privacy?" Mom asked.

"Says the woman who's impersonating a Villa resident," I said.

"With her blessing," Mom said.

"Nothing's illegal unless you get caught," I said.

"I can't even process that right now." Mom turned to Veera. "How's Dominic?"

"Preliminary tests show traces of poison, according to the nurse, but he's conscious and asking for a martini on the rocks."

Mom turned to me. "Oh, honey. This is too dangerous. I shouldn't have asked him..." her hand flew to her lips.

"Asked who?" Was she talking about Vincent? William?

"I asked Vincent about Sid. He got up and left, just like that." She snapped her fingers. "I should've gone after him, made him tell me more. I realize that now."

When my mother's hiding something, she chews on a fingernail, which is exactly what she was doing.

"Nana," I said. "What else happened?"

"Oh look, afternoon tea's being served." She pointed to the dining room.

"What are you not telling us?" I asked.

Mom studied her finger carefully.

"Something's happening right before my eyes and I'm blind," Veera said.

"If you must know," Mom said. "After Vincent left, I met with someone else."

Chapter Thirty-Five

Roundabout

"After Vincent left, I headed for the lobby." She lowered her voice and bent over slightly so that her hands rested on her knees. Veera and I did the same for a group huddle. "Then Peter texted me."

Had he been watching Mom on the sly?

"What'd he want?" Veera asked.

"A meeting, out front. When we met-up, he asked how I liked the Villa," Mom whispered.

"When did you meet?" I asked.

"Sometime after breakfast," Mom replied.

"Suspicious," Veera said. "Did you ask him about Sid?"

"I lost my nerve," Mom said. "I will, next chance I get. And I was doing so well."

"Were you with Peter when you heard about the explosion?" Maybe she noticed his hand in his pocket...if a remote detonator was used.

"I was at the front desk, asking about teatime," Mom said.

Talk about a one-track mind.

"You ladies look like you're plotting the overthrow of the government. May I join you?"

The hair at the back of my neck stood on end as Peter's low, raspy voice droned behind me.

We faced the little man. His lopsided smile leaned toward the devilish.

His dark hair was disheveled.

"We're worried about the explosion in the parking lot," I said.

His crooked smile didn't shift. "That was a terrible incident, but at least our Vincent is safe."

He probably cared as much about Vincent as he did the blades of grass he crushed beneath his feet.

"Most activities have been canceled today due to the latest misfortune. That's why I'm here." He stepped forward and extended an elbow to Mom. "To escort you to the dining room. Tea is served."

"Isn't that sweet?" Mom linked her arm with his.

I had to admit, she was an excellent actress.

Mom threw us a wave, and they drifted out of sight.

"I can't figure him out," Veera said. "Is he the wicked leader of a pack of old wolves or just an elderly gent out for some fun?"

"He's a suspect in a possible murder attempt, a hit and run golf cart incident, and now a car bombing." I turned toward the deep blue sea in time to view a ginger-haired woman cross the street. "Come on. Sofi's on the move."

She crossed the street and walked away from the Villa. The crowd near the parking lot had thinned to a handful of residents.

"Let's follow Sofi separately," I said. "It'll make us harder to observe."

"You think she'll be watching for a tail?"

"She's sharp-eyed, sharp-minded, and sharp-dressed."

"Add sharp-tongued to that list," Veera said.

"She's up to something I can't get a handle on."

We hustled along the shrubbery, far back enough from Sofi to avoid being seen.

"Looks like Sofi's headed toward the cart house," I said. Was she investigating the carts, too? How did she know about Holly's near miss? "You go ahead. I'll come in from behind."

I veered off to the side of the Villa, cut a right and ground to a halt. Ahead stretched an empty alley sandwiched between condominium complexes. Empty except for Lettie and Vincent chatting near a wall. Most of the words poured out of Lettie's mouth. She threw questions at him, I guessed, to which he'd nod or offer a short explanation. I flitted toward them.

"Didn't expect to find you two here."

Lettie glared at me while Vincent arched a brow, aiming a steely stare my way.

"What do you want?" Lettie gripped her clipboard like she was going to pound it over my head.

"Nana sent me to make sure Vincent was alright." I turned to him. "She was concerned." Vincent's silvery hair was askew and his crisp blue dress shirt untucked. He was a man shaken by events.

"That's kind of her," he said. "It was just an accident."

"Sir, someone planted a pipe bomb under your hood," I said. "That was no accident."

"How do you know that?" Lettie's cheeks puffed out and her lips receded, as if she wasn't miffed enough already.

"Officer Yamamoto told me."

"The police don't know anything for certain until the investigation has concluded," Lettie said. "I'll thank you not to bother us anymore."

"Seems like a strange thing to thank me for, but you're welcome." I turned to Vincent. "And you're welcome to borrow Nan's car any time you'd like." I threw that out, knowing he'd never take me up on it, but hoping he'd throw a crumb of trust in my direction. Why did I suddenly feel like a pigeon under a park bench?

His lips parted in surprise. "That's a generous gesture and I thank you, Miss." He turned to Lettie. "Pardon me." He took off toward the Villa and I quickstepped to join him. He didn't seem concerned about the bomb. Maybe he'd planted it himself. I slowed next to him.

"Lettie takes her job seriously." Could I get him to talk?

"She takes the reputation of the Villa seriously. The moment there's a vacancy for longer than forty-eight hours, she'll be terminated."

"Wow, that's intense." How did he know? Had Lettie confided in him? Is that why she kept tenants on who were late on rent? "Is that what Lettie said?"

CHAPTER THIRTY-FIVE

"That nugget of information came from another staff member."

Holly jumped to mind. "I don't know much about Lettie. Has she worked at the Villa long?"

"Lettie's family once owned the Villa property," Vincent said. "A financial reversal years ago forced them to sell to a company that develops retirement communities, with the proviso that Lettie run the place. Which she's been doing ever since."

My heartbeat quickened. Was Lettie behind the gambling? "Did she have any experience?"

"She'd worked in the hotel industry in Las Vegas."

As a card dealer. Did Vincent know that tidbit? Was it even true?

We walked a few steps in silence until my phone vibrated in my pocket. I'd nearly forgotten Veera.

"Nan really was worried after your car exploded," I told Vincent.

"I'll seek out Lucy Fay and explain. She is a lovely, fine woman."

"Thank you." I stopped in my tracks and he continued walking. "She's in the dining room with Peter."

He turned and waved. I even got a small grin out of him. I texted Mom with questions to ask Vincent and read Veera's text:

Sofi's lurking around the cart house. I'm gonna confront her.

I raced toward the cart house and nearly collided with Sofi as I barreled around the corner. She stood on the short cement driveway in front of the roll-up door, staring at Veera. Sofi pointed a taser at her.

"You're not making sense," Veera was saying.

Sofi whipped around toward me. "You two are up to something and I demand to know what."

"Okay. But stop pointing that thing at my sister."

Sofi backed up a few steps and lowered the Taser. "I'm listening."

"Nan's not the best judge of character, and that's why we came to the Villa with her," I said.

"We're making sure this place has good vibes," Veera added. "And good people."

"Is that why you were in Dominic's apartment last night?" Sofi asked me.

If she knew I was inside, that meant… "Why were you there?"

"It's my ask. Spill before I use this thing on your sister."

I wasn't worried. Veera would clobber her if she got within a foot. But I needed to convince Sofi to talk without Veera being accused of assault.

"We heard Dom cheated at cards," I said. "Since he wasn't around, and I'm proactive by nature, I went hunting for the deck he played with so he couldn't cheat Nan once he returned." I sucked in some air. Sounded legit to me. "She's an up and up player and she knows her way around a pack of cards, too."

"How good is she?" Sofi asked.

"The world championship poker match in Vegas," Veera said. "That's all I'm saying."

"Your turn," I said. Apparently, Sofi wasn't concerned about my breaking into Dom's place, which meant it was something she did regularly.

"Dominic took something of mine and I wanted it back." She pulled her cashmere cardigan tightly around her. Pearly accents dotted the black sweater which she'd paired with cream-colored slacks and pearl earrings. A pearl was missing at the bottom of her sweater.

"Was it the deck of cards?" I asked.

"I'm no cheater."

"You gonna tell us what you were after?" Veera asked.

"I am not." Sofi lifted her chin.

"How did you know I was in there?" I asked.

"I didn't. But when I leapt off the balcony, I ran like heck and hid behind a tree to catch my breath. I looked back at the balcony and saw someone slim with a ponytail shimmy down a palm tree. I just realized that someone could have been you."

"You poisoned Dom," I said. "And you're clearly no senior citizen."

"I did no such thing and yes I am. A very fit senior."

"Why should we believe you?" Veera asked. "You held me hostage here and threatened my life. If you'd used that thing you could've killed me."

"First of all, none of that is true," Sofi said. "Secondly, I feel threatened by you both. You could take down poor innocent me in an instant. You've been doing a lot of nosing around. Why?"

"As have you," I said.

"Dominic and I have a history," she said. "That's all you need to know."

"And we're protecting our grandmother. Wait a minute." Clarity lit up my mind. "You're the one who told Lettie you saw our Nana leave Dom's room."

Sofi's eyes rounded. "I don't know what you mean."

"You don't have a monopoly on snooping around here," Veera said.

Sofi lowered the taser. "Truce?"

Veera and I nodded. I stepped forward and extended my hand to Sofi. Veera and I locked gazes and, in two quick moves, Veera snatched the Taser from Sofi while I grabbed her purse. It was surprisingly heavy. What was she carrying?

When I pulled back, Sofi landed a roundhouse kick against Veera's wrist, which knocked the Taser to the ground. I swung the purse around my head like a lasso and she froze. My swing required two hands since the bag felt like it housed a couple of bricks. I continued swinging while I kicked the Taser out of her reach.

"You tricked me," she said.

"Where'd you learn that move? Man, that hurt." Veera rubbed her hand.

"You two should play nicey-nicey with a lady my age. I'm very fragile."

I unbuckled the purse and rummaged around. I didn't bother checking the wallet. I wouldn't find the kind of I.D. I was looking for. "You're not Sofi Reyes and you're not even a real senior."

Her lids briefly flickered and her shoulders straightened. "Maybe if you talked some sense, I'd listen."

A patrol car pulled in and parallel parked along the edge of the driveway. I tossed the purse onto the grass behind me just as a uniform stepped out.

"I'll need to see all of your identifications," he said.

"Ours are at the Villa," I said. "My sister and I are visiting our grandmother there." I held up my palms, as did Veera.

"You alright, ma'am?" He stepped up to Sofi.

She patted her dress. "Perfectly fine."

181

"Whose purse is on the grass over there?" he asked.

"Mine," Sofi replied. "You can hand my bag back to me."

"It belongs to our Nana," I said. "This woman is a thief."

The officer strolled over and picked up the purse. The Taser lay behind a rock, out of sight, thankfully. That might be a little tougher to explain.

"Mind if I look inside?" He held up the handbag.

"Go ahead," I said.

Sofi stuck her hand on her hip. "No, you may not."

What didn't she want the cop to view? I knew the answer immediately. It would explain the weight of the purse.

"There was a report about a disturbance," he said.

I glanced around. A curtain-free window from a condo pointed our way.

"Nan thought she saw this lady taking off with her purse while she did her business in a ladies room stall at the Villa Sunset," I said. "We followed her and when we arrived here, she tossed the purse on the grass and tried to attack us."

"It was scary 'cause it was so unexpected," Veera said.

"That is a lie." Sofi faced the cop. "Do I look like I could outrun these two, let alone attack them? Ha! Such a lie."

I waited for her to tattle on us, but she didn't. What was her game plan?

"What were these young women doing to bother you, ma'am?" the cop asked her.

Veera stiffened. My mental eye rolls made me dizzy.

"Plenty," Sofi said.

"I'm fairly certain, Officer, that if you search inside the handbag, you'll find who the purse belongs to," I said.

"Hogwash," Sofi said. If she had a projectile handy to hurl, she would have. "Do you expect him to believe that?"

"Officer, please," I said. "You found that purse on the grass. You don't know who it belongs to, do you?"

The officer took a few moments to stare at each of us.

"There was a small fire resulting from a car explosion in the Villa's parking lot about an hour ago." Here was the courtroom version of me talking again.

"You're welcome to ask Officer Yamamoto about me. She escorted me to the charred vehicle to ensure it wasn't our grandmother's car. Our gran is Lucy Fay Nightingale." If those juicy details didn't sway him, nothing would. "Please call to confirm."

He pulled out his phone and sent a text while Sofi grumbled. Veera sidestepped closer to me and muttered,

"Sofi was breaking into the cart house when I showed up. Should I tell him?"

I shook my head. Accusations would complicate matters more.

The officer looked up at us, and then at Sofi. "I'm going to search the bag for some form of identification, Ma'am."

Sofi huffed.

He stuck his hand inside the bag, pulled out her wallet and froze midway. "What's in the zipped pocket?" he asked her.

"My makeup, what do you think?" she said. "I need a lot at my age, sonny."

He unzipped the pocket and stared inside while extracting a glove from a little pouch beneath his belt. He stuck his hand inside and pulled out a revolver, dangling from his finger. That magic trick was no surprise.

"I'll bet it's loaded," I said. The purse was heavy enough.

"Nobody move." The cop backed away toward his vehicle and opened his rear door.

"I knew you had a gun in there," I whispered to Sofi. "The question is why? If you tell us, we'll help you."

"Shut up." She tapped her pump impatiently.

Veera whispered, "She's a firecracker wrapped up in one of those old-timey, lace handkerchiefs. Maybe she caused the explosion in Vincent's car just by touching it."

"Wouldn't be surprised," I whispered back.

Sofi marched over to the squad car with her hands in the air. She spoke quietly to the officer and he held up her wallet. She lowered her hands as he examined the contents. He removed an ID card from the inside and gave it a careful read, before punching in numbers into his phone. Sofi threw us a backward glance, pale hooded eyes narrowed into two slits, the corners of her lips tilted upward.

"Why do we keep underestimating these old people?" Veera asked.

The officer dropped the gun into the purse and handed it over to Sofi. He turned to us. "You ladies go back to the Villa, understand?"

"Yes, Officer," I said.

He returned to his squad car and pulled away.

Veera's lips parted and I muttered an expletive. Sofi sauntered back to us, nary a hair out of place, and a winsome smile to boot.

I faced Sofi. I raised my voice. "Who do you work for?"

"None of your biz whacks," she said.

"Nobody talks like that," Veera said. "How old are you anyway?"

"As old as I want to be." Sofi turned to me. "Who do you work for?"

"I'm flattered, but we're the real deal." I turned on my heel. "Just trying to help our Nana."

Veera shadowed me as I stomped away.

"Shouldn't we try and find out what she knows?" Veera caught up and whispered. "Why's a secret agent, or whatever she is, posing as a Villa resident?"

My exit was so perfectly timed and dramatic, I was reluctant to return. "You're right." We swiveled around. Sofi still stared our way, head tilted back, smirk deeply rooted on her lips.

"If we help each other out," I said, "we can speed things up."

"Go on." She fingered a pearlized button.

She was at the cart house for a reason. "You're trying to find the driver of the cart that nearly ran down Holly," I said.

"What?" She dropped the pose and straightened. "When did that happen?"

I just scored a touchdown. "You first."

"Why're you breaking into the cart house?" Veera asked.

"Because my dearies, someone tried to plow *me* down in a Villa golf cart."

Chapter Thirty-Six

Chances Are

Sofi inserted a pick the length of her pinky into the lock and popped open the cart house door. Looked like she used a wire from an old coat hanger. Even the Villa's cart house security was weak.

We scurried inside and conducted a self-guided tour with the help of flashlights. Apparently, the same matte black cart had targeted Sofi shortly before knocking Holly off her feet. Sofi scuttled out of harm's way, without a scratch. Was she an undercover agent with a lettered agency? Her primitive toolkit told me otherwise. But something about her made the cop back away. Maybe the Villa had hired their own snoop. Like Holly, she'd been asking questions that caught the attention of the wrong person. Sofi strolled over to the clipboard.

"You fit the profile of a typical Villa resident, but you're here doing undercover work. Is it because of the crime spree?" That was the best I could do to capture her attention.

She slowly rolled her head in my direction. Her eyes registered surprise. Did Sofi break into Dom's room seeking evidence that would connect him to the bank robbery?

"What's this?" Sofi studied the clipboard. "Carts are loaned out on the honor system?"

"We figured that much out already," I said.

She lit a small flashlight on the signatures. I slid over and pointed to the signature of the person who checked out the suspect cart.

"Pied Piper," she said.

Veera and I exchanged glances.

"We know that, too," Veera said. "Got anything new to add?"

"This signature belongs to someone short who could stand to lose a few pounds. It's someone arrogant, temperamental, and impatient."

Sounded like Peter. Which meant that he was her prime suspect. "What do you know about Peter?"

She tossed her head. "He's probably in the dining hall and that's where I'm going." She disappeared out the door.

"That was abrupt." Our questions were likely hitting too close to home. Or she truly didn't have answers.

"Peter passed out on our first day here," Veera said. "Think that was staged?"

"I think these geriatric delinquents are capable of anything."

Veera and I waited a few minutes before making our own exit. All the excitement from the explosion kept the residents and staff occupied enough so no one visited the cart house during our exploration.

My phone chimed. Holly texted me:

My cherished photo of Dominic and me is missing from my desk drawer.

I called her.

"The R.A.T. pack borrowed it," I said.

"How do you—?"

"What's the significance of Dom's T-shirt in the picture?" I asked.

"It's for fun," she whispered. "He likes wine, cards, and tennis. The picture isn't worth anything. Why did they take it?"

"When you visit Dom, ask him." I disconnected. "Make a note, Veera, in the P.I. handbook. Find ways to make the client useful."

Veera tapped her phone. "A good P.I. regards the client as a tool, to be used to progress the case, whenever possible."

We hustled down the path toward the Villa. I had a hankering to find Mom quickly. Worry wasn't an emotion that came naturally to me. Especially Mother worries.

"How old do you have to be to retire from a lettered agency?" Veera asked.

"Fifty's old for most agents. But Sofi lacks the sophistication of an FBI agent."

"Looks to me like she's wearing one of those *Mission Impossible* masks that you can peel off your face."

"Sofi's probably a little older than Mom's real age."

"We gotta watch out for that woman," Veera said. "She'll trip us up if we get distracted."

"We'll keep that thought close."

"Want to pay her crib a little visit?" Veera asked. "But we gotta be careful since she's probably got her apartment booby-trapped."

Those were my favorite kinds of places. The ones with thin red security lasers and tripwires. Like I had in my pad when I wasn't home. But that wasn't what I had in mind. "I'm taking a field trip to sections of the Villa most residents never see."

"Like the janitorial supply room? Or the security camera room..."

"The Villa is twelve acres of perfection except for a small, embarrassing backend that's overgrown." I knew as much from an aerial photo on the Internet. The book club held meetings somewhere private, out of earshot and out of sight. Maybe they met out back somewhere. Or did they use a bungalow? I was about to find out.

* * *

I left Veera in the lobby to watch Mom's back. Mom sat with the R.A.T. pack as afternoon tea inched closer to Happy Hour. I slipped out a side door and angled toward the recesses of the Villa. I barreled around a corner and made tracks until I could no longer view the residential buildings. A rich green lawn lounged on my right while a perfectly clipped hedge of yellow roses monopolized the other side, eight feet tall and thick as a big rig tire. The gardener must have attended barber's college to clip so precisely. From what I could tell, there was no getting in and out of the Villa at this end, thanks to a tall privacy fence serving as an extra buffer behind the hedge.

I slowed near the most lavish of bungalows, a vine-covered, walled-in, free-standing retreat, the size of a modest family home in the suburbs. I spun around at the sound of a grunt behind me.

Kyle stared my way, head cocked, bum eye half-closed. "You wander a lot."

"I'm exploring. Who lives there?" I pointed my thumb over my shoulder.

"Peter Cronkite."

"Seems like a big place for one person."

"Go big or go alone, that's what he says."

That didn't tell me much. "Does he host parties for residents here?" Maybe this was where they held the book club.

"No."

I waited, but that's all I got. "Okay." I strolled away.

When I glanced over my shoulder, he'd disappeared.

Minutes later, the landscape shifted. Crabgrass overran the manicured lawn and tangly growth populated the backside. I'd need a machete to slash through the thickness. Why would an establishment that prided itself on perfection, abandon this end of the property? Either to avoid unwanted visits or because of the cost of maintenance. Or both.

As I steered away from the residences, the grass paled, the hedges cut loose and the landscape turned unruly. Even the brick path narrowed and broke up, surrendering to sneaky-tough crabgrass. I'd left my machete at home, but I carried a three-inch blade that could split a strand of hair, figuratively speaking.

I waded into the heavy growth, knocking aside waist-high weeds and dandelions. Sunglasses shielded my eyes from dangling tree limbs and sharp branches. Did seniors ever tramp this way?

Time pulsed by until I reached an impasse. A chain-linked fence, overridden by ivy and sturdy vines, prevented forward movement. I climbed over it like a fox and continued my journey through the dense growth. A stucco wall peeked through and a train horn blared just beyond the Villa. The clamor grew faint until the only sound was the whoosh of cars traveling the 101-highway.

I followed the wall north a few yards and tripped over the knotty root of a towering ficus tree, landing on my knees. I wiped off the dirt from my palms, started to rise, and caught my breath. Just ahead, an arched opening appeared in a lower section of the wall.

Droopy tree limbs surrounded the opening. I picked my way forward. About fifteen feet in, I halted next to a vine-draped door with an old-fashioned doorknob, and a lock I could pick while blindfolded. The door belonged to a small cottage, painted green to blend into the surroundings. Brown shingles blanketed the roof and olive-green curtains covered the windows. Did someone live here? There had to be easier access to this end of the Villa.

I followed the perimeter of the structure until I reached a gravel path running parallel to the cottage. I hopped my way along the gravel to a gate in another chain-link fence topped with barbed wire. The gate was padlocked and led to the alley. This was a more civilized entry to the Villa's rear end.

I retraced my steps to the front door of the cottage. I knocked and pressed my ear to the rustic wood. I rapped on the door again. No answer.

My lock picker was begging to help and, in less than a minute, I stumbled inside a low-ceilinged living area, almost as small as the sardine can I called home. A cushiony floral sofa matched a quartet of armchairs. A brass ceiling fixture provided lighting. Two windows hid behind the thick curtains and oil paintings decorated the walls.

On my right, a kitchenette hosted a mini fridge and a single burner stove. Straight ahead, three steps led to a pocket-sized bedroom. A double bed dominated the space with barely enough room to walk. Was this a caretaker's cottage? Lack of clothes or personal items in the closet told me no. The place wasn't occupied full-time.

I headed back to the kitchenette. The fridge was nearly empty except for a hunk of gruyere cheese and bottles of sparkling water. Overhead kitchen cabinets hosted cans of chowder, crackers, and assorted tea bags. Enough grub for about two dozen people. Looked like a watering hole for the weary traveler, as long as the traveler didn't need a bathroom. Maybe there was an outhouse in the yard.

Uneven sand-toned rocks formed a wall behind me. I fingered the rough exterior. Three wine bottles adorned the wall, hanging in a triangular pattern. I wrapped my fingers around the neck of the top bottle. It stuck fast. So did the other two.

I headed for the entry, but stopped before reaching for the knob. What if the bottles weren't decor? I retraced my steps. Each one was corked like it had been opened, but the glass was too dark to view any liquid inside. I reached into my purse and extracted a latex glove. I pulled it on and grabbed the neck of the top bottle, tilting it to one side. Nothing happened, but I was surprised it moved at all. I tilted it the other direction and still nothing. I gripped the neck of the lower bottle closest to me and tilted.

"Bingo." A smallish click greeted me, like the crisp snicking of two marbles hitting each other. I reached for the center bottle and turned it. Nothing.

"Lucky number three?" I grabbed the remaining bottleneck and tilted until another click sounded. There was an order to the tilting. I pulled the third bottleneck toward me and the wall groaned softly as a thick door opened to darkness.

Chapter Thirty-Seven

Return to Me

I stared inside a darkened space resembling a cellar except it was above ground. The only light leaked in from my open door. A cement path rolled out in front of me in an area the size of a small dorm room. I switched on my penlight. A horizontal shelf jutted out on my right about four feet wide. No windows; no other doors. What was the point of a hidden, empty storage room?

I removed my sneaker and wedged it into the corner of the door to ensure an escape route. The air was musty, stale, and still. I shone the light on the floor. Dust-free, a meandering crack wandered through the cement. Why keep this room a secret?

One secret often leads to another.

Dad's voice chugged through my ears, as they often did during an investigation. I peered under the lonely shelf. Empty. I shined my light on the ceiling. No light source. Did Sofi know about this room? How about Lettie? Why was this cottage tucked away? I knelt, carving out pieces of darkness with my light. A large spider scuttled away to a cobweb-laden corner under the shelf. I aimed my beam toward the wall opposite the entry.

Black pegboard stretched from the floor to the ceiling. I inched closer and fastened the light toward the bottom of the board. A row of golf balls dotted the lowest border while neon green tennis balls ran along the vertical edge, all the way to the top. They were glued on so firmly that I couldn't pull any off without excess force. I paused halfway up. One tennis ball stuck out more than the rest.

"A tennis ball, wine bottles, and…" I shot up and pictured the T-shirt Dom wore in Holly's photo. He knew about this room. What was the message? I pulled out my cell phone and scrolled to the photo. "Tennis anyone?" What else? "Tricky play?"

I stared at the door.

"Aha!" I'd been wanting to say that since arriving at the Villa. Meaning I wanted to unearth a genuine, honest-to-goodness puzzle piece that would end all puzzle pieces. When is a tennis ball not a tennis ball? When it's hiding a doorknob. The one ball wasn't glued in place because it housed a hole big enough to conceal a brass doorknob. This cottage was jam-packed with surprises.

I turned the knob, expecting it to be locked, but it wasn't. Either the seniors were getting lax or they weren't worried about surprise visits.

I entered another windowless space dimly lit by nightlights. Wood-paneled walls blended in with tufted leather chairs and a plaid rug. An oversized red pendant lamp served as the centerpiece on the ceiling; the only splash of color among the subdued tones, if you didn't count the pedestal base table. A vintage mahogany table with a green velvet top and a wood border hosted brass cups, chip slots, and a Vegas-style dealer tray geared towards serious poker players.

No wonder Dom ran out of money. We were dealing with professional gamblers. Before I could poke around, the front door of the cottage creaked open.

"I'll only be a minute," Peter's low drawl drifted inside.

I dashed through the dorm-sized space, closing the door of the gaming room behind me. I pulled out my shoe from the secret entry before retreating under the shelf closest to the kitchenette. I'd figure out how to exit later.

A few clicks and the heavy door swished open. A beam of light lit the path for a pair of brown slacks and Gucci loafers. Peter had no problem closing the door behind him, which meant it didn't lock from the inside. The stiffness that mummified my body disappeared. There was an easy exit once Peter left.

He strolled in nimble-footed, like a man in happy anticipation. I lowered my head to watch his back, as his hand reached down to turn the tennis ball. He pushed the door open and waltzed inside like he owned the place. Did he? When he stepped out of my view, I leapt out, landing near the door. I edged closer. His head was blocked from view by a wooden panel that he'd opened. A panel hiding a safe, no doubt.

Dom's T-shirt hinted about this cottage. Was it to let the R.A.T. pack know that he might tip his hand at any moment? Was Peter a loan shark? That could explain why Dom robbed the bank. To get money to pay Peter back before he gunned him down in a dark alley or broke his leg. Or maybe I'd watched one too many Bogart films.

I scooted back just as Peter reached up to shut the panel door. I squeezed into the opposite corner. Peter sauntered by, but before opening the secret door, he stopped and slowly turned. I burrowed deeper into the corner. I'd probably destroyed the spider's web and was about to be bitten any moment. Peter swung around and left, closing the door behind him. The front entry shuddered to a close.

I waited before scuttling over to the decoy tennis ball. A minute later, I'd found the movable wooden panel, pressed it open and eyed a black electronic safe. A cheap model available at any big box store, opening it would be a cinch. Reaching into my purse, I pulled out a rare earth magnet, the size of my fist. I peeled off my sock and shoved the magnet inside. I stuck the magnet to a section just left of the safe's handle. Twenty minutes later, it finally clicked open.

"Wow." Wads of cash were jammed together in four side-by-side piles. "Gambling money."

I closed the safe and hurried out to the front door. Locking it behind me, I ran back to Peter's supersized bungalow. Slowing past his pad, I listened for sounds of life inside the walls, but all I got was the trickle of water from a fountain in the interior courtyard.

I switched direction and headed down a different path, one that curved along toward the self-parking lot. An urge to explore the area near Vincent's

Cadillac rose in me. It would give me a chance to recreate the pipe-bombing in my mind.

Just as I stepped through the hedges and onto the road, a solidly built guy bustled around the corner, knocking me back and onto the grass. I reached for my belt buckle and whipped out my Ninja star. I pressed it against his neck.

"Sorry!" he said.

I lit up like a firefly. "It's you!"

Chapter Thirty-Eight

Kissin' Cousins

I tucked my throwing star back inside my buckle.

"My life passed right before my eyes." Michael slapped a hand to the side of his neck. "But then I knew that you knew it was me, and everything would be just fine."

Michael was the lovable nerd and best friend everyone should have in their lives. And he was sweet on the eyes, too. I didn't need to touch his barely-there beard to know it was soft and kind and filled with warmth just like the rest of him.

"Why didn't you call? Don't answer that." That was a dumb question. My ringer was nearly always on mute.

He pulled away bits of leaves and twigs from my hair while I brushed them off my clothes. A large figure loomed behind Michael. We scrambled to our feet.

"Kyle. Meet my cousin," I said. "He's here to visit our Nana."

"Good to meet you, bro," Michael said. "I can see Nana's in safe hands."

Kyle grunted and pointed to the Villa. "Check in at the reception desk. You need a badge." He marched off into the night.

"Glad you found me before the big guy did." Michael's hazel gaze rolled over me. "Gee, it's sweet to see you."

"You came because—"

"I've got news." He stared down at me.

Was Lucy Fay giving us the go-ahead? Or the ball and chain? A rush of feelings jammed my circuits. Was I mad, glad or dizzy from the fall? I couldn't deny I tingled all over from seeing Michael.

"I had to see you. To be with you. What I told you over the phone was a lot to digest." He slouched slightly. "Hope I didn't give you heartburn."

"What Lucy Fay decides to do doesn't matter right now," I said. "I have to keep my head in the game. Someone's up to no good here and we've got to find out who."

"I totally get it. Don't even think about Lucy Fay. I'll handle her. She's asking questions, which I'm answering. We took an incredible deep dive into what was spoiling the goodness the Villa has to offer its residents. We were on the same page. Except..."

"What?"

"She said I needed to stop wearing my heart on my sleeve." The corners of his mouth stretched into a tiny grin.

"That's what I love about you."

"Lucy Fay's a little more cynical than I'd hoped, but I'm not going to stop chipping away at that hard veneer until she turns into a cuddly, bright-eyed and bushy-tailed bunny rabbit."

"Maybe aim a little lower for her transformation." Most cynics didn't realize they had the power to improve the lives of others and their own lives in the process. "I'm plowing ahead and I'll face the consequences, whatever they are." I sure sounded brave. "Meanwhile, let's examine a crime scene."

A quick embrace and a few covert kisses later, we trekked along the path to the parking lot. I told him about the pipe bomb and showed him where the Cadillac had been parked.

"That's two cars away from yours," he said. "Was the bomb meant for you?"

"Vincent was the target. It's connected to a gambling operation at the Villa." I told him about the cottage I'd stumbled upon, the R.A.T. pack, and their idea of fun and games.

"It's like you've been stepping back and forth to avoid getting hit by a sledgehammer. I should've come sooner."

"You got here just in time," I said.

"Murder attempts, a car bombing, and a hideaway cottage swarming with secret rooms," Michael said. "Just your average retirement community, right?"

We stopped near the empty space where Vincent's Cadillac had been parked.

"And, during their downtime, they're playing high stakes poker, robbing banks, and practically killing each other over croquet?" Michael asked.

"That summed it up nicely."

The clean-up crew had swept the area, but a small dusting of ashes and charred metal huddled against the parking marker. A border of dirt and greenery provided a buffer between the lot and the sidewalk on Channel Drive. Bushes and trees supplied enough camouflage to hide lurkers. I slipped inside the buffer and onto soft, springy ground, thanks to abundant leaves flooding the floor. The canopy of branches above us hid all but glimpses of the sky. Michael joined me.

"This is where the bomber hid?" he asked. "I'll bet a senior's behind the explosion."

"Not necessarily. It was detonated remotely, so the cop said. Could've planted it the night before or lunchtime. If the bomber crouched low, he or she wouldn't be seen, wouldn't be heard. He could either pop open the Cadillac hood or roll beneath the vehicle and plant it. Can the hood be popped without getting inside the car?"

"There's a latch on the backside of the radiator support," Michael said. "A long screwdriver could open it from underneath. But sliding under and using a strong magnet to put the bomb in place would be quicker."

Michael's mechanical and technical skills were top-notch. His being a gastronomical wiz was an added bonus. I was grateful to receive the benefit of his talents.

"This strip of land is called something." Michael scratched his head.

"It's a privacy border between the road and the parking lot." I faced the street. A luxury, gated condominium complex, Sunny Side, loomed across from us, walled in and with a 24-hour security guardhouse where a silhouette moved around behind tinted windows. "Let's introduce ourselves to our neighbor across the street."

* * *

"Excuse me." I addressed an older man with short gray hair, a stocky frame and pale eyes that reminded me of ice cubes. His white dress shirt, navy slacks, and matching tie looked freshly pressed. His name tag read Nate. The jacket hanging behind his chair hosted a security patch and logo.

"You're here about the car bombing." His voice was gruff and low.

Michael and I traded glances.

"You two were sneaking around the devil's strip. Wasn't hard to figure out why."

"Devil's strip? Is that what it's called? Because there's a devil of a gardener not maintaining it properly?" Michael flashed a charming smile with zero effect on the guard.

"That's where people go when they're up to no good," Nate said.

"Someone hid in there before the car bombing," I said. Nate was eagle-eyed, I could tell. His full focus was on his job. Not a book, magazine, or cell phone in sight. Even while he spoke, his gaze scanned the surroundings. He would make Veera proud.

"My shift started an hour after the car blew up."

Darn. I had such high hopes. "Whose shift is before yours?"

"Westie, but he has tomorrow off."

My hopes sagged around my ankles.

"If someone ran away from the scene, Westie would know," Nate said. "As would I."

"Because you were sitting in your car waiting for your shift to start?" Michael asked.

"Because we have security cameras."

Why hadn't I noticed? How could we get Nate to show us the footage?

"Wait a minute. There was a robbery where I work. Did you share the video with the police through Nextdoor.com?" Michael was on a roll. "Can we get a look?"

"We only share video with those wearing a badge," Nate said.

"There are residents who bully others at the Villa," I said. "We're worried about our Nana. Could be a senior behind the pipe bomb."

"Nana's sweet, but she's fragile and trusting," Michael said.

"Her car was parked next to the targeted vehicle. Nana drives a black coupe. What if the bomb was meant for her?" I asked. "These seniors don't see too well, which means they might have targeted the wrong car. Or what if it's a serial bomber? We want the bomber caught before any serious damage is done."

Michael scooted closer and whispered, "What if it's someone who lives at the Villa who was behind the explosion? Or maybe even someone in the Sunny Side condos."

The guard's brows softened and his jaw unclenched. "Small build, bulky and wore a hat. Moved slowly. I suppose it could've been a senior."

"You viewed the tape?" I asked.

Nate tapped a compartment next to him. "We keep hard copies here."

"It would put our minds at ease if we could have a look." Michael stepped closer. "We're just trying to protect Nana."

Without unfastening his stare, Nate popped in the tape. He fast-forwarded it and pressed play.

Grainy footage displayed an SUV ambling by and a man walking a small furry dog. Seconds later, a shadow appeared in the devil's strip, between the branches. I strained my eyes. Slightly stooped, neck projected forward, head down, like the person was staring at the ground. Why? The figure wore a bucket hat and possibly a bulky, longish coat. The shrubs parted as a little light shone through for a moment before the lurker disappeared out of range.

"Even Sherlock Holmes wouldn't get much out of that," Nate said.

"Was this footage just before the incident?" I asked.

"About an hour prior," Nate replied.

"Might have nothing to do with the bombing," Michael said. "Don't you have anything closer to the time the bomb went off?"

"Sorry, we have nothing in your size." He glared at Michael. "It's suspicious activity. If it happened during my shift, I would've questioned the loiterer."

"Thanks for indulging us." I flipped around and hurried across the street, Michael at my heels.

"Did you get anything from the video?" Michael asked.

"Average height, average build." I entered the devil's strip and put out my arm.

"Did you see something?" His head snapped around.

I pulled out my penlight. It was plenty light out, but I needed to take a hard look. "If I lost a button, could I find it here?" The ground was padded with layers of soft brown and green leaves, and speckled by sunlight streaming through.

"Might take a while," Michael said, "to find the impossible."

"What if the button is a pearl? A small white ball would stand out."

"Unless someone stepped on it and squashed it deeper into the ground," Michael said.

I knelt and surveyed the ground. Michael did the same.

"The person was wearing a bulky coat down to his knees." Or hers. "To hide whatever was worn underneath."

"To add bulk to his frame so he wouldn't be recognized," Michael said.

I inched closer to where Vincent's car had been parked. A stray branch poked against my head, but I kept my eyes downward.

"Why would someone be looking for a pearl in here?" Michael asked.

"Because in the tape, the person's head pointed downward," I said.

"That's what you do when you're looking for something. Why a pearl?"

"A resident hanging around Mom lost a pearl button." I remembered Sofi's sweater.

"Whoa," Michael said. "We're trying to find a needle painted white in a haystack that's been spread out which makes things easier. We can do this."

The natural light grew dim as we uncovered candy wrappers, shoelaces, and a heavy dose of impatience, which I shed all over the place. A two-inch wooden border separated the lot from the devil's strip. Just as I stepped onto the border, a tiny white ball appeared.

CHAPTER THIRTY-EIGHT

"Michael?" I turned toward him with the pearl between my fingers.

"Is this the part where we hunt down the owner of the pearl and confront her?"

"Sure is."

Chapter Thirty-Nine

The Great Pretender

I texted Veera and asked the whereabouts of Sofi. She called me before I tucked my phone back into my pocket.

"I'd been tracking the R.A.T. pack's every move. Then Holly walked by and we got to chatting. Next thing I know, most of them left the dining hall. Only your mom and Vincent stayed behind. I'm in the process of hunting down the rest of those slippery seniors."

"Where are you?" I asked.

"Front lawn. Sofi's got a habit of steppin' out. Peter headed toward the back of the building. No sign of William or Lil."

"I'll meet you in front." I disconnected and turned to Michael. "In the dining hall, you'll find Mom with a distinguished-looking gentleman sitting at a table." I grabbed Michael's arm and scrambled behind a stout tree. "William." I pointed in front of us. The man was fleet-footed, as he raced toward the bungalows. "Change in plans. Follow that man." Michael was the perfect candidate since William had never seen him before.

"The way he's moving, he'll be down for a nap soon." Michael jetted off. I headed for the main building. Veera texted me a minute later.

Still no sign of Sofi. Not at the beach or cart house.

I texted her back.

Eyes back on Mom.

I skipped along the brick path toward Peter's place. If he was Sofi's main suspect, she'd keep her eyes glued on him. That could be the reason for her lingering in the devil's strip, searching for something linking Peter to the pipe bomb. And if *she* was the prime suspect in the car bombing, I should keep my eyes on her because Peter could be next on her list.

I slowed when I rounded a bend. The heady scent of jasmine perfumed the air and an old-time tune floated around me. I plowed forward and surveyed the surroundings.

The hairs on the back of my neck prickled, and I turned. Peering out from behind a camellia bush, a head sporting gingery curls faced me. Sofi didn't bother ducking as I trekked closer. The identity of the pipe bomber became crystal clear.

"Why did you plant the bomb?" I asked.

Her lips parted and the corners curled upward. "Didn't you say you were an average girl looking out for a grandmother who doesn't look a day over forty?"

Boy, would Mom love to hear that. "Average? I'm offended."

She parted leaves and branches and stepped forward. "You're tampering with something big. I'm telling you to stay away for your own safety."

"Why would a pipe bomber worry about my safety?"

"Now see here..."

I held out my palm. The pearl glistened.

She sucked in a wad of air. "Where did you get that?"

"Where the pipe bomber left it."

"You idiot." She stomped a low heel. "My sweater went missing right after lunch yesterday. I searched all over, then Holly called saying it was found on the floor by a table. That's when I noticed the missing pearl."

"I can spot a liar like a hawk can spot a grasshopper." Was that even possible?

She turned her lips inward and lowered her voice. "Where did you find the pearl? Where exactly?"

"Do you want the longitude and latitude?"

I turned to leave and she grabbed my wrist in a vise-like grip befitting a mobster. It was that painful. I quick-stepped back, relaxed my wrist, and rotated it toward her thumb in one swift move. I ripped away my hand and grabbed hers in two seconds. "My next move will be a hard kick to your shin if you're planning a counterattack. You'll be in extreme pain, after which you'll have an ugly lump and won't be able to walk for days." Would I actually kick her? Probably not, but I'd twist her arm behind her until she cried uncle.

A curl fell over an eye as she glared. "Not necessary." She blew the curl out of her face.

I unlocked my grip and she massaged her wrist with her other hand.

"He sent you to keep tabs on me, didn't he? I'm sixty-two years young and fit as a fiddle. You tell him I'm going to bring in the ring leader and then hop up on my high horse and ride bareback into the sunset, at a gallop!" She blew another loose curl out of her face and mumbled, "It's just taking longer than anticipated. So what if I lost a pearl?"

Who hired her? Who was she even talking about? If I asked, she'd beat around the bush. I read between the lines. Sofi wasn't sure if she was up to the task. "There are seniors at the Villa committing crimes, from bank robberies to illegal gambling. You're here to find proof and turn them in."

"I'm the one who uncovered the heists and the gambling. You've only come this far because I laid the groundwork, Miss Junior Investigator. I'm at the final stages of finding the top dog. You'll set the whole operation back. Go away, already."

"We'll move ahead faster if we play nicely together."

"Nothing doing."

I turned and walked toward Peter's bungalow. Sofi fast-tracked after me.

"You've witnessed how I move things along," I said. "We should team up. All I want is for Nana to be safe." I wasn't letting go of my cover even if she did. "Who do you work for?"

"You don't know him."

I picked up speed and she trotted to keep up.

She dropped her hand to her side. "What do you propose?"

I must've looked like I knew what I was doing. "Tell me what you know, hang back, and let me finish the job by uncovering all the players."

She pointed her finger at me, accenting every other word with a rap on my chest. "I've perfected my cover. These ancient con artists don't trust you. But they trust me. They think I'm one of them."

They thought the same about Mom. "Why was Vincent's car bombed?"

"To send him a message." She dropped her hand. "He threatened to shut down the poker parlor after what happened to Dominic."

Just like I'd thought. The R.A.T. pack ran their own high-stakes poker games. They used the hidden cottage.

"They assigned me to pipe bomb Vincent's car, to show my mettle."

"And to hold that little act over your head if you decided to confess about the gambling," I said. "Why didn't Vincent call the cops or even Lettie?"

"High and mighty Vincent is a man of honor and reputation, on the surface anyway, which he doesn't want tarnished since he's a part of the gambling operation himself."

"Who assigned you the pipe bomb job?"

Her lips tightened and her chin lifted. "I don't know." She kept pace with me.

"Sid?" I slowed down. This could be the turning point.

Her eyes rounded. "That's right. Sid sends notes with assignments. I was given specific instructions about planting it."

"Where can I find Sid?"

"He doesn't want to be found. Listen, you should be happy I got the bomb gig. He left it for me in a hidden location and I made certain no one got hurt. I was nearly run down by a cart to show what could happen if I got cold feet or talked too much, get it? If your granny sticks her neck out, she's going to have to prove herself in a big way. Breaking into the staff office was a romp compared to the nasties to come."

"You know who Sid is?" I was beginning to doubt Sofi would ever provide any new information. I picked up speed again. Sofi ran after me.

"You're trying to prove yourself to your superiors just like I am," she said.

"I'm trying to make the Villa a safer place. How did the gambling operation start?" I was hoping for a clue leading to the ringleader.

"Flower arranging and bingo don't make the cut for people whose minds work fine, even if their bodies don't. These seniors want to live, to experience thrills, and kick regrets to the curb. Taking risks pumps lifeblood into their very core."

There's no progress without risks. I could relate to that part. "Is that why they turned to a life of crime?"

"Most of them have enough health issues to fill up a hospital ward. They want some real fun while they can."

"Going to prison's no fun." Look who's talking. Every time I played a part in bringing in a criminal, I risked arrest. The thing was, confronting criminals and restoring public safety gave me immense satisfaction. I wasn't stealing money from anyone. I was just cleaning up. Some people rode roller coasters for a thrill. I rode criminals into the ground. The seniors had crossed the line.

"It beats doing nothing worth remembering," Sofi went on.

"What about Dom's heist a few days ago?" I asked.

She started to speak then stopped. Sofi was tongue-tied, which meant I'd surprised her.

"Isn't that why you were in his room?" I asked.

We stopped just shy of Peter's bungalow. A text rolled in on my cell from Michael:

The guy with the thin moustache just left his apartment. I'm following him to the back of the Villa. I think he took a catnap before round two of prowling around.

I turned to Sofi. "Why were you in Dom's room?"

"Because of a robbery in Montecito. Jewels and watches were—"

Sofi ducked behind a bench and I dove into the nearest camellia bush. The gate to Peter's place opened and he sauntered out, pausing for a moment to light a cigar.

I pulled out my phone and searched for news on the Montecito robbery. There wasn't much printed, but enough for me to get a handle on what happened.

Peter took off, disappearing toward the backside of the Villa.

"Where's he going?" I whispered.

CHAPTER THIRTY-NINE

"How should I know?"

Sofi was lying again. Her eyes narrowed and her face grew bland. I grabbed her wrist and twisted it behind her.

"Okay! I'm meeting William in ten minutes by the Moreton Bay fig tree in the main garden," she spoke fast. "We're going to a private party."

I loosened my hold. "To play poker?"

She stepped out of the bush and onto the lawn. She spoke over her shoulder. "I won't tell. It's for your own protection. Leave the R.A.T. pack to me."

Like that was going to happen.

She trekked in the same direction as Peter; the route toward the hidden cottage. To prove my point, William came doddering along the brick walk a short time later, whistling a little ditty. He traveled Sofi's path. Before I could follow, someone else snuck around the corner at a gallop, as William slipped out of sight.

"Michael," I whispered.

He dove for the nearest shrub, which happened to be my camellia bush. In our second collision of the day, I landed on my back with Michael next to me on his stomach. He smiled goofily and rolled on his side.

"Little did I know that the prettiest flower was hiding on the inside." His dark lashes fluttered like palm trees.

My whole attitude shifted. I used to think Michael was too good-hearted to be involved in criminal investigations; that my life of crime-cracking would corrupt him. Now I had no doubts that I'd impacted him. In his ordinary life, he never scrambled into bushes to hide out. I was stripping away his innate goodness.

"Have you ever thought of what you want out of life?" I channeled my inner Socrates. Maybe some heavy-duty thought would wake him up to the kind of life he was meant to lead. The kind without me. Could we go back to just being friends? A piece of my heart broke off just thinking about it.

"What *I* want?" he asked. "You mean like world peace and harmony or like my own personal video arcade and a Ford GT?"

"You might wake up one day and regret not living a saner and safer life."

This wasn't exactly the best environment for such a heady discussion with sharp twigs jabbing our backs and bugs crawling up our arms.

"Are you kidding me? With you by my side…" Michael took my hand, "… I'll never be just another average nerd who's into computers and strawberry cheesecake. I'm so much more because of you. Heroes are people who stand up for those who can't stand up for themselves. I'm helping you help them stand."

"Oh, Michael." The broken chip raced back and glued itself onto my heart. We shared a kiss and I helped him up. "Let's go catch some criminals."

Chapter Forty

Devil in Disguise

We settled behind a hedgerow across from the entry to the hidden cottage. A dim light shone behind the thick curtains. Faint voices were punctuated by trickles of laughter. I hugged my knees. Michael balled up next to me, our shoulders touching, breath nearly pacing mine. Confident footfall crunched against dry leaves and Lil chugged past. She lugged a large, sagging purse and mumbled under her breath, "I'll show that no good cheater what's up." She banged on the door so hard, birds fled the tree branches.

"What's all the racket?" Light streamed out the door and Sofi poked her head outside.

"There's a fire out here that needs putting out," Lil said.

"I don't see any smoke," Sofi said.

"My cash roll's burning holes through my purse." Lil's chuckles scattered the few remaining birds.

"Ha-ha," Sofi said.

"Don't you be thinking the so-called men around here only have eyes for you. I'll be the one turning heads tonight, sister."

"Come on in, already." William stuck his head out. "Before you catch some communicable disease in the wilderness."

"The only thing I'm catching is your money. You might as well pour it out of your pocket into my purse right now and save us some trouble." She held

209

up her handbag.

Sofi retreated as Lil stepped up. The door closed quietly and their voices drifted out of earshot.

"How much money do they play for?" Michael whispered.

"Enough where they have to do it in secret."

Quick steps padded nearby and a couple streamed past. A steely-haired man led a blindfolded woman with one hand while the other draped around her waist. My heart leapt at the sight of the silvery bob and the crushed velvet cocktail dress. A puff of air seeped out through my clenched teeth. Tonight was Mom's initiation into the book club. Would she be alright? I nearly stood but Michael grabbed my hand. He shook his head quickly.

"We can't go after her," he whispered.

He was right. Where was Veera?

Vincent rapped softly once, three times, and once again. Did they have a secret handshake, too? The door opened and he guided Mom wordlessly through.

Seconds later, bushes rustled and twigs snapped. Veera emerged from between two scraggly olive trees. She crouched and tippy-toed toward the front door. I stood.

"Psst." I waved my hand.

Veera whirled around, dropped to her knees, and crawled into the hedge with us.

"Am I crashing a stakeout?" She turned to Michael. "Fancy meeting you here."

"No one would ever suspect this innocent-looking shrub of camouflaging covert activity," he whispered.

"What's Mom doing?" I asked her.

"One minute, she and Vince were strolling arm in arm and the next, he took out a fancy white handkerchief and covered her eyes. Seemed kind of kinky to me."

"Veera!" My impatience bubbled over.

"Your mom took it all in stride. She's our secret weapon," Veera said.

"She's no weapon," I said. "I've put her in a very compromising situation."

"Don't you remember?" Michael turned to me. "We have a strict policy of keeping mothers safe. She knows not to drink or eat anything, right?"

"She's got enough pepper spray on her to take down a band of Navy Seals," Veera said.

I needed to focus. "This cottage is kept secret. Mom's blindfold was to keep her from knowing how to get here since she's new to the R.A.T pack."

"She probably counted the steps and timed the turns," Veera said. "She's a human compass."

"Excuse me, but do we have a plan?" Michael asked.

"Maybe we should storm in and make them talk," Veera said.

"I'm going inside." I rose and Michael grabbed my hand.

"As Lucy Fay's granddaughter?" he asked.

"In stealth mode," I said. "To watch them in action."

The light behind the living room window darkened. I took that as an omen.

"They're heading to the poker parlor." I shot toward the door and pressed my ear against the rough wood surface.

Michael hot-footed over. "Corrie—" His breath warmed my cheek. "I'll guard the back door."

I pulled out my lock pick. "I don't think there is one. They're in a windowless room toward the rear. See if you can hear anything."

He squeezed my hand and took off.

"I'll be ready to bust inside when you give me the signal." Veera planted herself beside an overgrown hydrangea shrub near the front door.

"Text me if anyone else arrives," I told her. "My phone's on vibrate." The lock clicked open.

* * *

The laughter and yelps were exuberant enough to prick through the wall of the kitchenette. Gripping the neck of a wine bottle, I tilted it until the tiny clicking noise rippled the still air. I waited a minute and did the same to the others. The wine wall snapped open. I stared at the slice of light crossing

211

the cement walkway. The door to the poker parlor was ajar. Jokes and jabs flowed freely as did the odor of tobacco.

"Never snuff out a cigar," Peter was saying. "It needs to extinguish on its own."

"You're saying if it causes a fire, no firemen can touch it?" Lil chuckled. "I'll go for that. As long as you're in it."

I opened the door wider.

"I need to wet my whistle," William said to the tune of scraping chair legs.

"Your whistle's drowning already," Sofi said.

Closing the door behind me, I tiptoed into the corner closest to the game room. My heart thumped against my chest.

The poker room door squeaked open and William lumbered through, heading toward the kitchenette. Why did I have a gnawing feeling he knew I was there?He stopped by the exit. I held my breath.

"Your turn, William," Sofi yelled out.

"Get back in here, you ol' buzzard," Lil shouted, "so I can whip your sorry butt."

William swiveled and sauntered back toward the poker room, stopping again just short of the door. Was he just his usual drunken self? Or was something else going on?

He stumbled into the game room. I blew out a stream of air and crawled away from my corner, closer to the door. The jovial mood gave way to loud banter. Mom folded most of the time, which was smart. This was probably her first poker game.

"If you win again tonight, Shorty," Lil said. "We'll know the game is rigged."

"I win," Peter said, "using skill."

"Raise you five," William said.

"I'm out," Vincent responded.

A chair scratched against the cement floor and steps padded, like someone stood and walked around.

"I'll meet your five..." Mom said, "...hundred, is it?"

Did Mom even know how to play?

"Ha! Good one. I'll raise you another five grand," Lil said.

I sat up.

"Son of a gun," Sofi said. "I'm out."

"Well, pretty lady, looks like it's you, me, and the loudmouth," Peter said.

"Are you jealous of my towering frame and sexy lips, Shorty?" Lil chuckled.

"Maybe I should fold again," Mom said. "I've never played with so much money before."

"Don't let the dollar signs scare you, honey," William said. "They'll be dancing a jig in a little while."

"Hurry up and make your call," Peter said, "so I can finish Lil off."

"You ain't finishing anyone off, tonight, you pumpkin eater," Lil said.

"You listen to me, Queen Kong," Peter said.

"If you think, I'm gonna sit here—"

"Ignore him, Lil," Vincent said. "You know how he gets during cards."

"If you say so, Vincent," Lil said.

They were kindergarteners flinging sand in the sandbox.

"Is this where we show our hands?" Mom asked.

"Read it and weep, suckers," Lil said. Someone slapped the table. "Two pairs."

"Three queens," Peter said with a hyena laugh. "I win again."

Another slap followed and the room went quiet.

"What about these?" Mom said. Yet another slap against the table.

William whistled. "The lady's got a five-high straight. Madam, you just beat the pants off everyone at this table, which means a lot of sagging bare bottoms."

It was all I could do to stay in place. I should've hightailed it out of the pantry, back to Michael and Veera. The players would be ambling through any moment. But I needed to make sure Mom was in the clear.

"Lucy Fay," Vincent said, "looks like you'll need a larger handbag for all the cash you'll be carting off tonight."

"Cheater," Peter said. "You tricked us. You said you'd never played before, yet you not only caught on instantly, but ended up winning. How can that be?"

"I did watch *The Cincinnati Kid* a few times. And *Molly's Game*," Mom said.

"They had good tips."

"I'm a Steve McQueen fan myself," William said.

"Cheater!" Peter yelled.

"Listen, Mister," Mom said. "If I were cheating, everybody would know it. I have no secrets."

Boy, was Mom good. I'd probably inherited her lying genes.

"Leave Lucy Fay alone, Peter," Vincent said. "You know she played fair and square. Pay her off."

The room went silent, followed by a shuffle, then Vincent reversed out, leading Mom away. He never once turned his back on the players. What was he afraid of?

Mom and Vincent exited, while the others quibbled over money, over gambling, and over Dom.

"Don't think I don't know what happened to Dominic," Lil said.

"Let me see those cards," Peter said.

Did he think Mom marked them? Did she? My phone vibrated. I pulled it out and cupped it in my hands. Veera had sent a text.

Mom and Vincent just left. You coming?

I texted: *Not yet. Tell Michael I'll leave in a few minutes. You follow Mom and we'll all meet in in Lucy Fay's pad.*

"The cards don't look marked to me," Sofi said. "I'd say it's beginner's luck and call it a night."

I jerked back as Sofi scudded through and out the door.

"What are you going to do about her, Peter?" William asked. Gone was any lightness in his tone.

"I'm no thief," Lil said.

Quiet reigned a few beats.

"I watch the news," she said. "I know Dominic robbed that bank and you put him up to it. Well, I'm not doing it. I'd stick out like a raisin in a jar of mayonnaise." Someone thumped against the table. "I need money to pay my rent."

"That's not my concern," Peter said in a low drawl. "Find a way to get it. You owe the house plenty, Lil. That will not make Sid happy."

"Even your dime-sized heart must feel some pity," Lil said. "Can't you see I'm in pain?"

"Pain is part of the bargain," Peter said. "Play the game, take the risk. You know Sid is watching us, Lil."

Was there a hidden security camera inside that I'd missed?

"I won't steal," Lil said. "And I'm not going after Lucy Fay to get my money, you he-devil. You've got bad karma. You'd better watch yourself. I'd stay away from dark alleys and slippery slopes if I were you."

Lil stormed past me and slammed the front door. Only Peter and William remained in the poker parlor. My feet were ready to fly, but I had a feeling I'd miss something noteworthy.

A glass clinked against the table. "Well, old man," William said, "seems we're done."

Steps padded toward me and stopped.

"Want to tell me about last night?" William asked.

"You flatter me, William," Peter said. "I know as much as you do."

I was willing to bet Peter was hoarding all kinds of secrets.

"Dominic returned from his little excursion," Peter said, "wallet heavier. I know this because he called and bragged about the robbery. He won a good amount at the casino, too."

"The scent of money creates a powerful hunger." William shuffled out and slipped into the kitchenette. The cottage door groaned shut behind him.

I crawled forward on my knees and peeked into the parlor.

Peter's back faced me, but his hand gripped a stack of cash. Who got all the money? Did he play the role of the house and keep it all? That could explain how he lived in the swankiest bungalow. Peter divided the cash into bundles to stuff inside the safe. I debated confronting him. Would I get any questions answered?

A snapping sound, like the cracking of a knuckle, pushed me back to a dark corner. I wrapped my arms around my knees and pulled them close to my chest.

"William?" Peter yelled. "Is that you?"

Peter's pudgy frame filled the doorway to the parlor. He waited a few beats before retreating. Had someone entered the cottage?

Puzzle pieces floated through my head. To raise gambling money or to repay lost sums, a few Villa seniors braved daring deeds, like robbing banks. Did they steal from each other, too? What about the jewelry store robbery?

My little corner lit up as a high beam spotlighted me.

"Well, well, look what the cat dragged in." William gripped a flashlight. "Where'd you come from, little mouse?" He knelt and stared at me.

"Who's there?" Peter asked from the doorway.

I gulped. "I followed Nana." I raised my voice an octave and widened my eyes. "To make sure she's okay."

"One of these days," William said. "You'll step on a banana peel and slip into a deep pit with no way out."

Was he threatening me? I crawled out and stood between them. "I like you better when you pretend to be drunk." I'd turned back into Corrie Locke, runaway lawyer and case-cracking P.I. "Quite an operation you're running."

William cracked a smile. "You know what I'm thinking, Peter?"

"That we should smother her in chloroform and bury her body behind this shack?" He laughed in that half-cackling way of his.

What a macabre sense of humor. Or was he serious? Peter's neck disappeared inside his double-breasted dinner jacket. William's charcoal three-piece suit looked custom-tailored.

"I've been wanting to show you gentlemen something for a long time," I said.

In two quick moves, I gripped Peter in a headlock, a sharp point of my shuriken stuck to his neck. Before he could reach up to grab my arm, I twisted his wrist behind him with my free hand. He moaned.

"The little mouse plays rough." William's words sputtered and slurred. He talked like a drunk again.

"She must work for Sid." Peter coughed.

That was unexpected. I loosened my hold on Peter and pushed him away while I reached down to my ankle, pulling out a small pistol. I stuck my shuriken back in my belt buckle and pointed the way with my gun. "Inside, hands above your heads."

Two minutes later, they sat around the poker table while I stood facing them.

"Keep your hands on the table where I can see them. Who's Sid?" I asked.

They locked stares.

"The faster you talk, the faster you can leave." No one was going anywhere until I got some answers.

They both started talking at once.

"Stop!" I faced them. "You first, Peter."

"We've never met Sid. But he seems to know a lot about us." Sweat beads trickled down Peter's forehead. He wiped it with a napkin. "How do we know you don't work for Sid?"

"You don't," I said. "What I do know is that he collects the money after each game."

"Then you also know," William said, "that if we don't pay, we get punished."

"What does that mean?" I asked.

"What he's saying is…accidents happen," Peter said.

Holly had confirmed this part.

"Someone gets pushed down the stairs or nearly run over by a golf cart. If we don't play by Sid's rules…" Peter took a long sip of an amber liquid.

"Yes?" I took a step closer, leveling my gun at him.

"We are given assignments."

"Don't you dole those out?" I asked.

"He's just the messenger boy," William said.

"Shut up." Peter faced him. "You know why I play."

William blew out a puff. "Because it's the only game in Villa town."

"Make sense or I'll shoot," I said. Was my pistol even loaded?

"You first, sweetkins. Who are you and what do you want?" William asked.

"Information. I heard there's a rat who'll squeal on the others to save his own neck." I pointed the gun toward him.

"None of the rats here squeak your language. With or without their dentures." William reached for his pocket watch and checked the time. "Would you look at that? Dinner is served." He tucked his watch back into his breast pocket. "Why does Lucy Fay's grandkid carry a rod?"

"Because she's no grandkid," Peter said. "Who are you?"

"More importantly, ever shoot anyone before?" William asked.

"Actually, I'm looking for Sid," I said. "He sent Nana a message to meet him and didn't show up." I focused on William. "She ended up with you." These two struck me as the type that would sell their own hides to make a buck. How could I convince them to talk? I pitched my head toward the dorm-sized room. "How'd you know I was hiding in there?" Being outed didn't happen to me too often.

"I'm a bloodhound disguised as a dashing and witty fellow," he replied. "You smell pizza, I smell tomatoes, oregano, basil, and mozzarella. I can even tell if it's whole-wheat or white flour."

"What did you smell?" I asked.

"Metal."

William made me sound like a robot. I discreetly sniffed my shoulder. It smelled like lavender laundry soap.

"And now I know where the odor came from." His gaze dropped to my pistol and pointed to his nose. "I've got a super sniffer."

Where did he learn to do that? From his perfume company days? "Who's Sid?"

"I told you. We don't know," Peter said. "We leave money for him in the safe."

"Look me up when you get tired of playing with Sid and want some real help." I backed out toward the exit.

"Wait." Peter shot a look at William and back to me. "We hid out late one night to ambush Sid when he arrived to take the cash."

"He shows up a few times a month to collect the winnings," William said.

"From gambling or robberies?" I asked.

"The source isn't relevant, is it?" William regarded his fingernails.

"It's not always cash," Peter said.

My mind raced like a NASCAR competitor in the lead. "The jewelry heist of Montecito." I owed Sofi one for telling me about the theft. "A few months ago, two men and a getaway car driver took off with five Rolex watches and a sapphire ring. The thieves weren't caught."

"Must've been seasoned criminals," William said.

"The only lead was an abandoned rental car found in Ventura days later. You had another rental car waiting to bring you back to the Villa." The last part was guesswork on my part.

"You foolish girl!" Peter's eyes popped out of his head as if they were on springs. "You don't know anything." He dropped his head in his hands and sobbed.

William patted his back. "There, there." His gaze darted to me. "We try to avoid stressful situations. It's not good for the old ticker. Could give out any minute."

Did he just wink at me? There wasn't much I could do unless I located the goods.

Peter's head snapped up. "Look what she did to Dominic because he didn't follow orders."

She? "Are you talking about Lil? Or Sofi?" Or me? Where was this going?

"What he's trying to say is, Lettie," William said, "is Sid."

Chapter Forty-One

Ring of Fire

The "Lettie is Sid" bombshell was tossed at me with no evidence other than Lettie went from living the high life to working for a living. And, since she did a stint in Vegas before taking up the Villa gig, she knew the ins and outs of a gambling operation. Needing money and dealing cards didn't necessarily equal bilking seniors, but you never know.

The gamblers started as a handful of residents playing simple card games with play money. Rummy and canasta escalated into poker and blackjack, with stakes that climbed higher with every game. Only seniors willing to play big numbers were invited. The book club Veera and I had visited was a lighter version of the poker parlor games. They displayed books when outsiders interrupted them.

"Nothing like real cash to improve the blood flow in your veins," William said.

"Like heroin-induced euphoria." Peter wiped his face with his napkin. "The more one wins, the more one wants."

I got that same euphoria after binging on donuts. Where did Sid fit in?

Word got around about the secret gambling games, and the residents who'd played and lost started grumbling. That's when the games shut down, except they didn't. Invitations were circulated to hardcore gamblers, and a poker parlor was set up. Maps to the hidden cottage were provided to a group of six - hence, the R.A.T. pack was born.

"Who provided access to this cottage?" I asked.

"The cottage belongs to me," Peter said. "To do with as I please. It's included with my bungalow."

"And that, sweetkins, is how we know Lettie is Sid." William tapped his fingers across the green felt of the table.

Peter grinned crookedly. "It's the oldest structure at the Villa, which once was home to Lettie's family, as you may have heard. We made some..." His bulging gaze wandered the room. "...modifications, which Lettie verbally approved."

"She approved a gambling parlor?" Lettie seemed a stickler for the rules.

Peter gave a single, slow nod and leaned forward. "She approved a playroom."

"But we know she knows about the poker games," William said. "It can't possibly be anyone else."

"If she knows you know about her acting as the house, why does she collect in secret?"

"She's turning the other cheek," Peter said. "We've become quite good at playing ignorant fools."

What about the threatening note from Sid in Lettie's office? It didn't add up.

"None of you confronted her?" I asked.

"We are proud gambling addicts, plain and simple," William said. "We thrive on it. What's there to confront?"

"She rakes in ten percent?" This is where it got sticky. When there's a house involved, gambling turned illegal. Losers had to pay to play. Why would Lettie take that chance?

"Ten percent is nothing compared to what we can win." Peter stared at me. "But it's something to her. We pay her off and she keeps quiet. If you question Lettie, you'll see that we're right."

"If she questions Lettie," William said. "No more play-time."

"So what? We shut down for a while and start over again," Peter said.

"You owe money to the Villa. What if she tries to collect?" I asked.

Peter sank into his chair like a deflated balloon. "She won't."

"As long as her lucrative income stream continues, we have nothing to worry about," William said.

My phone vibrated. Veera texted me.

Mom's back. Hurry on up!

I took a step toward the door. "You're going to slip and then law enforcement will show up." The cops would be very interested in the robberies and attempted murder, as soon as I uncovered hard evidence. "That'll mean an end to your fun and games."

"Did you know Butch and Sundance were never caught?" William leaned back and grinned. "They were careful planners."

"Did you know them?" I asked.

"You're cute and funny."

"I'll be in touch." I backed out of the parlor and raced away from the cottage. Had I made any headway? I couldn't tell, but shadows hounded my every step until I reached the brick path. Were Peter and William lying to throw suspicion off themselves? Should I confront Lettie? As I headed toward Mom's suite, the seeds of an idea sprouted in my mind.

* * *

We sat on the floor in Mom's bedroom, the contents of her purse fanned out between us.

"That's a lot of dough," I said. "Mom, have you played poker before?"

"Oh, sure." She threw her manicured hand at me. "But this was the first time I played with real money."

Was she telling the truth? Maybe if I didn't lie so much, I wouldn't doubt so much.

"You had to buy in," Michael said. "And to end up with big bucks, you had to buy in big."

"How much cash did you have?" Veera asked.

"Vincent loaned me the money. Wasn't that sweet?" Mom's smile was super-sized. "I paid him back with my winnings. He said it was worth watching Peter get bent out of shape."

"If we turn them in right now," Michael said. "All our problems are solved. They're gambling illegally."

"The cops aren't interested in gambling seniors," I said. "They'll get a mild slap on the wrist. If we find whoever tried to poison Dom, we find the golf cart driver, the bomber, and Sid. I have a feeling Peter's playing a bigger role than he's letting on."

"That man's a criminal type," Veera said. "Ex-mobster maybe. I'd be willing to bet on that if it wasn't illegal."

"When is a book club not a book club? When it's a gambling operation," I said.

"Two other seniors were interviewed to be members of the book club the same night as me," Mom said. "They didn't make the cut."

"But you got in," Veera said.

"I dropped hints that I'd always wanted to play a real poker game," Mom said.

"Mom." I scooted closer to her. "I was hiding outside the poker room, listening."

Her mouth opened wide. "I knew it!"

"Did you cheat to win?" I studied her expression

She wiped the smile off her face. "I can't lie."

"See," Veera said. "She won because she played it straight."

"Actually, I played it crooked," Mom said. "I asked to shuffle the cards a few times because I was feeling nervous, which was true. Lil and William did the same. Except I used sandpaper on my thumbs to sand off itsy bitsy portions of the power cards. They were so busy chatting, no one noticed."

"Are you serious?" Michael asked.

"That's how you won?" Veera slapped a hand to her head.

"Honey, I know what I'm doing, and I never cheat when I'm playing with friends. These people aren't real friends. And I am on your payroll, wishfully speaking, so I had a job to do."

I'd officially met Mom 2.0, the upgraded version. "What if you'd been caught?"

"Never would've happened," she said.

"Do you always carry sandpaper in your purse?" Michael asked her.

"Won't leave home without it. I sand the soles of my shoes so I don't slip and fall."

"I sharpen my shuriken with sandpaper and polish my car headlights," I said.

"Sandpaper's good for filing fingernails in a pinch," Veera said.

"And here I thought sandpaper was for smoothing out wood," Michael said.

I told them about my conversation with William and Peter.

"Lettie does have a mean streak," Veera said. "Money brings out the worst in some people."

"How do we get evidence to turn her in?" Michael asked.

"Haven't figured that part out yet," I said.

"Does that mean they know you're investigating?" Mom asked.

"They're sharper than they let on, but not that sharp," I said.

"What about your winnings?" Michael turned to Mom.

"We'll return the money once our job is done," I said.

Mom pulled out a sticky note from her purse. "I made a list of who paid what, so they get their original shares back."

I turned to Michael. "You can crash here tonight. We could use your help. There's somewhere we need to go."

"Where to?" Veera asked.

"For starters..." I regarded Mom. "...what about dinner for you and Vincent?"

"Want me to ask him out?" Mom grinned.

"And keep him busy for about an hour." That should give me a chance to ransack his apartment.

"Why Vincent?" Michael asked. "Lettie's the money collector."

All eyes glued to me.

"Until we have proof, we need to watch them all." I wasn't sold on Lettie. "Let's sift through the suspects." I strolled around the perimeter of the room. "Peter, William, Lil, Sofi, Vincent, and Lettie." I turned to Michael. "Can you do deep background checks on them?"

He raised his right hand so his fingers touched his forehead in a salute. "Roger that. Can't believe I didn't do that already." He pulled an iPad out of his backpack.

I turned to Veera. "We're going to visit Vincent and William's apartments, and Peter's bungalow."

"What about the rest of the old folks? And Lettie?" Veera asked. "Shouldn't we split up and check them all out?"

That was an attractive option, but it would be safer if we stuck together.

"Lil's sitting out dinner tonight," Mom said. "She's got a sing-along at her place."

"She's rehearsing her TikTok video." That was my best guess.

"I'll sweet TikTok my way into her musical act," Veera said.

Lil sat lowest on the suspect totem pole. There was a certain honesty about her. "She'll be lucky to have your help, Veera."

"I'll sneak into Lettie's office afterward." Veera rubbed her hands together. "It'll give me a chance to test out my breaking-in skills."

"Let me know when you're ready to move on to Lettie." If I hurried, I could join her.

What about Sofi? "Mom, find out where Sofi lives."

"Okay. Vincent texted me." Mom stared at her phone. "We're having dinner on the terrace. Isn't that romantic?"

"Mom!"

"It would be romantic if I was Lucy Fay and he wasn't a suspect."

Michael's phone jingled and he glanced at the screen. He snapped up his head. Mom and Veera headed toward the door.

"It's Lucy Fay," he whispered to me.

"Answer it." Either she was going to call the cops or she was going to give us a greenlight, longshot that it was. Time was running out.

Veera and Mom poked their heads back in.

"What's the holdup?" Mom asked.

I hustled toward the door, ushering them down the hall. "Michael's working here." I followed in their footsteps.

Minutes later, Mom sashayed toward the dining hall and met up with

Vincent. Veera aimed for Lil's bungalow. I waited in the lobby for Mom to give me the go ahead that Sofi, Peter and William were accounted for.

My phone rang. It was Michael.

Chapter Forty-Two

Money, That's What I Want

"What did Lucy Fay say?" I asked Michael.

"She called with more questions." His voice upped several octaves, which meant he was either very excited or on the verge of hysteria.

"Questions like what the heck are we still doing here, or should I call the cops?"

"Details about the plan of attack." He practically squealed out the words. "I said an insider may be involved and we'll need her cooperation more than ever to clear the Villa of all the muck."

"Did it work?" I asked.

"Sort of."

"She's not pressing charges?" What was she going to do?

He turned quiet a beat and his voice dropped a few octaves. "We didn't get that far. She got another call and had to go."

"What just happened?"

"But it sounded like a yes to me," Michael said. "In the meantime, I'm running the background checks on the suspects."

"Let me know if Lucy Fay calls back. Gotta go." I disconnected and read a text from Mom.

Everyone's in the dining hall except Lil.

Perfection. I headed toward the back of the Villa with the full moon to light my way. Apartments stood stiffly on my left; along my right, trees and shrubs trembled, probably from all the nightlife teeming within. A low moan scattered my thoughts. That was no four-legged animal.

I cut across the damp grass, keeping in the darkest shadows. The moan turned into a whine, followed by a wheezing. A musky honey fragrance scented the damp air. I pressed my back against a chubby palm as a thicket of leaves swished together nearby. Were there bears in Santa Barbara? I tiptoed toward the shrubs.

"Don't you come any closer."

The voice was low and droopy, like a sad crab hiding in her shell.

"I gotta left punch that'll send you all the way to the beach. As in Waikiki."

Maybe more like an irate crab. "Lil? It's me, Cor… Lucy Fay's granddaughter."

Glossy green leaves parted and the moon lit up a black straw hat with a red organza bow. Lil lifted her teary face toward me.

"What are you doing here?" she asked.

"What are you doing in there?" I stepped closer. "You alright?"

"Of course," she dropped her voice, "I'm not."

I texted Veera that I was bringing Lil back to her bungalow. "Is this about the poker game?"

"I'm no sore loser and maybe Lucy Fay won fair and square, but this isn't about that." She wiped her eyes on her sleeve. "It's about the shame of my own wickedness."

"You don't seem wicked." I felt a confession coming on. I slipped on my kid gloves. "Did something happen?"

"I blew nine thousand dollars, which leaves me with four hundred ninety-five dollars and twenty-two cents. I'm so turned around I can't even lick my wounds."

"Do you have any investments left?" Did she blow it all on gambling?

"I got nothing." She sniffled and blew her nose. "The gambling bug sunk its fangs deep inside me." Her chin fell to her chest. "Gambling brought me here. I figured it would keep me going."

"You're a professional gambler?"

She snapped her head up. "The only thing I'm a professional at is cooking, which I did for twenty-two years at Cafe au Lil until I won the lottery. My winnings paved the way for me to make this piece of heaven my own. I've developed a taste for luxury, and for the devil."

The devil seemed mighty popular around the Villa. "I'd like to help."

"How much interest are you charging?"

"What? No, I'm not loaning you money. I'm going to get your money back," I said.

She took a giant step out of the bushes, sprinkled from hat-to-toe with leaves and twigs. "You have my full attention."

"How do you know the games are on the up and up?"

"I know they've been cheating." She gave me a squinty eye. "I'm so agitated." She pointed above my head at the apartments behind us. "I could kick in that second-story window from right here." She lifted a low-heeled pump to prove it. "I've been suckered by a bunch of rats. And I'm one of them."

"Nothing to be ashamed of, Lil. Someone took advantage of your fragile state."

She looked about as fragile as a steamroller on the outside, but inside? Maybe she was a delicate Christmas ornament. "I'm a lawyer and I'll find whoever swindled you out of your money."

"Pro bono?"

"Won't cost you a cent." I held out my hand and we shook on it. "When's the next game?"

"Tomorrow night. But I can't play without some serious cash."

"You'll be playing and I'll get you the cash." I knew just where to get my hands on plenty of the green stuff. I walked her to her bungalow.

"When I'm playing cards, my arthritis disappears. I don't notice the pain in these rickety old joints at all. I can't give up my dancing."

"Are you in any pain right now?" I asked.

"I've got a humongous pain." She held up her handbag. "The pain of an empty purse. When I moved into the Villa, I had three million dollars, until the poker parlor came along."

I slid closer. "When was that?"

"Five, six months ago." She bunched her lips. "I won forty thousand in three days, then in two weeks it disappeared." She made a left toward the bungalows. "And kept on disappearing. I'm a pathological gambler."

The hidden cottage was like a little casino, except without the cocktail waitresses and slot machines.

"We even had a cocktail waitress in the beginning."

I walked Lil up to her bungalow. Veera shot up from a bench near the door.

"I've been waiting for you, Miss Lil," she said. "I'm here to help with the TikTok video."

"You two don't look like sisters." Lil's finger waved between us.

"Never said we were twins," I said.

"Our parents worked at the U.N.," Veera said.

"Come on in." Lil waved us over.

Her bungalow was modest compared to the others at the Villa. Tidy, with only the bare essentials, Lil didn't even have a T.V.

"We'll talk in the morning, and I'll have what you need." I hustled away to my next stop.

Chapter Forty-Three

Ain't That A Kick In The Head

The closer I got to Peter's bungalow, the more I decided against breaking in. I'd get more out of the visit if he was at home, and it would make the visit infinitely more interesting. Same with William. But not so with Vincent.

Mom texted me the location of Vincent's apartment, and I made a brief appearance there. A larger second-story unit overlooking the massive Villa lawn, everything about his bachelor pad screamed luxury. From the imposing metal chandelier to a film projection room with original movie posters promoting the Golden Age of Hollywood. And as expected: his pricey art collection showcased Picassos and Chagalls.

Vincent's desk drawers were mostly empty and his safe beyond my cracking skills, mainly because I couldn't find it. Certain he had one, I searched but came up empty-handed.

I texted Holly and asked if residents kept valuables in a Villa safe.

No Villa safe. We are not responsible for the safety of residents' valuables.

I texted her again, letting her know I discovered the hidden cottage. I asked what she knew about Peter's remodeling it

He added a small den, I think. Lettie's been there once or twice. Dominic was a frequent guest. He never took me.

Oh brother. Holly never figured out that Dom wasn't the guy for her. I headed toward Vincent's bedroom and halted at the threshold. The antique furnishings were ornate, especially the intricately carved bookcase. The shelves showcased a collection of old clothbound books, vases, and candles. But an oddity made the top shelf look like it belonged in a children's room: a pale pink, brown felt-pawed Teddy bear with dark glass eyes, a button nose, and a hot pink bowtie with a black center. It was the black center that concerned me. The perfect spot for a hidden camera. A few more feet in and I'd be spotted by a wireless surveillance system hidden inside a child's toy.

"Motion activation." That was my best guess. Had his room been broken into before? Or did he have another reason for the camera? Maybe to keep an eye on housekeeping. What was he afraid they'd find?

I focused on two doors at either end of the opposite wall. One was slightly ajar; a walk-in closet from where I stood. The other door was closed. Mom needed to get closer to Vincent so we'd get closer to finding answers.

I was about to exit when I retraced my steps to his refrigerator. I ran my gaze slowly over the glass bottles of milk, fresh-cut fruit in ceramic bowls and flavored yogurts. Inside the doors rested butter, eggs, and… a single water bottle in the same cheap brand that Dom favored. Was it a coincidence?

* * *

Michael called just as I stepped back onto the brick path.

"Find any dirt on anyone?" I asked.

"For rats, they're squeaky clean," he said. "No records, top credit scores, and monied backgrounds. Lettie had money, but her family fell on hard times about fifteen years ago when her granddaddy cut every single relative out of his will, leaving his fortune to charity."

That could be the motive. All signs kept pointing to Lettie. How badly did she miss her monied life?

"I did find a colorful tidbit or two you'll find interesting," he said.

"How about we talk during an evening stroll?"

"I'll be right there." He disconnected.

It would have helped if I'd told him where to meet me. I texted him: *By the hidden cottage.*

* * *

"What's that noise?" Michael whispered.

We hid behind a clump of trees facing the cottage. A drawn-out growl, like the motor of a quiet scooter, grumbled nearby.

Michael edged closer to me.

"Just a raccoon, maybe an opossum," I whispered. "Listen for human sounds. They're more dangerous."

Light steps crackled across the gravel driveway on the side of the cottage, too light and unsteady to be man-made. Plus, the gait was uneven, like that of a four-legged creature. A cat, maybe. I rustled around some branches to let nearby wildlife know that we meant business. The crackling faded.

"Follow me." I stepped onto the soft earth amid squeaking and chirping. "Are those birds?"

"Rats." Michael straightened up behind me. "Not the human kind."

The hairs on my arms stood on end as shrubs stirred nearby. We dashed toward the front door.

"You sure no one's inside?" Michael asked.

"Fairly to pretty darn." What I really meant is I wasn't sure at all, but I didn't want to rattle him.

"Don't worry about me," he said.

The man was a mind reader.

"I'm ready for anything," he said. "I have my knife, a scream that could crack a mirror, and my gun."

Michael's pacifist tendencies didn't prevent him from bringing his knife and his gun, even if it was a tranquilizer gun. My own inner pacifist was alive and well, as long as no one messed with me or Michael.

Minutes later, we stood in the poker parlor, penlights in hand. The lingering odor of gin, lemon and tobacco powdered the air. Empty glasses and popcorn litter dotted the carpet. A cigar butt missed the trash receptacle.

I was reminded again that these seniors were teens in disguise. The mess must have driven my mother batty. Tidying up was one of her favorite pastimes.

I slipped into latex gloves and rapped my knuckles against the middle wood panels. The one on my right made a slightly higher pitch. I pressed my fingers against the wood and the panel popped open. The black safe faced me. I pulled out my earth magnet. "This'll take a few minutes."

"Mind if I make myself at home?" Michael unzipped his gray hoodie and hung it on the back of a chair.

"Go right ahead."

Nearly twenty minutes later, I pulled down the handle. The floor of the safe was lined with bundles of cash tied up in rolls of one-hundred-dollar bills bound together with rubber bands. I hadn't noticed the smaller pile behind the money on my last visit. I reached in and scooped up notes rolled up and held together with a blue ribbon.

Michael shot up next to me and gave a low whistle. "It's a miniature Fort Knox."

I eyeballed the parlor. "What'd you do?" The place looked immaculate. The trash bin was full, but all the litter was gone and the disorder a memory.

"You know how I feel about straightening up," Michael said.

"That was thoughtful." What would the R.A.T. pack think? That little elves tidied up?

"I should've checked with you first, but I didn't want to break your concentration. Want me to put it back the way it was?"

"You've made someone's life a little easier. They'll be silently thanking you."

He kissed my hand and I showed him the letters.

"Check these out." I coasted around while he untied the knot. The cabinet to the side of the poker table looked freshly dusted.

"Did you use furniture polish?" I asked.

"Found a can of Lemony Fresh polish." Michael hunched over the letters. "In the bathroom."

Bathroom? I whirled around. Wood panels covered the entire wall, but one vertical row near the side hosted a narrower row. I pressed my fingers along the top panel and pulled open a door. A toilet, sink and small mirror faced me. A horizontal wood window ran above the mirror. It had been painted shut. I stepped back into the parlor, and the door closed automatically. How could I have not noticed the thin seam? Sleep deprivation. My brain was running on fumes.

Michael held up the letters. "Big number IOUs."

I read over his shoulder. A name, a date, and the amount owed. "Almost seventy thousand dollars. Looks like most of them belong to the R.A.T. pack." And a few other names I didn't recognize.

"That means none of them are Sid?" Michael asked.

"It means Sid's playing hide n' seek and no one's found him or her." Yet. "What background intel did you uncover?"

"Oh my gosh. You won't believe this, but—"

I put up a hand. My ears perked at a slight click. "Close everything up." I shut the safe and the panel, grabbed Michael's hand and the letters, and pulled him into the bathroom. The door closed behind us.

"We're about to have company," I said.

Chapter Forty-Four

The Stroll

"Cozy, isn't it?" Michael grinned and snuggled closer to me.

"Shhh." I pressed a finger to my lips. "This isn't the time to get all romantic on me."

We faced the door in the tiny bathroom, waiting for confirmation of a visitor in the poker parlor. In the old days, Michael's bundle of nerves popped in all directions during an investigation. Now he barely broke a sweat. Cool and debonair, he even arched a brow. Silence expanded until a slow padding grew louder. The parlor door swished open. A chair squealed.

Gone was the cool Michael. A little yelp escaped his mouth. I put up a hand.

"Come out, come out, wherever you are." Sofi's crackly voice rang out.

Michael's eyes rounded and he stared down at me. Slightly jittery Michael was back. There were only two things for me to do. I kissed him soundly and yanked open the door.

"Well!" Sofi's pale blue gaze rolled over us, then back to me. "I had a feeling I'd find you here, but who's he? I won't ask what you two were doing in there."

"The real question is what are you doing here?" I asked.

"Oh!" Michael raised his hand. "I know the answer. She wants us to join forces."

"What are you? Psychic?" Sofi asked.

"I'm Michael. You're Sofi Reyes," Michael said and glanced at me. "She was expecting to find you in here."

"I'm impressed," I said. Did Sofi know this wasn't my first time in the poker parlor?

Her close-mouthed grin expanded and she batted her eyelashes at Michael. "What else do you know?"

"You're a sixty-two-year-old, ex-librarian who writes noir detective fiction. You haven't sold anything you've written yet, so you're investigating true crimes for inspiration."

Michael was back to his very useful, debonair self, so much so that he poured himself a glass of wine while he talked. Now I knew what intel he'd found on Sofi. He got extra points for adding his own logical take on her life.

"Don't you dare drink without me," Sofi said.

He faced her. "You set up shop near upper State Street and Las Positas, and within two weeks you snagged your first client." He poured a glass for Sofi.

"I've quite the reputation." She practically rubbed her knuckles against her chest.

"You're an apprentice to Karl Kruikshank, a fairly well-connected Santa Barbara P. I."

"He's your boss." Now I understood. She worked for a P.I., hoping to make enough waves to strike out on her own.

Sofi turned to me, "I know who Sid is." She downed her drink in two gulps and fixed her slinky stare on me. "Peter Cronkite. I found a typed note to Lettie in her office."

"That note's old news," I said. "Can't pin that on Peter without something more."

"Guess who has a vintage Smith Corona clipper?" Sofi planted a jeweled hand on her hip.

"Does the 'y' key stick?" I asked.

Sofi lifted her chin. "Maybe."

"'Maybe' isn't good enough." I was so over speculation. "Let's go, Michael."

"Wait." Sofi trotted after me. "Your psychic's right. Teaming up will be better for us both."

I pushed open the door to the kitchenette and we scrambled outside. Sofi kept pace with me and an eye on Michael who nipped at our heels.

"This way, we both win," Sofi said. "Take note that I don't care who you are as long as we finish this job."

"Who hired Kruikshank?" I asked her.

"Sofi's got a relative working here," Michael said.

I tossed him a long look. How did he gather so much intel? His face blushed in my favorite shade of pink. Michael never ceased to impress me.

Sofi's stare tripped toward Michael. "I don't know who he is, but he's right again." She squared her shoulders. "Kyle's my nephew, but that's not why I'm on this case. Kruikshank got an anonymous tip about the jewelry heist on Coast Village Road. The tip points to an inside job."

"As in inside the Villa? Kruikshank sent you here to check it out," I said.

"I told Kruikshank I'd lean on Kyle to get what I needed."

Nice plan. If Kyle helped uncover the thieves, he'd move up the security guard ladder himself.

"I've lived here for a few months gathering clues." Sofi hurried to keep up. "Somehow, you and Lucy Fay caught up to me in just a few days."

I beamed like a lighthouse leading a lost ship back to shore. Veera knew it all along. Mom's a huge help. She acted like a pro from the get-go. "Where'd you get the money to pay for your stay?" I asked.

"Kyle got me a discount and Kruikshank footed the bill. Do we have a deal?"

"First, you need to explain what were you doing in Dom's room." We hopped onto the brick path.

"Dominic and I shared a nightcap in his apartment the night before he left, and he loosened up. He confided that he'd hidden something valuable in his apartment. Something the R.A.T. pack wanted bad. Said they'd never find it."

"What was it?" I asked.

"I haven't located it yet. Dominic said it's hidden in plain sight. He dared me to look for it. He even trailed me while I checked his apartment. I got nothing." Sofi was breathless. "That's why I came back later. That's more information than you bargained for."

We made small talk until we got to Peter's plush bungalow. Only one exterior lamp shone above a bundle of bougainvillea spilling onto the entry gate. No other signs of life.

"He must be the House in the poker games," Michael whispered. "That explains how he can afford to live like this. I mean, sure, he was a B actor and owned a few radio stations—"

"Which he sold to a Wisconsin-based media company," Sofi said. "He's not in it for the money. I tried to tell you. These seniors are thrill-seekers."

My kind of people. A text rolled in from Mom:

Meet me at Peter's bungalow.

Somehow, Mom was one step ahead of us again.

Chapter Forty-Five

Yackety Yak

Mom texted again a minute later:

Behind you!

I spun around in time to view Veera and Mom jogging around the bend. The moment Mom laid eyes on Sofi, she held a hand to her chest and drooped.

"At my age, I'll get a heart attack running around like this." Mom pressed her lips together and stared hard at Sofi.

"She's helping us," I said.

Mom whispered in my ear, "Does she know who we are?"

"She knows all about you, Nana," I spoke loudly, "and she knows we're here to make sure the Villa's a safe haven for you and everyone else living here."

"Nana says Peter's acting strangely," Veera said.

"That's the very definition of Peter," Sofi said.

"He's on his way home," Mom said. "We took a shortcut. Here he comes now."

I turned. Peter staggered up the path toward his bungalow, massaging his forehead with his hands.

"For someone with the appetite of a buffalo, he hardly touched the buffet," Mom whispered.

"Did he drink anything?" I asked.

"Just about the whole martini pitcher," Veera said.

Peter tripped off the brick path and nearly fell over.

"Son of a gun," Sofi said.

"He's going down," Veera said.

"He's drunk." I turned to Veera. "According to Sofi, he's got a typewriter that's connected to the threatening note to Lettie." I looked at Sofi. "Let's take a look around his bungalow. Meanwhile, Nana needs to learn more about Vincent."

"Maybe she should pay him a late-night visit," Veera said. "With me lurking nearby."

"Good idea." I turned to Michael. "In my trunk, you'll find a bag filled with bills that Veera borrowed a few days ago." I'd nearly forgotten about the prop money Veera had snagged from the warehouse. I handed Michael my car key and the key to Lucy Fay's pad. "Find Mom's black duffel bag and stuff the bills inside. Dummy it up so the bag's overflowing with cash."

Michael's eyes lit up. "No one will ever know."

I motioned for Sofi to follow and zipped toward Peter. We caught up as he stood by the gate to his house.

"Can we help you?" I waited by his side. He pulled a handle and shook the wooden gate.

"Oh, why isn't it opening?" He slurred the end of his words. "I need to get inside. Do you know who lives here?" He turned to me.

"You do, darling," Sofi said.

He faced her for a moment before slowly blinking at me. "Have I seen you before?"

"I'm Lucy Fay Nightingale's granddaughter. We'll help you inside."

He dropped his key onto my open palm. I unlocked a small padlock attached to the gate latch. Slipping an arm around Peter, I gently guided him forward into a private courtyard brimming with lush plant life and a trickling water fountain. Sofi padded in behind us.

"I may lose all the contents of my stomach at any moment," he said.

I jerked my body away. "Did you eat dinner?"

His bulging eyes widened and his head tilted toward me. "I couldn't." His fingers flared over his mouth.

I hurried forward and unlocked the bungalow door. I stepped inside and they followed.

"Food is what you need," Sofi told him.

Perfectly appointed with pillows, artwork, and accents in all the right places, the living room looked poised for an *Architectural Digest* photo shoot. Not a goose-down cushion out of place. A window seat ran nearly the length of the room, interrupted briefly by French doors. The place hardly looked lived in.

Peter tumbled toward a large crystal decanter and empty glass sitting on a marble-topped cocktail table. Auburn-gold liquid filled the base of the bottle.

"I've been dreaming of this brandy." He grabbed the bottle by the neck and emptied the remainder into the glass. "Such complex flavors."

"Hey!" Sofi grabbed the glass before it touched his lips.

His face contorted into an angry frown. "That's mine."

"If you drink that, I guarantee you'll have paramedics swarming within an hour. Is that what you want?" Sofi asked.

He stared at her and leaned forward. "Your eyes are like..."

"I know limpid pools," she said. "My teeth are like pearls, blah blah blah."

"I was going to say angry marbles." Peter sank onto a yellow sofa.

I turned on a floor lamp and roamed the room.

"A little nip won't kill me." He reached for the glass. Sofi jerked it back.

"I forgot to add that you'll overwork your liver," she said, "and end up with pancreatitis, cirrhosis, and shingles."

"Shingles can be painful." He leaned back.

Sofi finally made an impact. I grabbed the decanter and strolled into the kitchen. I poured it out, rinsed the glass, and replaced the alcohol with water.

"Don't throw away that brandy," he yelled. "That bottle cost twelve hundred dollars."

"Oops," I muttered and searched the pantry. I found saltine crackers. I dropped the pitcher and crackers on the table by Peter.

"You need to hydrate and put something in your tummy," Sofi said. "Then you'll be as good as new."

"I'll never be new again." He nibbled the cracker. "I'm an old man weighed down by regrets." His head tipped downwards like it was too heavy on his shoulders.

"It's never too late to make amends," I said. Maybe now we could get him to talk.

Peter silently shifted his gaze to Sofi.

"What regrets?" she prodded.

He laid back against the cushiony comfort of the sofa and closed his eyes. "Nothing I can speak about."

"My grandmother..." What could I say to make him open up? "...is very fragile right now and I don't want anything to upset her."

Peter opened his huge eyes. "Hasn't she been treated exceptionally well here?"

"She has. But I hear that's about to end."

I wasn't sure where I was headed, but a pout dropped over his lips, which meant I'd hit a soft spot. Would Sid have any soft spots?

He grabbed the glass of water and guzzled it down. He held the empty glass up and examined it. "I didn't realize how thirsty I was."

"Maybe you're thirsty for something more than water," Sofi said.

Where was she going with that?

Peter's menacing eyes landed firmly on Sofi. "You're beating around a bush that's lost all of its leaves."

She stood. "You're looking pale. A warm shower is what you need."

I ducked into his office while Sofi helped him stumble down the hallway. When the water turned on full blast, I rummaged around a walk-in closet brimming with office supplies, books, pads of paper, and... bingo! In a lonely corner sat an old-school typewriter. I yanked out a sheet of paper from a nearby printer and typed a quick note.

"No sticky keys." Darn. Did this mean he wasn't Sid? Or maybe he had the typewriter repaired?

The water shut off and voices drifted my way. I inched toward the master bedroom.

"Did someone send you to talk to me?" Peter asked.

"Of course not," Sofi replied.

I peeked into the room. Oversized pillows scattered on top of the embroidered duvet of a large four-poster bed. Sofi's back faced me as she angled behind a small desk. She pounded away on a small vintage typewriter. I darted over and stared at the paper.

She shook her head. "Nothing sticky."

"I'm not to blame," Peter said from the bathroom. He spoke so quietly I could barely hear him. "I only give people what they want, but are afraid to go after themselves."

"You're like the Wizard of Oz." Sofi stood and tidied up around the typewriter.

"I'll need help dressing," Peter said.

"You don't need any help and you know it." Sofi pushed past me and whispered, "I do not want to see him naked." She strode down the hallway.

I sprung for the door. Neither did I.

Peter shuffled out and I prepared to avert my eyes, but I needn't have worried. Fully dressed in black silk pajamas, he swayed slightly as his slippered feet slid into the bedroom.

"Nan needs a typewriter repaired that looks just like that one." I pointed to the one on the small desk. "Know of any repair shops?"

Without looking at me, he said, "My machines haven't been used in years."

"How many do you have?"

"Two." He removed a nail file from a pocket and tended his thumbnail. "I hate typing."

"Why have a typewriter?" I asked.

"I was formulating a cookbook for retirees that I planned to publish, but never got past page four. I'm waiting for inspiration."

"Are typewriters popular at the Villa?"

"How should I know?" He paused near the bed. "Such a dull topic of conversation."

"Has Sid ever sent you a threatening note?" How was that for an interesting topic?

"You talk too much." He rubbed his temple and stared at my hand. "No gun today?"

Sofi wandered in with a cup of coffee she passed on to Peter. He clutched the cup and headed for the living room. He tried to sneak a shot of bourbon, but I grabbed the bottle before he spilled a drop.

"I'm feeling better." His eyes turned toward me, while he faced forward. "Why were you two so eager to help me?"

"We're like family here," Sofi said.

"A family of barracudas," Peter said and shuffled toward the kitchen, with Sofi close behind. She covertly pointed out a drawer beneath the window seat.

I darted toward the drawer and gently coaxed it open. Magazines, books, and newspapers overflowed. I pulled it open some more. Tucked behind the jumble lay the triangular edge of a letter. I pinched the corner between my fingers, gingerly pulled it out, and nearly finished closing the drawer just as the doorbell rang. I jumped up and hid the letter behind my back. Who'd be visiting at this hour?

Peter peeked out of the kitchen. "Answer that, won't you?" His gaze dropped to the partly open drawer next to my shins. "Looking for something?"

Oh boy.

Chapter Forty-Six

At Last

Sofi popped out of the kitchen next to Peter, took one look at me, and spun him toward her, blocking his line of sight. I opened the envelope and read:

If you don't collect it all, you'll be squished like a fly on the wall. Sid

Sid was a poet? There was that sticky "y" key again. I tucked the note back in the envelope and held it up for Sofi to view. I mouthed, "Sid."

The buzzer rang again.

"I'll get it." I strode outside and opened the heavy wooden gate. William's finger was glued against the ringer. His pencil-thin mustache twitched when he spoke.

"I knew you had a thing for us older guys." He brushed past me and into the house.

I trailed him inside. Back in the golden age of Hollywood, mustaches like his either belonged on a dashing hero or a dastardly villain. Which one was he?

William joined Peter and Sofi in the kitchen. They munched on tomatoes and celery, gnawing and chewing like rabbits. I passed the note to Sofi when they weren't looking. She read the note.

"What are you doing? That's personal." Peter's bug-eyed gaze landed on the paper in Sofi's hands.

She dug into her handbag and pulled out another note. "Let's play show and tell, shall we?" She held out a piece of paper. "From our pen pal, Sid."

Peter snapped it away, while William reached inside his jacket. He pulled out his note and held it out to Sofi. She read it and stared up at me.

"Looks like we three are in the clear."

She handed the notes over to me. All three had the same sticky key. They were hardly in the clear. If Sid was a member of the R.A.T. pack, there was a chance he or she would send a note to himself to throw off the stinky scent.

"Glad you're better, Peter." I backed out toward the door. "Sleep tight. I mean sweet dreams." I ran through the gate and didn't stop until I locked the door behind me in Mom's room.

Michael sat cross-legged on the floor next to a small duffel bag, big enough to stuff gym shoes, shorts, shirts, and even a pair of dumbbells inside. I texted Veera for a progress report. Michael unzipped the bag and leaned it toward me. I gasped at the bundles of hundred-dollar bills.

"Looks like the real deal." If one didn't look too closely at the small print in the lower right corner which said, *Play Money*.

"This should cover a few bets," he said. "What's next?"

"Have you heard from Mom or Veera?"

A frown etched a line between his brows. "No. Should we send out a search party?"

"Hold on." I dialed Sofi's number. She picked up on the first ring.

"Who is this?" she answered.

"The person who's going to help you solve a crime tonight," I said.

Michael's lips turned up into a megawatt smile.

"Go on," Sofi said.

"Get Peter to invite the R.A.T. pack to a surprise poker game at midnight in the hidden cottage," I said. "Imply that Sid suggested it. Don't take no for an answer."

"That's in almost an hour," Sofi lowered her voice.

"They can come in P.J.s if they want," I said. "Sweeten the pot. Tell them Lil got her hands on a big chunk of change."

"I can do that," Sofi said.

"See you soon." I disconnected.

Michael picked up the money bag. "Time for another stroll?"

"Almost." I needed to get ready. Weapon ready, that is. "Check to see if you can find a local typewriter repair shop. We need to find out if they repaired a vintage one with a sticky 'y' key." No one would be open at this hour, but at least the ball would start rolling.

Michael snapped his fingers. "Brilliant."

He picked up his phone and I aimed for the bedroom.

Mom's luggage held enough outfit changes to last two weeks for all three of us. In a few moments, I'd found the perfect get-up. It was nothing like the rest of her elegant wardrobe. This was handpicked for me. A black, fitted hoodie and satin tactical pants with enough zip pockets to stash almost all the weapons I'd brought along. My phone vibrated. Lil texted me,

I need money to play at midnight. You got it or not?

I texted back: *Coming right up.*

Turned out I wasn't the only one with pockets galore. Michael wore a four-pocket, military-inspired jacket in dark gray.

"Santa Barbara has one typewriter repair store, Dedham Office Works," he said. "I left a message. The address was a P.O. Box."

"Good, that means you called a cell phone."

"Hopefully they'll call back right away. I told them it was an emergency police matter, which it could become at any moment, due to any number of reasons." He ran his fingers through his hair.

"We'll try Vincent first, then head over to Lil's."

I held the door open. Michael stomped through and stopped. He pulled out his phone, staring at the screen.

"It's the typewriter shop number." He pushed a button. "Yes?" He clenched his teeth and stretched out his lips. A few beats went by as we strode down the hallway. "You did?" His gaze hit mine. We headed toward the stairs at the opposite end. "You don't?" He paused a few beats. "How long will that take?" A few more beats. "This could be a turning point in a breaking case. I'll be waiting." He disconnected and slapped a palm over his heart. "I am so grateful she didn't ask any questions. She just answered mine. Someone did bring in a typewriter with a sticky key. She didn't know which key."

I squeezed his hand. "We're getting closer. We'll get more questions answered momentarily."

Chapter Forty-Seven

Games People Play

"It's too quiet." I pressed my ear to Vincent's door.

"Maybe they left for the poker parlor," Michael said.

That would explain why there was no sign of Veera. But why wasn't she responding to my texts? "Maybe." I stuck two paper clips in the lock, jiggled them around and we tumbled inside. I didn't care who saw me anymore. Finding Mom and Veera was my priority. "Wait here." I pointed toward the front door. Too many potential booby-traps to risk Michael tripping around.

The apartment was dark and quiet. Two empty wine glasses perched atop circular brass coasters. The lavender-scented perfume meant Mom had been here.

I hustled into the master bedroom. This time I ignored the teddy bear cam and headed straight for the walk-in closet door on the opposite wall. Neatly arranged racks of clothes filled the space, color-coded and hanging together by item type, just the way Mom liked it. No wonder they got along. Plenty of velvet jackets and ascots, too. Vincent liked the luxurious, orderly life. He wouldn't put up with a sticky typewriter key.

I tried the second door. It was locked. A fast tapping down the hallway sent me diving for cover. Michael ran in.

"I know you told me to wait, but I couldn't. The typewriter repair shop owner called back. I was right. The owner works from home. She said someone brought in an old Mercedes Prima typewriter with a sticky 'y' key. It was fixed two days later and picked up by the customer. Paid in cash. No name, no phone number, no address."

"Description?"

"Eightyish. Cowboy hat, button-up shirt, and jeans. Never took off his shades."

Why were disguises suddenly so trendy? "What else?"

Michael gulped. "I snooped around while I waited. There's a Mercedes Prima typewriter in Vincent's den."

"I knew it." My gaze dropped to a spot under the bed. I sank to my knees and picked up a yellow sticky note. "Mom's been in here. What was she doing in his bedroom?"

"Maybe he wanted to show her something." Michael backed out. "Something perfectly innocent. Hopefully."

My inner mercury rose chin-high.

"I'll investigate some more." He ran down the hall.

I poked my head back into Vincent's closet. He had plenty of jeans, but no cowboy hat. If he was involved, my gut said he was too smart to leave any trace.

I examined the knob of the other door. The slit in the middle was short and slim, a nearly unpickable lock. Vincent was hiding something important behind the door. Something suspicious.

"Maybe that's where he keeps his safe." Michael returned by my side. "No other sticky notes lying around."

"The kitchen." I jogged down the hallway to the fridge.

"What's in there?" Michael landed next to me.

"Evidence." Of what I wasn't sure, but it had to be linked to something. I pulled open the fridge door and grabbed the water bottle that resembled Dom's stash. I shook it and water sloshed around. I grabbed another bottle from another brand and did the same thing. What was different?

My phone pinged. Lil texted me,

Why am I still waiting on my money? You trying to torture me? I got a game to play.

I stuffed the first bottle into my pants pocket and texted Lil that I was on my way.

"Is the water suspicious?" Michael asked.

"Not sure." The case had suddenly accelerated and I still wasn't certain of anything.

"Your mom and Veera," Michael said, "they can handle themselves. You know that, right?"

Veera should've texted me back. Wasn't like her not to. A nagging worry clawed at my insides. I called Sofi to let me know when Nana arrived. "Let's scram."

* * *

We landed on the brick path and had nearly reached Lil's bungalow when I slowed. I whispered to Michael, "We're being followed. I'm going to disappear. Walk toward the parking lot. Lose the tail and double back. I'll take the phony Benjamins."

"I... we..."

"We can do this." My insides had turned to steel. My mind primed for action. No room for worry...or error. I grabbed the duffel bag and waited until we'd reached a dark section before parting ways with Michael. I ducked behind thick bushes, watching him saunter off, whistling a little tune. Whoever shadowed us wasn't on the bricks. The padding steps were soft and quick. Stopping and starting to keep pace with us. Did the tail notice that I'd slipped away?

Heavy breathing invaded my space as the shrubbery nearby rustled.

"You're in my hiding place," a husky voice said.

Why was Lil always hiding in bushes? She eyed me beneath a chic ribbon-style hat with a fabric bow. She wore a royal blue dress and matching fuzzy cardigan. "I hope you don't plan on doing any illegal deeds in there, like smokin' weed."

"That's actually legal now." Was Lil the shadow? "Have you seen my moth...grandma and sister?"

"I haven't seen anybody. I was on the lookout for you. Took you long enough."

"Heard from Sid lately?"

Her brows rose so high, they added two more inches to her height. "How'd you know I got a note?"

"Because Dom got one, so did Peter, William, and Sofi." I had to move things along.

She snapped open a purse straight out of the sixties and pulled out a small white envelope. She held it out.

I took the envelope and unfolded the note. Lil snatched it from me.

"Any reason I should be trusting you?" she asked.

"None whatsoever. Except that I want to stop whoever's behind this. For Nana's sake."

"Is that what lawyers do?"

"Lawyers are troubleshooters. If criminal activity is involved, I find the proof to put the criminal away."

Lil grabbed me and held tight. "God bless you, you real-life Perry Mason. When you catch that sucker, I'm gonna tan his hide so bad, he'll look like a fruit leather, one that's all black and blue."

"You'd get hauled into court for doing that unless it's self-defense."

"That's what you're gonna tell the judge."

"How do you know it's not a woman?" I asked.

"I'm laying my money on a man. Women don't cheat as often. It's the odds." Lil showed me the wrinkly note. "Got this three days ago."

I flashed my penlight and read:

You'd better find an income stream fast before your toilet gets clogged with your organs.

The creativity was unique.

"Nasty, isn't he?" She wrinkled her nose. "I can't even do my business without picturing a kidney or a spleen floating in the toilet bowl, and I don't even know what a spleen looks like." She crossed her arms over her ample middle section.

"This is ruining a perfectly wonderful senior community," I said.

"What'll we do?"

"What would happen if nobody won tonight's game?" I asked.

"Somebody would get real mad."

Which meant that somebody might slip up. "We've got to stop your losing streak."

"I'll whop everyone's butt. You watch and see," Lil said. "I'm a superstar when I'm playing poker."

"Could be one of the players sending the notes," I said. "What about Vincent?"

"Fat chance. He throws a hissy fit when we don't play by the rules. You saw him storm off during combat croquet."

"Yet, he's gambling illegally."

"He's hooked like the rest of us." Her stony expression softened.

Was she sweet on him? Maybe Veera was right. "I say it's Vincent."

"Beneath that hunky exterior, that man has a heart the size of the planet Jupiter." She snapped to. "Not that I would know."

I still had my money on Vincent. "What about Peter?"

Lil's lips pinched together. "He gets plenty mad when he fills out his own IOU."

Then again, he'd been an actor. He could be fooling everyone, while filling his pockets. Maybe he sent William in to repair his typewriter. They could be in it together.

"Remember when the paramedics carted Peter away? He'd lost ten grand the night before." Lil narrowed her eyes and looked around before she continued. "Some money-grubber empties our wallets while feeding our unholy habit and his own greed."

Thankfully, Mom's days were numbered here. I stepped back onto the grass. Lil joined me.

"You got my money?"

I held out the bag.

Lil unzipped the top and swore. "How much is in here?"

"All that you need."

"I'll win with the good Lord's help." Lil's eyes shot skyward.

I planned on lending a hand, too.

Chapter Forty-Eight

At Last

Where were Mom and Veera? That question played front and center in my head as we plowed our way toward the poker parlor. I listened for Dad's voice to pitter-patter through my head with sage advice, but all I had was a strong gut feeling that Mom and Veera could take care of themselves just fine.

Michael caught up to us on the brick path.

"Lil was shadowing us," I told him.

"Hey now, I'm nobody's shadow." She stopped in her tracks.

"Wasn't her," he said. "Whoever followed us had no hat and he was taller. He trailed me until I lost him near a gardening shed."

"Probably that no good security guard," Lil said.

"Was he about seven feet tall?" I asked him.

"All I know was the dude panted a whole lot," Michael said.

Which meant the tail was a senior.

"I would've knocked him to the ground and sat on his back until the police arrived," Lil said.

"Gee," Michael said. "My job was to lose him and come back to help find Sid."

"And find Nana and my sister," I added.

Lil narrowed her gaze. "I'll side with you two on that."

We followed Lil down a more cultivated route to the hidden cottage. About fifty feet past the staff parking lot, a narrow dirt path twisted between manor homes and led to the rear of the Villa...and to the old cottage. Using a key, Lil opened a padlock to the wild wooded backside.

We finally arrived a few minutes to midnight. Everyone was seated around the table except William...and Mom and Veera.

"Where's my grandmother?" I asked Vincent.

He rose, gazing from Michael to me. "You shouldn't be in here. This is a private gathering, by invitation only."

"I invited them," Lil said. "To make things a whole lot more interesting."

In one giant step, I stood forehead to chin with Vincent. "Where's Lucy Fay? She was last seen in your apartment."

"That was a while ago," he said. "We shared a glass of pinot and I invited her to play tonight. She said she had other plans."

What? Did Mom and Veera go rogue? Were they trying to solve the case on their own?

"I kindly ask you to leave so we can commence playing our game." Vincent sat behind the table.

The bathroom door opened and William tripped inside.

"Oh, hello," he said to me, straightening himself out. He flicked his gaze to Michael. "Were boyfriends optional tonight? I would've brought someone, had I known."

"Did I mention," Sofi said, "that I won't be playing?"

"Why not?" Peter asked. "This promises to be an exceptional game."

"Miss Nightingale will be playing in my place. I can't think straight with all the hot air in here." Sofi fanned herself and stood, holding out her chair for me. "Be easy on her, kids."

"I need to find—" I said.

Michael stepped behind me and whispered, "I'll locate Lucy Fay. I promise." He raced off.

"Who was that unmasked man?" William asked.

"Shut up and play, loser," Lil said.

"Sit." Sofi placed her hand on my shoulder. I sank onto the seat.

"We only need four chairs." William took his seat. "Lil's run dry. She won't be playing."

"The hell I won't." Lil pulled the chair out from under him. "You'd better watch yourself."

William stumbled to the floor, gripping the table's edge. He slowly rose, dusting off his bottom. "Not to worry. This new hip of mine broke my fall quite nicely."

"William's right." Peter stared at Lil. "You don't have the funds, or do you?"

Lil opened the black duffel bag, exposing the rows of Benjamins, "What do you call these?"

Peter's eyes nearly popped out of their sockets. Even Vincent's jaw dropped open while William blinked to make sure he wasn't hallucinating.

"Picking on poor defenseless females," Lil said. "No wonder Sofi doesn't want to play." She snapped shut the bag and dropped it between her fuzzy slippers.

William took the seat farthest from Lil. He cleared his throat. "Shall I shuffle?"

"I'll shuffle," Sofi said. "My fingers aren't nearly as sticky." She pulled an alcohol wipe from her purse and cleaned her hands before shuffling the cards like an old pro. She must've spent hours practicing.

"Before we start." I showed them the water bottle I'd nabbed from Vincent's fridge. Vincent ignored me and examined the cards Sofi dealt his way. I spoke louder, "I'm thirsty."

Vincent gazed my way and did a double-take when he saw the water bottle.

"Hope you don't mind, Vincent." I uncapped the bottle. "I helped myself to your refrigerator when I visited your apartment."

"You what?" His face turned an unholy shade of ash gray.

"Nana let me in." I clasped the bottom of the bottle and twisted. "She explained why she wouldn't be here tonight." Years of lying eased the falsehood off my tongue.

Vincent rose to his feet and arched a brow, old-school villain style. "She couldn't have let you in. How did you really get inside?"

"The suspense is killing me." Sofi continued dealing.

The bottom portion of the bottle detached and a watch tumbled onto my palm. Peter slowly rose to his feet. "Why, it's a Rolex…" His wide-eyed gaze turned to me. "What's it doing in there? Where did you obtain that, Vincent?"

"It was originally in Dom's fridge," I said.

"I remember that bottle," Sofi said. "In front of the Artesian spring water."

"This bottle's a diversion safe. An ordinary object you'd never suspect of hiding valuables." Dominic's last words to me, "watch, water, safe" had finally made sense. I stood and focused on Vincent. "Dom owed Sid money. Sid got angry every time Dom disappeared and returned with pockets full of dough because Dom never paid Sid a dime." I inched closer to Vincent and glared down at him. "One night you and Dom got drunk and he told you about the Rolex."

"Dom said he dropped it when he ran out," Peter mumbled.

"Didn't you leave out a vital part?" Sofi asked me, passing the cards around.

"Yeah, like when's our game starting? My fingers are getting itchy." Lil wiggled them.

"Why was Dominic hiding the Rolex?" Sofi spread the remaining cards along the table, face down.

"I never drank with Dominic," Vincent said. "And I am not Sid as you insinuate. I owe money to him just like the rest of you. That bottle showed up in my refrigerator. I thought the cleaning crew left it there. You can check. I expressed my great annoyance to Lettie about it."

He was going to be a tough nut to crack.

"Why does a closet in your apartment have a special lock?" I asked him.

"You should be arrested for trespass," Vincent said.

"We're all ears," Sofi said.

Vincent slammed a fist on the table. "If you must know, I'm a closet artist. I don't want anyone seeing my artwork until it's ready."

Maybe Mom could verify that.

"I hate to interrupt this funfest, but…" William swayed to his feet. "I'm feeling faint. I need my beauty rest mattress."

259

"You're not going anywhere until after we play, you old fool," Lil said.

"Sit down." I pointed my Glock at William. He slowly planted his bottom onto the chair. I turned to Peter. "You, William, and Dom were the jewel thieves. Five Rolexes and a sapphire ring were taken. You ended up one watch short. This one." I held up the Rolex.

"All I know is that's a high-quality Rolex with a two-carat diamond dial. Very attractive piece." Peter strolled around to my chair. "I heard about the theft in Montecito. A band of bold thieves struck early in the afternoon. The driver seemed especially clever. He secured a phony Puerto Rican driver's license to rent a car, then abandoned the vehicle, after which they disappeared without a trace."

"You have more details than the news reports." It was Peter's way of bragging that he was the driver. Michael texted me,

Mom and Veera are safe!

I heaved out a breath I'd been sucking in since Mom went missing. I spun toward William. The heaviness in my head had lifted. "It was you."

"I haven't the foggiest notion what you're babbling about." William's feathery brow arched. "I don't own a Rolex. Though I wouldn't mind having one."

"I'll bet he arrived in the poker parlor just before we did," I said.

"Come to think of it, he did," Sofi said.

"And it was William who followed Michael and me tonight." I finally had clarity. "And he sent himself a note from Sid."

"Don't tell me he's Sid," Lil said. "That man couldn't even find his ear if he had an itch to scratch."

"Flattery will get you nowhere," William said.

"He's keener than we think," I said. "He was the brains behind the jewel theft, he drove the golf cart that nearly ran Holly and Sofi down, and sent Vincent in to fix a typewriter with a sticky key." Vincent resembled Bob Dylan now that I took a hard look at him. And he had something the others didn't.

"I'm the only one among us with my own transportation. It's only natural I go on errands when needed," Vincent said. "William had borrowed my typewriter. When I noticed the sticky key, he offered to take it in, but I went there myself. He even paid for the repair."

"I always pay my debts." William patted Vincent on the back. "You did me a big favor, old man. That repair shop reeks of perfume of the cheapest quality, which causes my super sniffer to run incessantly."

"Your super what?" Lil asked.

"Where did the cowboy hat come from?" I asked Vincent.

"I keep it in my car," Vincent said.

"That part's true," Sofi said. "I borrowed it once when we went for a drive."

"Bet that cowboy hat would look real nice on my head." Lil patted her hair.

I wasn't finished with Vincent. "Why was your car targeted with a pipe bomb?" I asked him.

"Because," Peter said, "a note appeared beneath my gate from Sid, instructing me that Vincent was about to blow the whistle on our poker games. Sid wanted to teach Vincent a lesson. I shared the note with everyone, but Vincent. Per the instructions."

"You never said anything to me," Vincent said. "I thought we were close friends."

"About as close as Santa Barbara is to Palm Beach," Lil said. "You should never have trusted these lying, cheating old fogeys."

"I'm deeply hurt," Vincent said.

"Did you say cheap perfume?" I turned to William. What was I missing? "When did you collect the money from the games?"

He squeezed his lips together. "What balderdash."

"I'll tell you when." Lil stood and swung around her arms like she was prepping for a boxing match. "After the first few games I waited in the bushes so I could jump Sid and sucker punch him. I ran into this loser each time. He said he was hidin' for the same reason, to meet up with Sid. I believed the conniving buzzard."

"Dom knew you were Sid," I told William. "Not only did he not pay you the money he owed, but you paid him a cut to keep him quiet because he threatened to turn you in for the Montecito robbery, the gambling, and who knows what other criminal activities. You finally decided to end that relationship when you poisoned him with an ingredient only a perfumer would know." I ad-libbed the last part, but it had a powerful ring of truth to it. "You had access to a chemical lab which made it easy to request a sample." Wait a minute. What poison smells sweet and burnt at the same time? I'd studied poisons after Dad's death. "Acetonitrile. An ingredient used in perfumes. It dissolves in water and quickly changes...to cyanide."

Sofi rose to her feet and used her phone to take videos. "Oh, this is good."

"It causes shortness of breath and if the victim gets to the ICU in the first twenty-four hours, he stands a chance," I said. "Otherwise..."

Peter gripped his throat with a hand.

Michael raced in with Mom and Veera in tow.

"He did it." Mom pointed a finger that circled the room and landed on Peter. She ran up to him. "The jig is up." She turned to me. "Isn't it?"

"Close, but no cigar." I gave Mom a quick hug. "It's William."

"What?" Veera said. "That man can barely stand without falling."

In one rapid-fire move, William grabbed Mom's arm and twisted it behind her, his hand at her neck. A hand that gripped his dirk, the old military knife Veera heard him mention at the beach. I pointed my gun at his chest.

"Don't make me use this," I lied. I had no clear shot.

"You've gone too far, William," Peter said.

"My lovely companion and I are leaving now." William backed toward the door using Mom as his body shield.

Lil huffed and squinted at him. "You're going to flub this up and you know it."

"After I'm gone, you'll remember me as the mastermind I really am." He continued the retreat. "I don't know how you knew about the poison, but I don't care because I'm going to escape. If you're a good little girl, I'll throw your granny out the car somewhere, so you'll have a body to bury."

"William!" Peter said. "You don't have a vehicle."

"You think I didn't plan an escape? You're wrong, my bloated little comrade."

I matched William's steps out into the connecting room.

"You can't get far with her," Vincent said. "Let Lucy Fay go and none of us will come after you."

"If anyone follows, I will slit this charming lady's throat." William grinned wickedly. "I have a fondness for carving knives." His crazed gaze fastened onto mine. "It'll be slow and painful, I promise." He dragged Mom out the door and slammed shut the secret entrance with a few loud clicks. I turned the handle and rammed my body against the door, but there was no give.

Michael did the same. Veera even banged a chair against it.

"No use," Peter said. "If you turn the bottles in the opposite direction, the door locks down. The stones are a facade over thick adobe. Impossible to break through without proper tools and machinery."

I shoved my way back to the poker parlor and kicked open the bathroom door. The window above the sink was just wide enough for me to squeeze through. "Stand clear." I turned my back to the window, aimed over my shoulder, and shot. Glass shattered and clinked to the ground.

Michael threw his jacket over the bottom of the window frame, seconds before I hopped onto the sink and dove outside, landing hard on my hands and chest. It took a minute for my lungs to reactivate. I tumbled around and sprinted toward the front, grabbing a small pistol from a holster beneath my hoodie.

I rounded the corner. William dragged Mom out to the alley, slamming the gate shut behind him. He secured the padlock to keep me at bay. Barbed wire ran along the top of the fence. How to get to Mom? She pivoted to look behind her, but William wrenched her forward. She tripped, landing on her knees. I took aim, but he jerked her up and pressed her against his side, stumbling along beside him. About twenty yards away, a souped-up golf cart awaited.

"Oh, no." I reversed and thrashed through the thick growth along the back perimeter, the same direction as William. Then I saw it. A break in the barbed wire. I dashed toward the opening, climbed up, and hurled myself over, my hands a bloody mess, my clothes ripped and studded with foxtails and burs. I raced toward the cart.

William pushed Mom into the passenger seat, all the while gripping her wrist. She kicked him hard and earned a slap across her face. I ran like my feet were on fire and launched myself toward the cart, moments after it sped off. My hands flew toward the curved bars at the rear. I grabbed hold as William accelerated. Fat tires and a lifted body meant higher speeds. My sneakers dragged and one hand slipped. Mom yelled and reached back toward me. William waved his knife and Mom jerked her arm away. She yanked off her wig and threw it at his face. He let up on the pedal long enough for me to pull myself aboard and swing my legs onto the back platform. He still clenched the knife pointed toward Mom. I lunged toward his hand, grabbed it, and jerked it up so his own fist knocked him under the chin, snapping his head back. I conked him on his crown with the butt of my pistol while Mom took hold of the steering wheel. William slumped to the side, dropped his knife, and moaned.

Mom snatched the wheel and turned toward the self-parking lot. William's suede lace-ups had eased off the pedal and he fluttered open his eyes, staring at the knife on the floor. I pinned my pistol to his temple.

"Told you I smelled metal," William said. His head lolled back onto the seat.

* * *

Fifteen minutes later, a small crowd assembled in the parking lot, including the remaining R.A.T. pack members. Michael had managed to help Sofi squeeze through the bathroom window of the cottage. She'd circled around and freed the rest of the players. Then they formed a search party.

"I had the winning hand tonight," Lil said to me. "And I made Peter pay up. Wasn't worried about your Nana getting hurt. I knew that heathen was going to hell. You got spunk." She adjusted her church hat and ambled toward the Villa, just before the cops arrived.

"That may have been the first compliment that ever crossed her lips," Veera whispered. "When your Mom and I arrived at the cottage, I broke inside on my own."

We shared a high five. "What happened to you and Mom? You didn't answer my texts."

"After she left Vincent, we nosed around some, then went to Lucy Fay's apartment and found a note under the door. From Sid. He said if Lucy Fay didn't hightail it to the utility office, her chick would be fried."

William-slash-Sid definitely had a way with words.

"We figured he'd gotten to you, so we went. As soon as we walked inside the utility room, somebody locked the door behind us. We banged on it, but these seniors don't hear too well." Veera focused on Michael. "He freed us."

Michael's hearing rivaled that of the African elephant. He'd heard the pounding from the opposite end of the Villa.

"It was teamwork. I used a screwdriver—" Michael said.

"So did I," Veera said.

"We dismantled the doorknobs." Michael fist-bumped Veera. "Simultane-ously."

"Where would I be without you all? Thanks for sticking so close to Mom, Veera," I said.

"Didn't keep her from being taken hostage." Veera dropped her chin.

"Veera noticed the fresh tire tracks of the escape cart," Michael said, "in the alley. That's how we found you so quickly."

Police and paramedics finally arrived and carried William away on a gurney, babbling about the smell of hospitals.

"Hey, psychic." Sofi waltzed over, cool as a wintry stream. She pointed her pale blues to Michael. "I could use you on some of my cases."

"Oh, I'm not really a—"

Veera jabbed him in the ribs. "We'll loan him out, for the right price."

Sofi turned to me. "Wanna tell me who you really are?"

Lettie marched up and glared my way. "Why are you always in the thick of things? What happened tonight?"

I told her what I told the cops. William threatened and kidnapped my grandmother, and I gave chase.

Peter hid in the shadows, listening. He spoke up, "William frightened us all. He was a menace."

We stared at Mom. Her wig was back in place, but her silver bob looked war-torn. Vincent rubbed her hand while a paramedic fixed up her cuts and bruises.

Paramedics had patched up my hands, but Michael insisted on rubbing ointment on them.

"Your hands'll be like new tomorrow," he said.

They were feeling better already.

Mom barely spoke and when she did it was like she sat in a library. Inside voice and brief answers. She leaned over to me. "What's the word?"

"Mum," I said.

Vincent sidled over and whispered, "Are you turning us in for the gambling?"

"What gambling?" I had my own problems. We'd located Dom and uncovered an illegal gambling operation, but still had to answer for impersonating a resident and her family. How to overcome that colossal hurdle?

Chapter Forty-Nine

The End is Near

Nothing beats the high of unveiling a criminal, especially when it restores a safe haven for vulnerable senior citizens. Okay, so the delinquent, thrill-seeking seniors were part of the problem, but saving Mom was the crowning achievement. Granted, I was the one who put her in a risky situation, but still.

The high seeped away by sunrise thanks to my prickly conscience. We'd found Dom, kept him alive, and unmasked Sid, but now there were consequences that could turn our success into failure. And there were criminals still running loose at the Villa. How to sort through it all?

Analyze what you want to happen and conquer what's preventing you from making it happen.

"Piece of cake." I tossed, turned, and wriggled around in my rollaway bed. I finally shot up. There was only one thing for me to do.

I threw back the covers and slipped into my sneakers. Where was Michael? I grabbed my phone and texted him, asking him to put me in touch with Lucy Fay. She'd be the priestess in my glass confessional.

"Where do you think you're going?" Mom jumped in front of me, blocking my path.

"I've got a bridge to cross," I said.

"Not dressed like that you don't." She ushered me to her bedroom. Veera trekked close behind us, yawning.

"Did I dream last night or did we crack our case WIDE OPEN!" Veera's arms reached for the sky.

"You don't realize—" I started.

"No. *You* don't realize what you've done," Mom said. "A Villa criminal is facing charges or will shortly, thanks to you. And any others contemplating underhanded activity will think twice." Mom sliced one hand into the palm of the other hand. "This case will put you two on the map."

"Except we can't advertise what we did, working undercover and all." Veera plopped on the bed.

"Who needs advertising when you've got something more powerful? Word of mouth." Mom rushed to the closet and flung open the door. "Lil and Sofi are going to be singing your praises, and don't forget Holly and the rest of the Villa staff. You might have even thawed out Lettie enough to make her appreciate your accomplishments. Get dressed girls. The dining hall awaits."

"How could we possibly eat anything?" My upper eyelid twitched at the pace of a drumroll.

Veera dropped her head. "Corrie's right."

"We'll talk through everything over breakfast," Mom said.

If she were a balloon, she would have popped from the excess air inside of her. What was Mom up to? "What did you tell your Villa pals?"

"That I'm moving out." She pulled out a V-neck, floral print jersey with a bold print. "Veera, I've got just the pick-me-upper."

"I don't feel like..." Veera lifted her head and bobbed up to her feet. "...are those tiny crystals along the neckline?" She stroked the dress and held it up against her. "Ooooh, I should probably see if it fits, since you went to all the trouble of packing it." She disappeared into the bathroom.

"Where's Michael?" I asked Mom.

"He'll be back in time for breakfast." She held up a floral print chiffon with a ribbon tie at the waist. "For you." The powerfully feminine dress was her home run pitch, but I wasn't up for it.

"What I wear won't matter," I said.

"Oh, honey. Nothing's ever so bad that it can't be made better."

"I don't—"

Mom's burner phone rang. She grabbed it before it finished ringing and trotted out to the living area. She was giving herself quite the workout this morning. Veera emerged wearing her new frock.

"I'm ready to face the Villa world." Veera twirled around.

We took over Lucy Fay's identity, her new home and her potential friends. Why would she cut us any slack? And there was Lettie to contend with.

Mom strolled in. "Downstairs, twenty minutes." She pushed me and the chiffon dress into the bathroom.

"Who called?" I asked.

"One of the residents saying goodbye."

I popped my head back out. "I texted Michael and he hasn't responded."

"He will. Now get ready."

She was definitely up to something.

* * *

The Ocean Vista was nearly packed when we arrived. Mom didn't bother waiting to be seated. She homed in on a corner table with an ocean view. The only problem? It was already occupied.

"Mind if we join you?" Mom asked.

A snowy-haired woman motioned for us to sit. Glittery stars dotted her mint green dress. Her neck, ears, arms, and fingers hosted enough gold jewelry to fill a fine jewelry store case. Her topknot was textbook chic; her light smile floated around the table. Mom and Veera sat, but I remained standing.

"You live here?" Veera asked her.

"Yes," the lady replied.

A blue bomber jacket was slung over the seat closest to her. Where had I seen that jacket before? I sucked in my breath. It was Michael's.

"I'll be back," I said, but Mom grabbed my arm.

"Steady now," she spoke out of the corner of her mouth.

I sank onto a chair.

"There you are!" Michael flew up to us, head cheerleader smile etched on his lips. He stared at the woman and gestured toward me. "This is Corrie Locke. We love her to pieces."

"You know each other?" I asked.

He wrinkled his nose in glee. "Lucy Fay drove all the way here to meet you in person. I mean she hired a driver, but she came for you."

I snapped to attention, heart pounding. "Came for me because…" Was my arrest imminent? No cops in sight. That was a good thing, right?

"You're her?" Veera half rose.

We were about to face the music.

Lucy Fay stared up at Michael, then me. "I became very upset when he told me what was happening. I called the authorities."

Veera and I teetered at the edge of our seats, shoulders nearly touching our earlobes.

"By authorities, do you mean the FBI?" Veera asked. "Or SBPD?"

"Villa security." Her voice was low and slightly sing-songy.

Veera fanned herself with her hand. "That was a good choice."

"They knew nothing," Lucy Fay said.

"The residents involved covered things up well." I never thought I'd be sticking up for Kyle, but it was true.

"That's to be expected from sophisticated retirees with too much time on their hands." Lucy Fay regarded Michael. "Take me, for instance. After Michael first called, I did my own investigating." She zeroed in on me. "I know more than you probably know about yourself."

"You investigated the investigator?" Veera asked.

"I did my homework. Or should I say, I hired people who did. Michael convinced me of the importance of your work. His integrity and sincerity were compelling forces in my decision. What you all did…you repaired things no one even knew were broken."

Mom half smiled and half teared up. "I feel like I'm watching my favorite kind of T.V. movie, only now it's starring my daughter and her best friends."

"I don't mean to rush to the ending…" Veera leaned toward Lucy Fay, "…but are you going to call the police? Because if you're not, we might have business to discuss."

I jabbed her in the side with my elbow.

Lucy Fay turned to me. "I know about your investigative agency idea. It is a good one."

"It is?" Veera beamed and stuck a hand into her purse. "Here's our business plan." She handed Lucy Fay a sheet of paper. "I've been refining it to where it's ready to go."

"I am interested in learning more," Lucy Fay said.

"But we—" I started.

Mom kicked me under the table and then I knew. She and Lucy Fay had already talked.

"Music to our ears." Veera slapped the table with her hands.

"When did you two speak?" I stared at Mom.

"Veera and I chatted when we were locked in the utility closet," Mom said. "As soon as Michael arrived, I had him call Lucy Fay, pronto. I needed to make sure she was good with what was about to go down. We talked on the way to the poker parlor. We had a nice conversation about the Villa gardens, the food, and I told her you were minutes away from finding the ringleader of a series of felonious criminal activities." Mom turned to Lucy Fay with a grin.

"I updated Lucy Fay on the jewelry store robbery, too," Michael said.

"We have a lot in common." Mom patted Lucy Fay's hand. "We're gourmet cooks and fashion hounds who play a mean set of billiards."

"I won the Dubai classic in 1992," Lucy Fay said.

Mom leaned back to whisper to me. "Here's the story I gave Lettie. I'm Lucy Fay's younger sister who arrived early to check out the Villa and, with Lucy Fay's blessing, I pretended to be her."

Between Veera, Mom, and Lucy Fay, there was enough wattage to power the southern half of Santa Barbara County.

"I called that one." Veera pointed to the opposite corner of the room.

Vincent and Lil sat at a cozy table for two, all smiles and handholding. He sure got over Mom quickly.

"They have my approval," Mom said. "I gave Vincent the same story I told

Lettie."

"Excuse me." Holly paused by our table and stared at Lucy Fay. "Welcome to Villa Sunset. We are at your disposal."

Lucy Fay bowed her head slightly. "Congratulations on your new post."

"What post?" Veera asked. "You leaving the Villa?"

"Holly's replacing Lettie as Villa Director," Lucy Fay replied.

"For a little while," Holly said. "Lettie's going on a leave of absence. Something about recuperating from too much-unauthorized activity."

Veera did a fist pump and whispered to me. "We're in the clear, right?"

"Keep that thought," I said.

"I am proud to have lent my identity and my apartment to such a worthy group of investigators," Lucy Fay said.

We were so indebted to Lucy Fay, we'd have to name all future children and dogs and cats after her. How would we ever pay her back? The answer popped into my head moments later. "I've got the perfect name for our new agency."

"Better than the Locke Head Agency?" Veera asked.

"The Nightingale Agency," I said. "Nightingales are small birds with powerful voices. Who sing night and day."

"Just like we work night and day to crack our cases," Veera said. "And we are powerful. I'm down with that."

"Me, too," Mom said.

"Me, three," Michael said.

"With your permission, of course," I said to Lucy Fay.

We stared at Lucy Fay.

"It would be an honor if you used my name," she said.

I turned to Holly and spoke low, "I've been meaning to ask, exactly who told you to call me to help locate Dom?"

"A man I once knew. Tall, good-looking, dreamy. You work together."

"We *worked* together. Past tense. Dad is no longer—"

"What? Not your father. Wayne, the director of your film studio security department gave me your information."

"Wayne?"

"He used to be an L.A. private investigator, a real go-getter, which is what I wanted. I called Wayne, and he suggested I call you."

"But I'm not—"

"You're a lawyer and an investigator who solved an important case for him. He told me about it and about the cases you'd solved with your father."

"You didn't call my father's office number?" It still didn't make sense.

"I never lie, but I lied to you about that," Holly said. "Wayne told me you were angry with him, so I got creative to get your attention. When I called, I substituted your father for Wayne. I was desperate."

"It's a pity you had to resort to lying," said the liar to the liar.

"That was before I knew you'd lost your father. Can you forgive me?"

"I'm okay with everything." There wasn't anything I wasn't okay with at the moment.

She patted my hand. "Thank you." She looked around the table. "Thank you, every one of you."

Sofi sauntered up. "Good news. Dominic confessed from his hospital bed about the Montecito jewel theft in exchange for house arrest for his role in it." Sofi basked in doling out news hot off the press. "And Peter was just arrested."

"Couldn't go down any other way," Veera said.

I had to agree.

Sofi's gaze rolled over Lucy Fay. "Who are you?"

"My sister," Mom said. "Lucy Fay Nightingale."

"You have the same name?"

I pointed to Mom. "Meet Vicky Fay. It's a long story."

"I've got time." Sofi stared us down.

"Not us," Veera said. "Now that our great auntie is back, we gotta go."

"Not so fast," Sofi said. "I want to borrow your psychic. I'm serious."

"We don't have a psychic," Michael said.

"He's so modest," I said. "What do you want him to do?"

"I'm a computer science professor—" Michael started.

"Who moonlights as a psychic." I was not about to let a potential gig escape from us, especially now that we were closer to opening up our agency.

"Who's the client?"

"A friend of mine." Sofi stood. "I'll be calling with details. Ta-ta."

Sofi sashayed away and Michael scooted over.

"Corrie, I can't—"

"Yes, you can. You're observant, have super-duper research skills and hearing, not to mention a logical, hyper-intelligent mind. Plus, we'll send you to psychic boot camp."

"I guess I can do that. Wait, I won't be seeing dead people, will I?"

"I promise to keep them away." I kissed his cheek. How hard could it be to pose as a psychic after posing as the family of a real-life wealthy senior resident of the Villa? Especially for seasoned posers, like us.

Acknowledgements

So much gratitude to:

My sharp-eyed beta reader Kim Pendleton who generously paused pursuing his passion for restoring his beloved cars to read my early draft. Thank you for sharing your valuable time and insights with me.

The real-life Sofi Reyes who in no way resembles the fictional Sofi Reyes, except they've both got plenty of spunk. Real Sofi is kind, thoughtful, and lovable. Thank you for lending your name to a character (not just any character, mind you) and for your support and enthusiasm for my work.

Marilyn Metzner and Judge Thomas Anderle who give me a lift every time I'm in their presence, and for always asking about my books. It means so much to me. I'm so very appreciative for your support.

Mike Hadley for also always asking about my books and for spreading the word that my mystery series is worth reading. Thank you very much.

The Level Best Books Team: My amazing publisher and wonderful editors, Verena and Shawn, two hardworking, lovely ladies who help me whip my books into the right shape.

My fellow Sleuths & Sidekicks: Authors Tina deBellegarde, Jen Collins Moore and Carol Pouliot. Banding together, we turned book marketing in a pandemic year into an absolute joy.

My family who are my true sidekicks in life: I am so fortunate to have a family that supports my book endeavors and who are ever willing to help me make time to write. Because they know it means so much to me, they make it mean so much to them. My husband, sons and daughters-in-law, and my lovely sister. Extra thanks to Dr. Nikki for letting me bounce off my fictional characters' medical issues when they pop up.

My readers: As always, my deepest gratitude goes to you. Thank you for your continued support. There are too many marvelous people to name, but I have to make special mention of special readers, Wayne & Ruth, who've been there for each and every one of my books. Thank you, thank you, thank you so very much.

About the Author

Lida Sideris' first stint after law school was a newbie lawyer's dream: working as an entertainment attorney for a movie studio…kind of like her heroine, Corrie Locke, except without the homicides. Lida was one of two national winners of the Helen McCloy Mystery Writers of America Scholarship Award and a Silver Falchion Award Finalist. She lives in the northern tip of Southern California with her family, rescue dogs and a flock of uppity chickens. To learn more, please visit: http://www.LidaSideris.com

SOCIAL MEDIA HANDLES:
   https://www.facebook.com/lidasideris
   Twitter: @lidasideris
   Instagram: @lida_sideris
   https://www.bookbub.com/profile/lida-sideris

AUTHOR WEBSITE: www.LidaSideris.com

Also by Lida Sideris

The Southern California Mysteries (in order of appearance):
Murder & Other Unnatural Disasters
Murder Gone Missing
Murder: Double or Nothing
Slightly Murderous Intent

And don't forget the picture book for kids – *The Cookie Eating Fire Dog*

CPSIA information can be obtained
at www.ICGtesting.com
Printed in the USA
BVHW071704160322
631197BV00001B/1

9 781685 120863